NS BR

NS Brooks, a qualified Chartered Accountant, spent over 40 years working In London as an accountant in practice. He started his writing career on retirement. This is his second novel.

Also by the author

Betrayed

REVENGE

N S BROOKS

ISBN 978-1-7398094-0-9

First published 2021 by NS Brooks
www.nsbrooks.com

ACKNOWLEDGEMENTS

I am particularly grateful to my editor, Mark Leggatt, for his patience and insight in reviewing and correcting several iterations of my manuscript.

CHAPTER ONE

Marius Vassily pulled up the collar of his jacket that covered his scrawny neck. His gaunt features matched his body, thin and long, and his eyes darted from side to side, watching everyone and everything as he neared the prison entrance gates. If there was one thing that Marius hated, it was prisons. The seen and unseen eyes that scrutinised him as he passed through security. The irrational fear that he may never be allowed to leave.

His shirt was damp with sweat as he made his way to the designated seat. The face that looked out at him through the hazy perspex screen was puffy and almost translucent, framed by long, lank hair, receding at the middle parting.

"Boss, how's it going?" asked Marius.

"Lousy, what do you fucking think? Look at me," he indicated with his hand.

"Why do you want to see me, Boss?"

Spittle sprayed onto the partition as the Boss spoke, "before they put me away for life, I was collecting a lot of money owed to me. He still owes me." He swatted a newspaper on the shelf between them as if he were killing a fly. The Boss looked around to ensure he had not attracted any attention and leaned forward close to the screen. Marius could smell stale breath through the small holes.

"I want you to find the bastard who stole my money and kill him," he said, stabbing his finger on a heavily ink-circled name on the newspaper. "It's all in here."

"But if we kill this man, you will never get the money that's owed to you.

"Can't spend the fucking money in here, but it will make me feel better if that bastard is dead."

Marius sat back in his chair, trying to distance himself from the rage distorted face that still turned his blood ice cold. He said, whispering, "do you know where he is?"

"Course, I don't bloody well know where he is. He should be in here for nicking my money, and then I would deal with him myself without having to trust you idiots." He wacked the paper again. This time the warder did look across in their direction.

"Okay, I got the message. Is there anything else I can do, Boss?"

"Apart from getting me out of here, which you ain't going to do. Naw, just kill that man."

The Boss rose to show that the conversation was at an end. Marius stared through the screen at the folded page of the paper with the circled name. The headline read 'The Missing Millions.'

Head down and deep in thought, Marius made his way back through security and out onto the street. Out of habit, he checked behind him to make sure no one was following him. He had left his car a few roads away, so CCTV would not pick up the number plate.

Marius slumped into the driver's seat.

"How was he?" asked Marius's companion, Christophe Wesinivic, a chubbier version of Marius with similar coarse features.

"He looked like shit. Pale and thinner, and he has let his hair grow long. He looked a mess."

"What did he want?" asked Christophe.

"He wants us to find the man who stole his money and kill him."

CHAPTER TWO

Acid churned in the pit of his stomach. He began to read. He didn't want to but knew he must, like the nightmare that sucks you into its fearful darkness, slithering forward, hiding in the shadows, where you cannot avoid the inevitable. Will Slater's handsome aquiline features were distorted by a grimace as the words slowly filtered into his brain.

He knew the article had been coming but seeing it in black and white made him realise that this would rekindle old memories and hatreds. His life was now in danger.

He turned the pages, his fingers fumbling as he read the damning words. He had read many newspaper investigative reports and wondered how the subjects had felt, words condemning and maledictory. However, this article was not about someone else; it was about him.

"You look awful darling, what's wrong?" said Jay, entering the room in her sweat-stained exercise suit that clung to her svelte physique.

"That piece, the investigative reporter called about a few weeks ago, it's in today's paper, a long article in the magazine section."

"You were expecting it. The journalist asked if you wanted to comment, and you declined."

"Yes, but when you see it in black and white, it looks bad. Very bad, it doesn't portray me as the victim, quite the opposite. The implication is that I stole all the money. But there was nothing I could do. The money was all in that blasted Java company which ended up belonging to me. No one seemed to care, certainly not SO15. Well, you know that. They were just pleased to arrest the terrorists and the people behind the whole operation and move on. There was no one to whom I could give the money. You can't just write a cheque for twenty million pounds to the Government."

"That's true. I think everyone forgot about the money."

"I know, but if I hadn't worked out the password to unlock the bank accounts and transfer the money, SO15 would never have caught Michael Bore," said Will, looking down at the article again. "The whole thing has ruined my life, ruined my practice, my reputation and mentally scarred me. The only good aspect, and it is an incredibly good aspect," he said, looking up at Jay, "was meeting you."

"Well, all things have a price attached," she replied, smiling, "what else does the article say?"

"The journalist suggests that it seems very unlikely that I could have been surrounded by all these people, who eventually betrayed me, and yet I didn't know? It is easy for him to say that, but I didn't. I hadn't a clue."

"You and I know that, so who cares what he thinks?"

"That's not what's worrying me; everyone involved in the whole ghastly affair will now know that I still have the money. Everyone thought the taxman or," said Will shaking his head, "the Official Receiver had the money. Now they know that is not the case, it will encourage them to come looking for it. They are desperate people."

"They are criminals, and why would they risk anything else

by harming you? Look, you acted incredibly honourably. Without your diligence and perseverance, the authorities would not have caught these despicable people whose actions would undoubtedly have caused many deaths in the future. Anyway," said Jay putting her arm around Will's shoulder and running her fingers through his wavy, dark brown hair, "they are all in prison or dead."

"I wish I had your optimism, but I still think this article will act as a reminder and stir up hatreds. Also, that blasted policeman, Dawkin, I suspect, still thinks I'm guilty. And who knows, he might still be trying to put together a case against me. This article will probably just encourage him."

Will shook his head as if trying to axe something from his mind, but like a lot of unpleasant thoughts, they appear like wet knots, difficult to untie.

"Did the article mention me? I hope not?" asked Jay.

"It just talks about a mystery woman going to the Virgin Islands with me. That's it."

"Good, anything else of concern?"

"Well, it covered the shooting of Peter Crombie by my ex-business partner, Sara, his wife. The trial of Michael Bore and his sentencing, along with that horrendous criminal gang leader, for their terrorist activities. To think I had known Michael all those years as a client and didn't suspect anything."

"People are strange. You can never be sure of anyone."

"I suppose you're correct, but a bit of a depressing thought." Will paused. "What is strange is that the article says that the Crombie children – Justin and Chloe – were in court for their mother's trial and Bore's case. Why would they want to sit through Bore's case? What could their interest be? Once Sara was sentenced for the manslaughter of their father, surely their interest was over?"

Jay shrugged her shoulders. "Perhaps they wanted to work out how their parents fitted into the whole sorry affair."

Will couldn't work out why this last piece of information

disturbed him. He let the thought slide away. "We need to get out of London, and we need to do it now, somewhere remote. We can't wait any longer. Someplace where we'll see anyone coming first."

"Well, we have already looked at a lot of houses in Scotland from a dozen different agents, but don't you think you are over-reacting?"

"No, I don't. It may even be too late, now that article is out. I have an awful feeling about this. We must be extremely cautious. I'm now definitely a target."

Again looking down at the paper, the headline staring back at him, 'The Missing Millions.'

CHAPTER THREE

Tie undone, paunch pushed tight against the desk, one hand rubbing his close-cropped hair, Inspector Jim Dawkin sat flicking through a file with his chubby fingers when his phone rang. Irritated by having his concentration disturbed, he grabbed the receiver. "Hello, Dawkin."

There was a slight pause, "ah, Inspector Dawkin, my name is Chris Melody. I'm with the Financial Services Commission in the British Virgin Islands."

"How can I help you, Mr Melody?"

"We have been investigating a man called Justerini in connection with his banking activities on these islands. He was connected to a case that I believe you were dealing with involving a London solicitor called Will Slater."

"Yeah, that's correct," said Dawkin, sitting bolt upright in his chair.

"We found a sheet of paper in Justerini's desk, which was headed Java Plc, that was the company that collected all the terrorists' cash."

"Yes, yes, I know all that. I was the senior officer on the case."

“Well,” continued Melody, “the piece of paper had two telephone numbers on it. The first number belonged to a Michael Bore, whom we understand has been convicted under terrorism charges in the UK. The second number was not traceable. Pay as you go, I imagine.”

“And?” said Dawkin, drumming his fingers on the desk,

“As far as I can tell from the reports that I have read, everyone involved in the case is either in detention or dead,” replied Melody.

“That’s correct, with one exception, I suppose, but what has this to do with this second telephone number?”

“Well, I was just coming to that. Out of curiosity, I have just phoned the second number again, and it was answered this time, but whoever it was didn’t speak. I wondered if you had any idea who that might be?”

Something close to excitement surged through Dawkin’s veins; his round face became florid.

“I’m afraid I have no idea, sorry I can’t help. Good luck with the case. Let me know if you make any progress. Bye,” replied Dawkin dropping the phone into its cradle.

He pushed himself up from the desk and shouted to his empty office, “I knew it, I knew it, Slater has made fools of us all.”

CHAPTER FOUR

Jay was hunched over her laptop, swearing under her breath.

"What's wrong?" said Will.

"Blasted internet, it's so slow, it's as if we are sharing it with the whole of the street. Are you sure you password protected it?"

"Of course."

"Are you sure you haven't got anything running in the background?"

"No, nothing."

"Anyway, these house details have just popped up," she said, pointing an elegant finger at her computer screen. "I think this may be the ideal home for us; look at this blurb. It appears to be very remote, tucked into the back of nowhere in Scotland. End of a loch with little access from anywhere. Should suit us very well."

Peering over Jay's shoulder, Will read out aloud the property details from the screen. "*Situated at the edge of Loch Rannoch, Gaur House is a large country home with spectacular views down the loch and sits in 2000 acres of land, with a long lochside frontage. Very secluded, well off the beaten track, would appeal to those who want to get away from the hurly-burly of city life. The house consists of a lounge, library, dining room, kitchen, snug and games room, nine bedrooms and three bathrooms. Large garage and various outbuildings. In need of some modernisation. Offers in the region of £1.5m.*"

"It sounds the best by a long way. I think we should take a look."

* * *

Will and Jay packed their bags for a few nights' stay in Scotland. Even if Gaur House didn't turn out to be what they wanted, they would take the opportunity to search the area for other suitable options.

Once they had landed at Glasgow airport and picked up a hire car, they headed for Loch Rannoch.

"You know the only time I have been to Scotland was when I followed you up here to protect you," said Jay.

"How could I forget that trip? I think it was the coldest I have ever experienced. The wind was howling around the car, blowing huge clouds of gusting snow across the frozen landscape. I remember I struggled to keep the car out of the ditches along the side of the road. If only I had known what was waiting for me at journey's end." Will paused. "If it hadn't been for you, it would have been a one-way trip. That assassin hired by Michael Bore and his associates would have killed me. I must have been mad, thinking I could sort it all out by myself."

"Well, good thing I was there," replied Jay.

Although the sun's warmth washed through the car windows, Will felt a chill of apprehension envelop his body. Yes, Jay had saved him that day, and somewhere deep down, he had the feeling that there would be another day when he would need her special skills again.

Jay looked down at the map. "Listen to these exotic names of villages that we are going to pass through - Luss, Inverbeg, Ardlui, and Crianlarich. It's so exciting. I can't wait to live up here."

They needed somewhere where they could get lost. Still, the barren landscape in winter, the isolation, and the solitude were not appealing to the city boy in Will. Having lived and worked in London all his life, the fresh air and space felt unnatural. He would get used to it and perhaps even enjoy it eventually, but now it was a means to an end.

As the car rumbled through Glen Coe, Will noticed that a black Range Rover seemed to be following them. Will kept looking in his mirror as the road meandered towards their destination. As they approached the picturesque town of Killin on the banks of Loch Tay, he said, "there's a black Range Rover about two cars behind; I think it is following us. I'm sure I saw it at the airport."

"I can see it," said Jay, swivelling in her seat, "but there aren't too many other routes, and it's probably just heading the same way as us."

Will acknowledged that there were very few turn-offs on this road. Perhaps he had become paranoid since the article in the paper. "Let's stop for an early lunch in Killin and see if it drives past."

They parked just after the little bridge that crossed the Dochart Falls at the entrance to Killin.

Jay wandered back to an information sign by the bridge. Will stood by the car, peering at a map. Both waited for the Range Rover to drive past.

The bridge was narrow, so all vehicles had to proceed slowly. Will had a good view of the car, and there appeared to be only one occupant, a man, who had his head turned away as it passed. There was something familiar about the man, but Will couldn't quite recall where from.

Will watched the car drive past and disappear into the distance.

"There you are," said Jay, "just going the same way as us."

"Maybe, but it was hardly going to stop next to us and wait for us to drive on. I thought I recognised the driver, but it was only a vague feeling. I don't know. I think this whole article thing is getting to me."

Jay took Will's arm, "come on, darling, let's have lunch. This little town is beautiful."

Will smiled, "okay, it is beautiful, and you are probably right. It was just on the same road as us." However, deep down, an anxiousness gripped like a steel band around his stomach.

As they continued their journey, the road took them through Aberfeldy, crossing another bridge over the River Tay and then north to Pitlochry.

They passed through the town and turned onto a minor road towards Loch Rannoch. On the left, the River Tummel became Loch Tummel, its water sparkling in the late summer sunshine, and on the right were the tall green firs of the Tay Forest Park. For twelve miles, the view did not disappoint. A landscape of green forests, brown mountains, and clear blue waters.

Will kept his eyes on the ribbon of road that they had left behind, but it remained empty. The stiffness in his neck eased as he rubbed hard with his hand. The tenseness that had invaded him earlier seemed to be seeping away as he looked at the scenery. He had a tremendous urge to stop the car and walk up one of the hillsides as if that would somehow resolve his problems in the clean mountain air. But it was going to take more than a long walk to get him out of this perilous situation.

They then passed a small inn, and soon after, over a small bridge, which the map described as the Bridge of Ericht and turning to the left at the western end of Loch Rannoch, Will slowed down. "We must be close now, on the left somewhere."

"There it is, Gaur House. Look, the sign has come off its post," said Jay.

Will turned the car through the run-down entrance, the gate propped up with some old tree branches and continued up the drive towards the house.

The trees that lined the drive had now overgrown into a tunnel. Dappled sunlight reflected off the water in the puddles. The car bounced over the pothole-filled track, and a sharp spasm of pain shot up Will's spine. What was left of the top surface was just two lines of earth interspersed with deep holes. He could hear the water splashes collected in the hollows as they made halting progress towards the house. Will opened the car window and smelt the slightly sweet aroma from the pine trees and the more stringent odour of damp nettles and ivy. Although the sun shone, it seemed dark as they continued to lurch up and down through the potholes. A narrow bridge lay ahead, and it looked just like a few railway sleepers lain across a gap in the track. He approached at a crawl and sat forward in his seat to check whether it looked safe to cross.

"Do you think that's okay?" asked Jay, surveying the bridge with some concern.

'We are about to find out," as Will manoeuvred the car across the bridge and over the small burn underneath.

The selling blurb about being off the beaten track appeared pretty accurate. Then the tunnel of trees suddenly disappeared, and Will caught the first view of the house and the loch. At that moment, a strange sense of curiosity enveloped him. It was as if the house was calling him to enter and seek out its secrets. He couldn't tell Jay as she would have laughed. He got out of the car and looked up at the façade of the house. The opening line from Daphne du Maurier's novel Rebecca drifted into his mind 'Last night I dreamt I went to Manderley again.' He shivered and was sure it was not because of the cool breeze blowing off the loch.

Will looked around. The house was situated on the loch's

western edge, with the back of the house facing directly eastward up the long stretch of water. No one could approach from that way at speed. The immediate area around the house was open, and anyone coming would be seen, at least during daylight.

Jay stretched her legs and back and said, "the estate agent's details said that the house required some modernisation. Well, if the house is anything like the drive, they were not wrong."

"Quite so," Will replied, rubbing the small of his back to ease the pain caused by the jolting from the drive.

Will could see from Jay's expression that she liked the house from this first sighting. Will felt something different, not quite sure what. The hairs on his neck were standing on end. He had a feeling that someone was watching them. He looked around but couldn't see anyone, although there were plenty of places where they could have been viewed unobserved.

"I'm speechless. Look at the house, look at the view, Will, it's unbelievable," said Jay grabbing his arm, "don't you love it?"

"Let's take a look at the inside before we reach any conclusions." The sighting of the Range Rover had made Will realise that just being off the beaten track would not be enough. Other security measures would be needed if they bought this house.

They walked up the three stone steps to the solid oak front door, and Will tugged at the wrought iron doorbell pull. In the distance, he could hear a bell in the house.

The signal would have been for a liveried butler or a frocked maid to scurry to greet an important house guest in the past. He suspected now the only signalling would be to the owner.

Will looked across to Jay, whose face was alive like an excited teenager.

After a minute or so, the large metal door hinges creaked. The door opened to reveal a small, pleasant-looking man dressed in brown corduroy trousers, a yellow cardigan with holes in the elbows, and a pair of carpet slippers from which his big toes poked out. His clothes made it difficult to assess the man's age, but Will thought he was probably younger than the image he portrayed. There was also a faint peppermint smell hanging around him.

"Will and Jay Slater," said Will, "we've come to view the house, which we understand is for sale. The agents should have informed you of our visit."

"Aye, it is so," and after a slight pause, "Dougie Gordon, please come in," proffering a grubby looking hand. "Before we start the tour, would ye like a wee dram?" asked Dougie.

"Could we see the house first, please?" asked Jay, as whisky was not her favourite tipple.

"Aye, can do that," said Dougie.

Sweeping his hand around in a circular motion, he said, "well, this is the hallway."

The floor consisted of large, roughly hewn tiles, some cracked and chipped in the corners, but looked as if they had been there since the house was built.

"Those are the stairs," said Dougie, indicating quite a grand staircase in the middle of the hall.

"When was the house originally built, Mr Gordon?" asked Jay.

"Please, call me Dougie. There's been a building on this site since afore the uprising in seventeen forty-five. It was a wealthy man's home then, but it was never really enlarged, unlike many Scottish homes. A wee bit was added here and there through the early eighteen hundreds, but it is largely unchanged since then."

Will was hoping some improvements and repairs had been made since that date; otherwise, the renovations would be more extensive than they already appeared.

"This is the drawing room or sitting room as modern folk like to call it," said Dougie, indicating double doors immediately to their right. Dougie stepped forward and threw open the doors in a rather theatrical manner.

Will pictured in his mind a butler doing this when summoned

by the owner for another wee dram or more baccy for his pipe. In the background, he heard Jay asking various questions about the heating as Will looked around the room. It was undoubtedly a drawing room and not a sitting room. Double doors led onto a flagstone terrace that wrapped its way around the house. A wide ornate mantlepiece and surround framed an enormous fireplace. No modern log burner was going to fill that space.

"Come on, darling," said Jay, cutting through Will's reverie as Dougie led them through another set of double doors into the library. An oak-panelled room greeted them with floor-to-ceiling bookshelves on three walls, but the shelves were empty.

Will realised Dougie must have seen the surprise on his face, as Dougie said quickly, "I was never much of a reader, prefer the TV myself,"

Will followed Jay and Dougie out of the library, but Will experienced a strange sensation as the tour continued from room to room. It was as if he was somehow being held back. He could hear his breathing accelerate as if he had been jogging. That was until they reached the billiard room when he mentally re-joined Jay and Dougie as if this was the room where he had to be. It was the same sense he had had from outside the house. The air seemed easier to breathe in here, and his breathing slowed down. Will shook his head and concentrated on the conversation between Dougie and Jay.

"Darling, it's a pity that we don't play," said Jay indicating towards the full-sized snooker table.

"Yes, it is. Perhaps we should learn?" replied Will.

Will followed as Dougie led them out into the hall again and down a corridor that led under the main staircase to the kitchen, pointing out, as they passed, the main fuse box for all the lights in the house.

"Lovely kitchen," said Jay, "might make one or two alternations if we were to buy the house."

Gut the lot, Will thought, save the Aga, providing it works.

The tour went on, the breakfast room, the scullery, and the snug with its vinyl tablecloth and enormous TV. Will almost laughed out loud when he saw it, as it was the most incongruous thing in the whole house.

The bedrooms upstairs were next on the tour, together with the antiquated plumbing in the bathrooms. At the end of the landing, another flight of stairs led to the top floor of the house. Will could hear Jay and Dougie fussing over something in one of the many bedrooms, so he decided to walk up the stairs.

The boards creaked under his feet as he mounted each step. Will stood at the top of the stairs and looked along the dark and uninviting corridor. A wisp of air brushed his cheek as if someone had breathed on him.

Will reckoned that these would have been the servants' quarters. All the doors were closed apart from the one at the end. Stopping at the first door, the handle cold to his touch, he pushed gently, but the creak made him start, and he threw open the door, half expecting to see something or someone in the room. The hairs rose on his neck again, and he felt a tingle down his spine. Absurd, he said to himself, stepping into the empty echoing room. Dust caught at the back of Will's throat, making him cough.

A small skylight window was angled at the top of the wall where it met the ceiling. Will tried jumping to see if he could get a clear view outside, but it was too high. He entered all the other tiny, drab rooms as he walked down the corridor. The last door contained a lavatory, which looked Victorian. The pan was built into a wooden construction, like a low cupboard with the lavatory seat on the top. The flush consisted of a pull handle to the left of the pan.

On re-entering the corridor, Will thought he heard someone behind him. "Hello," he called out, but there was no one there. It was just his steps magnified and echoing on the wooden floor.

The wisp of air had become stronger as he approached the

open door. A rhythmic tapping noise was coming from the room. Will peered around the corner of the door.

"Ha," he thought, it was the bathroom with a dripping tap, and the breeze was coming from the open window on the far side of the room. Will noticed a curious smell; he didn't recognise it. It wasn't particularly unpleasant, perhaps the odour of cleaning materials, although it seemed to be masking another underlying odour. A puddle of water had formed on the window ledge from the open window. Will stepped around the old roll-top bath, stained brown with water drips, to close it. He gazed out at the view of the loch. It was a beautiful artist's canvass apart from the malevolent addition of a black Range Rover, its windows like dark eyes steering over the loch towards him.

* * *

Will hurried away from the window and descended quickly to the next floor to meet Jay and Dougie at the foot of the stairs.

"What's up there?" asked Jay.

"Just more empty rooms," Will replied, "let's go downstairs and take up Dougie's offer of a drink."

Jay looked at Will curiously. "Oh, okay then."

"Excellent," said Dougie, "excellent idea indeed."

They all descended to the drawing room, and Dougie said, "take a seat while I pour some drinks. Perhaps a wee dram while we talk about price."

On a table in the corner of the room stood glasses and a decanter half full of brown liquid, which Will hoped would be a malt whisky, but suspected it wouldn't, and he was right.

Will watched Dougie pour three large glasses. Distributing two, before he took a large swig from his glass, making a sound that indicated a degree of pleasure before wiping his mouth with the back of his hand. He then launched himself backwards into a comfy chair without spilling a drop from his glass. Well-practiced, Will thought.

Sipping indifferent whisky, corralled in a claustrophobic prison of brocade, feathers, and broken springs of Dougie's settee, Will noticed that a wind had sprung up outside. The window frames rattled, and the whistling seemed like a voice speaking to him.

He had never thought of himself as a person who believed in the paranormal. He was a lawyer, for goodness sake, feet on the ground, symbolic scales of justice in his hand. But something abnormal had occurred. As Will sat there, once again closeted in his world, he remembered his father telling him that he and his mother had looked at buying a house in the country when Will had been very young. But his father had noticed a strange sensation in the garden during the viewing. Later the estate agent had told his parents that the previous owner had hanged himself from the very tree under which his father had stood. Perhaps, that extra sense ran in the family.

The whistling of the wind echoing in Will's head convinced him that it was telling him to buy the house. He should have felt spooked in some way, but he was calm.

"Will, are you listening to me? You seem to be miles away?" said Jay.

Will shook his head to clear it of imagery. "Yes, sorry I was. Now, what do you think, should we make an offer for the house?" Will said, smiling at Jay.

"Yes, I think we should."

Turning to Dougie, Will said, "looks like we have a starting point, Dougie, but I don't much like the asking price. There is a huge amount of work needed, which is going to cost a lot of money."

"Aye, a wee bit of modernisation needs to be done, but your lassie here says you have the money to do it."

Will frowned as he was annoyed that Jay had made mention

of his wealth but let it pass. "That's not the point, there has to be value for money, Dougie, or we will walk away."

"No, no, don't do that. What had ye in mind then?"

"Well, the asking price was one point five million. I will offer you one and a quarter million, no negotiating. That is to include all the contents, save anything you want to take to your new home. The money can be in your bank as soon as the legals are complete."

There was no hesitation, "agreed, and that calls for another wee dram," said Dougie and sprang up to recharge the glasses.

Jay looked across at Will, smiled, and winked.

Dougie managed again to juggle the three huge glasses of whisky across the room.

"So, when would you be moving in?" asked Dougie.

"We have sold up in London, so we would like to move in as soon as possible," replied Jay.

"Grand, grand."

"Do you have a map of the estate, Dougie?" Will asked.

"Aye, I do that," he said as he jumped up again, spritely for a man of his age and full of whisky.

Will thought Dougie was a likeable character, slightly roguish, but something else didn't seem to fit with the house.

Dougie scampered back from the bureau in the corner of the room, waving a tattered document.

"Quite old, but it does the job," he said, spreading the map out on the coffee table in front of them. "You see, the land's almost like a horseshoe in shape. It stretches around the edge of the loch until you get to here," he said, jabbing his finger down aggressively on what looked like the south side of the loch. Will peered at the map, and there was a large cross where Dougie was pointing.

"What happens here, Dougie?" Will asked.

"Well, this land used to be part of the estate, but this chap, Roddy Neath, asked if he could buy it so he could open a water sports centre. The cash was quite useful. It is only a wee strip, with frontage onto the loch for his sailing dinghies and kayaks. Waste of time if you ask me. You never know he might want to sell the land back to you," laughing, Dougie got up and poured himself another large glass of whisky.

"Anyway," he continued, "the estate is about a couple of miles or so, towards the southeast. Then it follows the road in a big loop up to the west, back towards the north across the drive, with the end of the land just abutting the road by the inn. There's a wee path that runs up to the road with a gate right opposite the inn. Two thousand acres, mainly wood and moor, but beautiful frontage onto the loch. If it weren't too big for me, I wouldn't be selling."

"Fantastic, I can't wait to explore," said Jay.

"And me," Will said. "Do you have any help to manage the land?"

"Aye, I do, Angus Mack, the ghillie, worked on this land all his life and his father 'fore him."

"Do you think he would continue to work for us?" Will asked.

"Aye, Mack's a good pal, can't see why not, provided you pay him," said Dougie laughing at his joke.

"I would like to meet him. Where does he live?"

"He has a caravan on the land. If you follow the track towards that water sports centre, you can't miss it. About half a mile that way," said Dougie waving his arm.

"What does a ghillie mean, Dougie?" asked Jay.

"A ghillie, historically, was responsible for looking after the game on large estates, fish, game birds, and deer. Often acting as a gamekeeper protecting against poaching and controlling the predators like foxes and otters, and generally taking care of the wildlife," replied Dougie.

"Sounds like an essential person on the estate," said Jay.

"Aye, but we don't have a lot of game on the land now, and

Mack mainly helps to keep the estate tidy, cutting down fallen trees, mending fences, and the like. Now, another wee dram, for both you folks?" asked Dougie waving his empty glass.

"No, I'm fine, thanks, Dougie," replied Jay.

"I guess we had better get going. What about the inn by the loch? Any good?" asked Will, "Jay and I have to stay somewhere tonight."

"Aye, the Lochside Inn, run by Hamish and Lydia MacInnish. Great name for an innkeeper," said Dougie and roared with laughter again. "Good little pub, great food; Lydia is one of those cordon bleu chefs. I've never stayed there. Nice people."

"Great. Thanks, Dougie. It's time we were moving. We need to get the lawyers motivated to doing this deal quickly. Do you have the name of the solicitor whom you will be using?"

"Aye," said Dougie removing a surprisingly crisp business card from his pocket. Suppose he was expecting the request, thought Will as he fingered the card before putting it into his own pocket.

"You sure you don't want a final wee dram for the road? I certainly could do with another wee one after all this excitement," said Dougie.

"No, I think we are both fine, thank you, Dougie," said Jay, looking across at Will and nodding.

"Don't worry about showing us out. We can find our way and look forward to seeing you again very soon, Dougie," Will said.

"Yes, goodbye, Dougie, and thank you very much. We are both very excited," said Jay hugging Will's arm.

"Okay, cheerio for now," came the reply.

Will and Jay retraced their steps back to the car.

"Wow, can't believe we have just bought this place," said Jay.

"Well, not quite, still a few legals and I think we should do a survey if only to highlight areas of work that need attending to. Let's not 'cross our bridges' quite yet."

"Spoilsport, can't a girl dream?"

“What makes you like the house so much?”

“There is so much we can do here; stamp our mark on it. Bring it back to life, to its original standard. What about you?”

Will thought hard about his reply, “yes, bringing it back to life.” Or maybe find out what died originally, he added to himself. “I found the place,” he paused, “haunting.”

“Well, it’s incredibly old. There have probably been some mysterious goings-on over the years. Strange deaths.”

“Sure, but I don’t think it is haunted as such. That wasn’t the sense I felt, more that something needed to be discovered. I don’t know; I’m probably being stupid. Anyway, talking of strange things, while I was upstairs looking out of a window, I spotted that Range Rover again. I told you it was following us. Someone now knows where we are.”

“How do you know it was the same one?”

Will cocked his head to one side as he looked at Jay, “I don’t, but it sure looked like it.”

“Okay, perhaps you are right. Let’s keep a watch out for it. There is nothing we can do immediately. Come on, time to find this inn. I’m exhausted from the excitement and Dougie’s whiskies,” said Jay.

CHAPTER FIVE

The thick, dog-eared file taunted Dawkin as it lay staring at him.

He knew every case note, every witness statement, in fact, every word in the file, so there was little point in rereading it. It had been his case. He had been commended for putting a leading terrorist arms dealer in prison and breaking up the gang of Eastern Europeans who were supplying the arms. In many ways, it had been his most successful case. High profile in the press and throughout the Met. In the end, everything seemed to fit into place. The guilty were either dead or in prison. But there was still a nagging in his head, like dull toothache, always near the surface but not enough of a pain to keep you awake at night. The only person to come out scot-free was Will Slater, and he had been central to the whole case. He told everyone that he had been betrayed by those around him and knew nothing about the arms dealing. Dawkin had always been sceptical, but Michael Bore had admitted everything, and there was no case against Slater. There was still a nagging suspicion that he had missed something which would prove Slater was guilty.

He stretched back in his chair, frustrated that he couldn't find the answer, and dispirited because no one else thought the same way as he did. As he stared at the cracked and peeling ceiling in the hope that some bright idea would float into his mind, his office door was flung open.

"What's up, Guv?" asked Sergeant Edkins as he strode into the office.

Dawkin was annoyed by the unruly interruption, "don't you ever fucking knock?"

"Sorry, Guv just wondered if we had a new case to get our teeth into? What's that you've got there?" said Edkins looking at the unopened file and peering at the name on the front. "Not the Slater file, Guv, thought that was all tied up and finished."

"Well, it isn't. Not in my opinion. It was all too clean at the end. There are always loose ends in every case, but not here."

"But Michael Bore admitted everything, and he is in prison and will be for a long time."

"Well, there has been another development," said Dawkin.

"What's that then, Guv?"

"I had a bloke on the blower from some Financial Services Authority in the Virgin Islands. When they arrested the banker involved in the Slater case, the man who collected all the money from the arms deals had two telephone numbers on a sheet of paper pertaining to Slater's company. This banker said that he was told that he had to phone both numbers in the event of a withdrawal of the money. Well, Slater, so he said, worked out where the money was and tricked the banker into moving it into his account. So, the banker had to make the two calls."

"I remember, Guv, one belonged to Michael Bore, but they never found out who the second one belonged to," replied Edkins.

"Yeah, yeah. It turns out that the second telephone number has now been answered." Dawkin paused.

"Well, who answered it, Guv?"

"The bloke didn't know. Whoever answered the call didn't speak. He asked me if I knew or at least had an idea."

"What did you say?"

"I didn't say anything. Said I didn't know, but of course, I do know."

"You do?"

"Yeah, it can only be one person. Will Slater."

"We have been here before, Guv. This is not a new development."

"Of course, it is a development. We now know that the other person is out there, somewhere."

"But we can't prove it's Slater any more than we could during the case. Anyone could have picked up that phone and answered the ring. If the phone had been chucked away, anyone could have picked it up. It could have been a child or someone in the street. So I can't see we have any grounds for spending any more time on this Guv."

Annoyed by his presence and because he disagreed with him, Dawkin flicked his hand, indicating that Edkins should leave, and said, "go on, you must have some work to do."

Dawkin stared down again at the unopened file. Edkins was right. He was no further forward even after the call. He rested his hands on the tired brown manila cover in the hope some divine inspiration might permeate through the cardboard. Then something did occur to him. What was it Edkins said? Something seemed important. Closing his eyes, he tried to recall Edkins' exact words. 'Anyone could have picked up the phone and answered it. It could have been a child….' That's it. I'm sure that's it.

Pushing his chair back and oblivious to the crash as it hit the wall, he kept saying out loud, "that's it, that's it." Then, lurching out of his office, he bellowed, "Edkins, Edkins, I think I have got it. The children, we never did any checks on them. What about Crombie's and Slater's other partners' children. Do we know if

Bore had any children? Do some checking and let me have the details."

Dawkin watched Edkins shrug his shoulders and slope off to his desk. Dawkin smiled in satisfaction with his discovery and returned to his office.

CHAPTER SIX

Will and Jay checked into the Lochside Inn. It was run by Hamish and Lydia MacInnish, a husband and wife team. Rather than take one of the newish chalets at the rear of the hotel, they booked one of the older rooms with views across the loch.

After a good dinner, lying on their bed, iPad balanced on her lap, Jay watched Will standing in front of the window, staring across the loch. "What can you see, darling?"

"That's just it. I can't see anything. There's the reflection from the hotel lights across the edge of the loch, but apart from that, absolutely nothing. Just coal black."

"Not even a flicker of a candle from the ghost walking the floors of Gaur House?"

"Ha, ha, very funny. Whatever you say, there is something about that house that I must discover. It is a strange feeling. I can't describe it. I have never felt anything like that before. It doesn't unnerve me, though. I don't feel frightened; it's…" he paused. "It's as if it's a puzzle that needs to be solved."

"Well, I'm sure we will, whatever it is."

"What did you make of Dougie?" asked Will.

"Rather long-winded but charming, just as I imagined he would be. Why do you ask?"

"Nothing concrete, but I had this image that he didn't feel comfortable in the house. He seemed more like an agent selling the place rather than a loving owner. It was all so tidy too. No personal things, apart from that horrendous telly. No books on the shelves. Didn't that strike you odd?"

"Well, he explained that by saying he was not much of a reader."

"Yes, but he isn't the first owner of the house. Surely an earlier member of the family would have stacked the shelves. I don't know, call it a lawyer's nose, but there was something not quite right about Dougie. How old do you think he is?"

"I don't know, late sixties, early seventies perhaps."

"I think he is younger than that; late fifties would be my guess. But he wanted to give us the impression that he was older."

"Why would he want to do that?"

"I don't know. Another little mystery about the house. Anyway, I'm going to have a shower."

Jay closed her eyes. She could hear the water from the en-suite. It was a normal and reassuring sound so different from her dangerous past. For ten years, she had been a specialist anti-terrorism officer working for SO15. Before that, a police officer since university.

What would life have been like if Paul, her husband, hadn't stepped on an IED in Iraq? Would they have been happy? Lucy would have a father, but then Jay would probably never have met Will. That would have been a shame. He was a kind and resourceful man that had been trapped in an evil scheme through no fault of his own. Perhaps he had been a little too gullible and naïve, but that's not a crime, indeed nothing that should have caused such a monumental change to his life. Jay's mind wandered back to the assignment when she had first met Will.

Her job had been to protect him. Keep him alive. She had killed two men to ensure that the man showering in the room next door stayed alive. It was inconceivable that an SO15 officer should fall in love with someone they were protecting, but she had.

She was brought out of her reverie by the single ping of her mobile. As she read the words of the message, a frown formed on her forehead. Even in the most dangerous missions, she had always been in control or at least could take control of her own volition. It seemed different now. As she re-read the message, Jay realised that she was no longer in control, and it was like turning the pages of a novel. She didn't know what was going to happen until she read the next page. The one thing she was sure about was that they were both in a lot of danger. But before she told Will, she wanted to find out the exact nature of the threat.

* * *

The following morning, Jay said goodbye to Will. She had arranged to drive to Fettes School in Edinburgh, where Lucy would start her final two years.

"Have a good trip. I'm going to trespass on Dougie's land in the hope it will be ours soon," said Will.

"Perhaps you should call him first, just to let him know you will be roaming on his land. You wouldn't want his ghillie to shoot you."

"Yes, good idea, I will."

Jay had a stop to make before she travelled to Edinburgh. Heading first for the village of Kinloch Rannoch, she pulled in beside the statue of Dugal Buchanan. She gazed into the face of the man who helped to orchestrate the peace in this hitherto dangerous land during the eighteenth century. Jay switched off the engine and waited. A couple of minutes later, a black Range Rover pulled up. Jay watched as the driver's window lowered. She got out and walked back towards the other car and exchanged a few words. Frowning as she got back into her car, she reached across and slid a package into the glove compartment. As the Range Rover sped off as she pondered on the conversation she had just had. She looked up again at the statue of Dugal. Not much had changed in all the intervening years. There were still a lot of bad people about. Shaking her head, she started the car.

CHAPTER SEVEN

Will called Dougie as soon as Jay had left, but there was no reply, and he wandered downstairs to see if the hotel could rustle up a packed lunch to take on his walk.

Hamish was in the bar clearing up after the night before.

"Good morning, Mr Slater, 'trust you had a comfortable night?"

"Yes, good, thanks, Hamish. Please, call me Will, as I'm hoping we will be neighbours before long. We have put in an offer for Gaur House."

"Grand old house, that one. 'Am surprised Dougie Gordon's selling it. It has been in his family for years. We've not seen Dougie in here for a couple of weeks. What did you make of him?"

"Seemed a nice bloke, quite affable. Likes his whisky, though!"

"Hmmm, maybe, he never drank much when he came in here. Half a pint of heavy or occasionally a wee dram, and then he was away doon the road."

"Thought I might try and find his ghillie, Mack?" said Will.

"Aye, Mack it is, lives in an old caravan on the land somewhere. Never seen it myself."

"Don't suppose your wife could rustle up a sandwich and a bottle of water for me to take as lunch?"

"Aye, of course, she will. Hold on here, and will pop into the kitchen to ask her."

He returned a few moments later. "It'll be about ten minutes."

"Great, thank you. I'll sit outside until it's ready."

Will stepped outside. It was a beautiful late summer's day. He closed his eyes and let the warmth from the sun momentarily dull his anxiety. A cool breeze brought him back to the stark reality that he could not lower his guard. He crossed the road that separated the inn from the loch and stepped over the low boundary wall. The shingle crunched under his feet, and the aroma of seaweed invaded his nasal passages. He sauntered the few feet to the water's edge. The sun was shining on the water, lighting up the crests of tiny waves that meandered in higgledy-piggledy patterns across the loch. However, it looked dark and somehow foreboding, the deep black water matching his inner turmoil.

Will turned back to look at the inn. The morning sun reflected on the white pebbledash walls and blue wooden shutters. There were some seats outside interspersed with tubs of summer flowers. As he shielded his eyes with his hand, a slight movement caught his attention. A curtain twitched in one of the upstairs bedroom windows. He was sure it was in the room next to their bedroom. Cupping his hand to shield his eyes from the glare, he stared up, and although he could not be sure, he thought he had seen a shadow at the window. Being watched again, he thought, and with that, a notion filled his mind. Hurrying across the road, he entered the car park, convinced he would see a black Range Rover. Nothing, just a few non-descript cars.

"There you are," called out Hamish waving a little carrier bag, "thought you had gone without it. One of Lydia's specials, I suspect."

"Thank her very much. Tell me, is there anyone staying in the room next to ours?"

"No, it's empty. Why do you ask?" replied Hamish.

"No reason really, just thought I saw someone at the window but hadn't heard anyone in the room last night."

"I expect it is one of the cleaners checking everything is okay for the next guest. I will ask."

"No, don't bother. It's nothing, probably just my imagination."

"Okay, see you later."

Will made a mental note to mention it to Jay later.

* * *

The path that led directly to Gaur House was protected by an old gate that appeared not to have been opened in years. Flaky brown metal showed through the peeling black paint of the rusted wrought iron. The hinges sagged and were no longer acting as support. The earth smelt damp as Will kicked an accumulation of nettles from the bottom of the gate. He could have climbed over it but set himself a small challenge to try and get it open. He was going to have to lift it on its hinges and push it open. He bent his legs, trying to keep his back straight and getting his hands under one of the lower metal bars. He drove his legs upwards, pushing the gate at the same time. The blood pulsed in his head, his ears buzzed, and dribbles of sweat trickled down his face and back. He was defeated for a few seconds, but then slowly, the gate shuddered open a few inches. More exertion, more buzzing, more sweat, and then it opened with a rush, and Will just managed to keep his balance as both he and the gate propelled forward.

The promised path was no more than a slightly less dense part of the wood. Picking up the lunch bag and donning a pair of gloves from his pocket, he started walking in the direction of the house.

He soon realised that he had come ill-equipped for the journey. The paper lunch bag was soon in tatters, its contents now stuffed into his coat pockets, his trousers were ripped, and his gloves were inadequate protection from the thorns and the vicious nettles. The air was oppressive, laden with dampness and woody smell, and after a couple of hundred yards, he had to stop for a break. His breathing was ragged, and sweat was now streaming down his back and collecting in the waistband of his trousers. He removed his coat and struggled on. Mud clung to his shoes in lumps and acted as suction on wet parts of the track and, on several occasions, pulled the shoes off his feet. Bedraggled, hot, and increasingly annoyed, Will tramped on believing that he was now lost. Stopping to get his bearings, he could hear gurgling water. Stepping forward through some more nettles, the ground under his feet disappeared. He started to fall; twisting his body, he grabbed an old tree root. Swearing loudly, he scrambled back up the bank and looked down at the sheer side of a narrow but deep burn. It was too wide to jump across, and he wasn't about to paddle. Traversing upstream along the side of the burn, Will discovered a thick tree branch that had fallen across from one bank to the other. The branch didn't look rotten and having tested it with his foot, he sidestepped across the gap. He hoped it was the same burn that the bridge crossed in the drive, in which case, he was not far from the house. A surge of optimism revitalised his spirits, and his steps seemed to lighten even with the encased mud. After a few more minutes doing battle with nature, he stepped out into the open. In front of him was Gaur House looking even more impressive than it had yesterday.

Will looked down at himself. He looked like a tramp. He brushed off some loose debris and stamped his feet to remove the mud, but it didn't change his overall appearance. Bugger it, he thought, I might as well continue as planned. He climbed the front steps and pulled the ancient doorbell. No response. After a minute, he pulled again, this time placing his ear against the rough wood of the door. Still no response. Perhaps Dougie was in the kitchen? Will walked around to the back of the house and knocked on the kitchen door, listening again. Nothing. The polished brass handle felt cold as he turned it and pushed the door. It opened with a loud creak.

"Dougie, it's Will Slater. Dougie, are you there?" Still no reply. Perhaps Dougie was watching morning tv on his enormous telly. Will listened, but the only sound was the buzzing of a blue-bottle. Stepping into the kitchen, Will noticed that everything was tidy and in its place. He liked a tidy kitchen, but this was unnatural. A touch of the kettle told him that it hadn't been used recently. Will wondered if Dougie had been taken ill and called out again, "Dougie, are you okay? It's Will Slater." There was no reply. Everything was still; a shaft of light from the kitchen window reflected dust particles dancing in a frenzy. Instinctively, Will was sure he was not alone in the house. He had read that people transmit vibrational energy even when you can't see them. Whatever it was, he sensed someone now.

"Hello, is there anyone there?" The only sound was from the birds through the open back door. Now on his guard, Will walked out of the kitchen into the snug and ran his fingers down the back of the TV. Cold.

"Dougie," Will called again. He stepped back into the kitchen. The hairs on his neck were doing handstands. The tiled floor felt sticky under his feet as he opened the ancient fridge. The inside light startled him and glared into his eyes in the gloom of the kitchen. The fridge was empty. Entirely empty. How could anyone live in a house with an empty fridge? As Will turned to contemplate his discovery, he caught a fleeting movement out of the corner of his eye, and a shadow rushed towards him with something raised in the air. Will threw up his arms as protection and ducked to one knee. He felt the hair on his head ruffle from the downward draught of the shadow's arm before the crack on his head that sent him into a crumpled heap of legs and arms, his face resting against the cold, damp tiles as he glimpsed his attacker scurry out through the back door.

"Aargh," he cried out, "what the fuck?" He felt the trickle of blood making its way down his cheek, and gingerly he sat up and propped himself against the fridge. Nausea was rising in his stomach. Supported by the kitchen table, he pulled himself up and staggered outside, taking deep breaths. He leaned against the door frame until he thought he could take a few steps. The attacker would be long gone, or at least he hoped that would be the case. His head ached. He dabbed the wound with his handkerchief. There was a lot of blood, but bleeding from a head wound was not indicative of the severity of the damage. He made his way over to a bench that faced the loch and sat down. Sips from the bottle of water helped settle his stomach, and his breathing returned to a steady rhythm. His hands shook as he tried to replace the top on the water bottle. He had a ringing in his ears; he shook his head, but the ringing went on, and he realised it was his phone.

"How are you, honey, not getting up to any mischief?" asked Jay.

"I have just been attacked at Gaur House."

"What! Are you alright?"

"I have a slight cut on my head and feel a bit shaky, but otherwise, alright."

"Who attacked you? Is Dougie with you? Have you called the police? Do you need an ambulance?"

"Hold on, hold on, too many questions. I didn't see who attacked me and Dougie isn't here. It is all bizarre. The house is empty; nothing in the fridge, and the kitchen hasn't been used for a while. Yes, my head is a little painful, but I have had some water and will eat Lydia's lunch. So, should feel better."

"Okay, I'm on my way back. It will be another ninety minutes or so. I will meet you in front of Gaur House. Don't go back inside. Stay in the open and call me immediately if you see anyone."

"Okay, call me when you get a bit nearer. Love you. See you soon."

"Love you too. Remember, stay in the open."

Will sipped some more water and had a bite of sandwich, but he wasn't feeling very hungry.

Not wanting to sit in the open for the next ninety minutes, he decided to see whether he felt able to continue on his journey. Stuffing the rest of his lunch in his coat pocket, he got up. His head swam for a few seconds, and he thought he might be sick, but it passed. He wondered if he had concussion but could remember the day, the date, and birthday, so he decided to press on. He headed towards the track that Dougie had indicated would lead him to Angus Mack's caravan.

Up ahead, the track entered the woods. He picked up a stout branch to act as a weapon and continued. The way looked well-trodden, and progress was a lot quicker than his earlier trek. After a few minutes of walking, a distinct aroma of burning wood drifted on the breeze. Will thought he must be near his destination. The track opened into a clearing and in the middle was a ramshackle caravan. The tyres were flat, and several piles of bricks supported the frame. There was a large tarpaulin covering the roof, and the windows were crazed. Will doubted whether anyone could see out. At the front of the caravan, a wood fire smouldered. A washing line hung from the caravan's side to a nearby tree, and an axe rested against a pile of logs.

Will felt a chill breeze in the air. The temperature had dropped several degrees under the dark canopy of fir trees. He could hear himself breathing loudly, and the dull pain in his head had momentarily disappeared and been replaced by a cold shiver down his spine. The clearing looked like a set from a murder mystery TV programme. As the breeze changed direction, the smoke swirled, his eyes smarted, and the acrid smoke caught in the back of his throat. He coughed. How stupid he was. Suppose Mack was his attacker, and he had just walked into his lair? He thought about quietly retracing his steps, but he had got this far, so he decided against it. Gripping the rough bark of his makeshift weapon more tightly, he called out.

"Hello, Mr Mack, are you there? Hello?"

There was no reply for a few moments, and then suddenly, a voice came from behind Will. His heart missed a beat as he turned to meet the owner.

"And who might you be, pal?"

Standing behind Will was one of the biggest men he had ever seen. He was too big to have been his attacker, and no one would be standing up after a blow from this giant. He was about six foot eight in height, probably eighteen stone, and looked all muscle. Difficult to tell his age from his leathery, weather-beaten face.

"Hi, I'm Will Slater. Are you Angus Mack?"

"Aye, that'll be me."

"Great, I'm hoping to buy Gaur House. I have put in an offer which Dougie Gordon has accepted," said Will offering his hand in greeting.

Will could see the suspicion on the ghillie's face as he hesitantly extended his arm. Will's hand disappeared into an enormous palm, the size of a dinner plate.

Will could see Mack looking him up and down, staring at his appearance. "I had a fall this morning on the way to the house, hence the state of my clothes."

"Hit yer head too."

Will put his hand up to the wound, "yes, but not from the fall. When I was at the house a few minutes ago, someone rushed at me and hit me on the head." Will paused, expecting some comment, but Mack just continued to stare at him. "You didn't see anyone around, did you?" Mack shook his head slowly. Will thought he would remain silent, but then he saw words forming on the ghillie's lips.

"Been a stranger on the land these past few days. Caught sight of him, but he was moving as if he knew how to run in a wood."

"Maybe that was my attacker. Unfortunately, I didn't get a good look at him. Perhaps you can keep an eye out?"

Will paused but again got no reaction, so he went on, "the strange thing is that the house was empty. It didn't look as if anyone was living there. When did you see Dougie last?"

"I haven't seen Dougie for a couple of weeks."

"Oh, I see. Anyway, I just wanted to introduce myself and say I hope you will continue working for my wife, Jay, and me after completing the purchase. Dougie tells us you know the estate very well."

"Aye, I know the estate well, brought up here and me Daddy afore me."

"So, assuming the purchase goes through, will you continue to work for us?"

Mack raised his head as if pondering the offer. "Aye, I will, Mr Slater."

"That is great news. Please call me Will. I understand you like to be called Mack."

"Aye, Mack's fine."

"If you don't see Dougie very often, how does he tell you what work needs doing?"

"Well, recently, he's been letting me get on with whatever I think needs doing. Occasionally he leaves a message on the barn door."

"A bit odd," Will replied.

"Aye, but I'm used to it," replied Mack.

"Okay, think I had better get back to the house as my wife is picking me up shortly," Will said, looking at his watch. "How do I contact you? Leave a note on the barn door too?"

Mack smiled, tilting his head to one side and pulled his mobile phone out of his pocket.

Will laughed. "Of course." They exchanged numbers, and then Will headed back.

He had almost reached the house when his phone rang. It was Jay saying she had just arrived.

"Stay in the car, don't get out. You don't know who's around. I will be a couple of minutes," said Will.

As Will got into the car, Jay said immediately, "let me have a look at your head."

"It's not too bad, it has stopped bleeding, but I have a bad headache."

"I've got some painkillers in my bag," and after a moment's rummaging, she extracted two tablets from their packaging. "Here, take these, and here's some water. So, what happened?"

"It's all a bit hazy. There was no answer from the front door, so I walked around to the kitchen and the door was open, so I went in. I called out, but no one answered. What is strange is that it doesn't look as if Dougie is living there. The fridge is empty."

"That is strange. Dougie didn't imply he was living elsewhere when we met him. But what about your attacker?"

"Just getting there. I was looking in the fridge when the attacker rushed me and hit me. I ducked, so the blow glanced my head."

"Did you get a good look at him, I assume a man?"

"Not really, yes, it was a man, and although it was quite dim in the kitchen, I got the impression that he may have had red hair."

Jay screwed up her face.

"I know what you are thinking. I have issues around men with red hair."

"Well!"

"Can I remind you that last year I was almost killed by being pushed in front of a Tube train in the London Underground by a man with red hair. I can still feel the shove on my shoulder and continue to have nightmares of falling off the edge of the platform as the train thundered into the station."

"I know, I know," said Jay trying to sound sympathetic.

"I only survived because another passenger grabbed my collar, and he had seen a man with red hair immediately behind me just before I fell."

"But we know that was Sara Crombie's husband, Peter, and he's dead, killed in front of your own eyes by Sara. So, he can't have been in Gaur House an hour or so ago."

"Yes, I appreciate that, but that doesn't mean there isn't someone else out there."

"Why would anyone want to attack you then? You didn't know they were there. Whoever it was could have stayed hidden and then just walked out after you had gone."

"I know. What was the attacker doing there in any case? The house is pretty empty. It doesn't look as if there is anything to steal. I reckon the family flogged the silver a long time ago. It must be to do with the so-called missing money. I'm sure of it. I told you that article was going to be a big problem."

"Maybe, but we have only just got here, and we haven't even bought the house yet. So, if he wanted to hurt you, he didn't do much of a job."

"Very reassuring, thank you. Mack, the ghillie, said he had spotted someone on the land but didn't see who it was."

"We should report it to the police?"

"Yes, perhaps, although I'm not sure what they will be able to do. Let's get back to the inn. I could do with a lie-down."

CHAPTER EIGHT

The room was at the rear of a café in East London. Condensation from inside and damp from outside had created brown patches on the magnolia coloured paint. The smell of old frying fat hung in the air like an invisible cloud and attached itself to everything. Marius Vassily and Christophe Westinivic sat opposite across an old scoured and scratched kitchen table that now functioned as a desk. Marius, arms behind his head, leant back in his chair and gazed up at the patched and peeling ceiling and said, "a bit different from the days when the Boss was free."

"Yeah, fucking right. As soon as the Boss went inside, another gang was always going to take over. A sniff of weakness, and then they're in," replied Christophe.

"Well, we ain't going to make much from protection and minor drug supplying."

"I have been thinking about that. Maybe the answer is this bloke Slater."

"How?" asked Marius

"Look, the Boss is in prison, and there is nothing he can do to us. This Slater bloke owes the Boss a lot of money, so perhaps we can suggest that he gives it to us instead. The Boss won't know."

"It might get out; Slater might even get a message to him as revenge. Then we would be the targets."

"Not if we kill Slater after we get the money."

"That would work," said Marius nodding his head.

"The question is, how do we find Slater? We haven't been successful so far. He seems to have disappeared - no forwarding address from his previous home. The new owner of his house, this woman, gave me the solicitors' telephone number. Waste of time. Can't see them giving us his details."

"Naw, anyway, we don't want to put him on guard that we are looking for him," replied Marius.

"So, the only lead we've got is that this woman gave the impression that Slater may have moved to Scotland."

"Scotland's a big place. We've got to narrow the area down. Let's try the internet first." Marius tapped a few keys on his laptop. "Look, there is some stuff about Slater."

Christophe peered over Marius's shoulder at the screen.

"This was about the shooting when the Boss got caught," said Marius.

"What about that? There's a link to an article by a journalist," said Christophe.

They both read the 'missing millions' article from the Sunday paper.

"Didn't know much about that. It looks like Slater has got a lot of money. More than he owes the Boss. This could be our lucky day, Marius. Perhaps this journalist, David Fringell, might know where Slater is?" suggested Christophe.

"I would have thought so. Fringell must have tried to contact Slater about the article. We could try, but what can we say without incriminating ourselves or arousing his suspicions?" asked Marius.

"Not sure, but maybe the direct approach is the best. Is there a number?"

"Yes, and an email address," said Marius.

"We don't want to contact him using our email address. Let's give him a call. I will use this new burner and throw it away after we have spoken to him."

Christophe dialled the mobile number and got a voicemail. "Mr Fringell, I wonder if you would call me. I would like to talk to you about Will Slater and your article in the newspaper. My number is…."

"How long before he phones, do you reckon?" mused Marius.

"If he bothers," said Christophe.

They both sat transfixed by the phone that sat silently on the table between them. Eyes willing a flashing screen and a vibrating shuffle. They didn't have long to wait.

"Mr Fringell," said Christophe, confident of whom it was, "you don't know me, and it is probably wise that you don't ask any questions. I'm very keen to find out where Will Slater now lives."

After a pause, Fringell replied, "why would I want to give you this information? Why do you want to contact him?"

"I thought I said that it was not wise to ask any questions, Mr Fringell?"

"Seems that we have reached an impasse," Fringell replied.

"I don't understand, Mr Fringell. I just want to know where Will Slater is. However, I'm sure I can find out where you are."

"That sounds like some type of threat."

"I'm just saying; it would be helpful to us both if you could give me Slater's address."

There was a short silence.

"Okay, I don't have the exact address, but he has left London and moved to Scotland. The Highlands, somewhere quite remote near Pitlochry."

"How do you know that?"

“I found out from the new owners of his house which removal company he had used. I phoned them on the pretence that I was moving to Scotland and a friend had just used them. They let it slip that the move was close to Pitlochry. I don’t know anymore and hope that will be the end of this conversation?”

“Thank you, Mr Fringell. I suggest you forget this chat and it would be very unwise to tell Mr Slater that we called. Do you understand?”

“Yes, perfectly.”

Christophe finished the call, removed the sim card from the phone, and fed it through the shredder.

“Looks like we will be taking a trip to Scotland, Marius.”

CHAPTER NINE

Roddy Neath looked out of his office window towards the loch. In front of him was the slipway for his water sports centre, where he launched his kayaks, canoes, and small sailing vessels for the hiring punters. The trade was very seasonal and weather dependent. Still, he was pleased with the development of the business since buying the land from Dougie Gordon.

Roddy thought he might get a few more weeks of trade if the autumn was kind. It had been in the past. Autumn's weather could be more tranquil than summer. He liked the autumn and how the sun caressed the flowers with gentle rays, picking out the colours without the harshness of the high summer sun. The trees with various hues of red, yellow, and green; the crunch of the fallen leaves underfoot as winter made its stealthy approach. Today, however, it was all different as the rain was hammering it down, being blown in gusts across the loch in clouds of mist. There would be no clients today. Roddy was not disappointed; he had had a good summer so far, bookings up on last year and money in the bank.

The phone rang. "Hello, Water Sports Centre," Neath said

into the handset. The voice at the other end was quiet, but Roddy recognised it immediately, and he listened intently.

"Roddy, we need your help," said the voice down the phone, "can we meet up, so I can explain what needs doing? What about tomorrow at my place?"

"I suppose so," and after a slight pause, "okay, see you tomorrow, about midday?"

"Perfect."

Slowly Roddy lowered the phone into its cradle and leaned back in his chair. He was not happy about the conversation. Even though he didn't know what was needed, it would be a distraction from his business, but he saw no alternative but to comply.

The call had unnerved Roddy and brought up dark memories. Tremors started in his hands as they rested on the desk. Panic spread out like the roots of a tree, slowly covering his whole body. Heavy limbed and glued to his chair; Roddy stared out of the window at the rain ricocheting off the concrete like bullets.

He was crouched behind an armoured truck while machine gun bullets danced across the dirt road towards him, creating small eddies of dust. He could hear them hitting the side of the vehicle, deadly metallic twangs. He crouched lower, praying none would dance under the vehicle. He couldn't move; he daren't move. If he did, he would be hit. That would be quick. He wasn't afraid of death. It was the fear of that mind-numbing pain as a limb is ripped off or a huge abdominal gash that the body armour can't protect. Holding your guts in with bloodied hands until someone injects you with morphine and tells you that you will be fine, knowing they were lying.

Then the firing stopped. Everything was suddenly still. A voice called out, shattering the silence, "Neath, Neath, two injuries, get the fuck out there. We'll give covering fire."

"Yes, Sarge, on my way," Neath shouted back and adjusted his medic armbands so they were visible. He removed the medical pack from his back and peered out from the side of the armoured

vehicle. The wounded soldiers were lying on the dirt road about twenty yards away. Lying flat and calling out "covering fire," he pushed the medical pack in front of him and inched out from the cover of the vehicle. With the taste of sand in his mouth and the smell of gunshots hanging in the air, he concentrated on each movement forward. He could hear the covering fire, but that seemed to be in a different place, another part of the hell that is Helmand Province. He felt in a vacuum. All he could hear was drumming in his ears and his combat smock and body armour scraping on the uneven road. He edged forward towards the fallen men. No enemy fire yet. Just concentrate, keep moving, don't think. His knees and elbows were rubbed raw by the road. Each movement sent a spasm of pain to his brain. One final push and he would be there. He reached out his hand and felt the coarse material of the first soldier's trousers.

Wounded soldiers lie still until the medics get to them, so there is no knowing the extent of the injury. "Where does it hurt, mate?" Neath asked quietly. No reply. Neath eased himself forward, so he was now lying parallel with the soldier. He reached up and felt for the pulse at the soldier's neck. Shit, no pulse, dead, he thought. He crabbed his way around the dead man to perform the same routine on the second soldier, the same result. He would have to leave the bodies here until they had secured the area from the Taliban. He couldn't risk dragging them back. Anyway, what would be the point? They were dead.

Lying face down on the ground between two dead soldiers, Neath wanted to scream. He was lying in the middle of a filthy road, in a godawful place, fighting a battle for someone else's cause and waiting to die.

"Neath, get the fuck back here," the Sergeant shouted. Slowly Neath inched backwards away from the dead men until he was behind the armoured vehicle. He called out, "no good, Sarge, both gone."

"Get back over here, Neath; there's more work."

"I can't; I can't move, Sarge. Legs won't work."

"What do you fucking mean? Legs won't work. Have you been shot?"

"No, Sarge, but the legs won't move."

Neath smelt sour breath tumbling over his face a few seconds later as the Sergeant crouched beside him. "What's up, lad?"

"Sorry, Sarge, can't do it, can't move," as he fought back the tears.

"Okay, lad, we'll get you out of here."

He had never recovered from that day, and others like it. The constant fear seeped into every pore of his body until it took over, and he could barely take a step. Being invalided out on medical grounds was a relief, but that is only the beginning of the long hell of recovery. The regiment had been good, and especially the Sarge, who said, "don't forget we're here for each other. There may be times when you will be asked to do something to help, don't forget, we have to act."

CHAPTER TEN

Will's mobile phone rang, "hello?"

"Will, it's George McCorkney."

"Hello, George, how are you?"

"Well, thanks, thought I would call to tell you that we have just exchanged and completed the purchase of Gaur House. It's now all yours."

"That's fantastic news. I can't wait to tell Jay. She is driving her daughter, Lucy, to her new school in Edinburgh at the moment. Were there any problems that I should know about?"

"No, all went very smoothly. I was surprised by how relaxed the other side's solicitors were. Very well prepared, too."

"I expect Dougie Gordon had teed them up to make sure it went through quickly."

"Well, that's the strange thing, the house wasn't owned by Dougie, or at least not overtly. A company owned it."

"Dougie might be the majority shareholder, or perhaps the house is owned by a family trust?" Will replied.

"Maybe, difficult to tell as the shareholders were all overseas companies in tax havens. Anyway, it's yours now, so it doesn't matter who previously owned it."

"Thanks, George, for dealing with it so speedily."

"No problem, I will put all the completion documents in the post, including the deeds. I will send them to Gaur House. Speak soon. Bye for now."

"Yes, bye, George." Will flicked off his phone. Dougie didn't strike him as a person who would be involved in overseas tax planning. Yet, something about Dougie still niggled at the back of his mind. Had they done the right thing in buying this house? Too late now, he thought, it was theirs.

He dialled Jay to give her the news.

"That's wonderful. That means we can move in tomorrow."

"There are certain basics that we need to arrange first, like a bed, but broadly it is ours to do with what we wish. So, I suggest we head over tomorrow morning and start planning. When will you be back at the inn?"

"I've dropped off Lucy, and I'm on my way back, so about an hour."

"Okay, we can have a celebratory drink in the bar later. Drive carefully and see you soon. Love you."

"Love you too, bye."

* * *

The next morning armed with two pack lunches from Lydia MacInnish, pads of paper, coloured pens, tape measures and torches, Will and Jay set out for their new home. Will explained his plan for the path leading directly to the inn.

"It will make it much quicker than by road," he said.

"You can walk or ride if you like, but I'm still going to use the car. Now, what about keys to the house?" Jay asked.

"The solicitors are putting everything in the post, but I'm told there will be a key under a pot by the front door."

"Doesn't sound very safe."

"Well, it's not like London, there aren't any passers-by, and anyway, there are probably quite a few places where someone could break in if they wanted to. I intend to look at security as a priority."

As they pulled onto the track that led up to the house, Jay said, "think this drive must be one of the first jobs, or it will wreak any vehicle we buy. Look at this bridge; God knows whether it will take any removal trucks or builders' merchant lorries. The bridge looks as if it has been in place since the eighteenth century."

"Yes, agreed, will get it on the list of priorities. Hopefully, something Mack can deal with." As they pulled up to the front of the house, Will spotted the pot, which he hoped would provide their entry to the house.

They both got out of the car and stood silently for a moment in their thoughts, letting the ambience of the place envelop them. The water in the loch darkened as the sun disappeared behind a Turneresque cloud formation. A breeze rustled through the rhododendron bushes, and a couple of seagulls screamed as they swooped over the surface of the loch. The peace and solitude should have pleased Will, but somehow it only added to his anxiousness.

Will wandered over to the pot, where he hoped to find the key. But as he was about to bend down, he had the distinct sensation of being watched. He turned around quickly but saw no one.

"What's wrong? Aren't the keys there? asked Jay.

Will lied, "I thought I heard something, that's all."

"Probably the wind. Come on, let's get inside; I want to explore."

Will bent down, feeling under the pot until his fingers touched something solid in the gravel. "Here it is; looks like just one old and very large key for an old and very large front door."

Will turned the key in the lock and opened the heavy door into the hallway. The creaking door echoed through the whole of the house. Will could tell Jay was excited by the prospect of working on the building, but he could feel something different, a pull, the need to find something.

"These floor tiles will have been down since the house was built. It would be good to keep them, even though some are a bit cracked. We could cover the worst with rugs. Let's look at each room and make some plans," suggested Jay.

"Let's start with this room," he said as he swung open the door.

"Yep, okay, let's have a look at the billiard room," said Jay pushing past him in her excitement, "I'm not sure we should have kept this," indicating towards the snooker table, "neither of us plays."

"I think you might be right; Dougie didn't say he was leaving it. I suspect this wouldn't fit into his new home, wherever that may be. This room would make a nice study for both of us. We could build some shelves. Maybe we could store the snooker table in one of the outbuildings until we decide?" Will said.

"I wonder whether we should keep all this brown panelling; it is all very drab, although I guess it was here originally?" said Jay as she walked around the room. The panelling was in two sections. One section ran from the ceiling to a shallow ledge about three feet from the floor, and another section ran to the floor. "Solid wall behind it, we could remove it and re-plaster," Will said, tapping the nearest panel with his knuckles and continued to tap the panels as he walked around the room. Will stopped. "Shush, listen, this one sounds hollow. Listen." He rapped the panel again and then the next one to get a comparative sound.

"You're right. There must be a gap behind it. Perhaps it is a secret compartment," said Jay, who was now on her hands and knees examining the panel. "I think it is this lower section that is hollow. Let me get a torch from the bag."

Will got down on his hands and knees too and turned his head so his ear was up against the natural join between one panel and the next. "There's a draft; I can feel the hairs in my ear move." He ran his hand across the wood, looking for a catch. Jay passed him a torch, and he shone it at the edge of the panel. "The light isn't reflecting off the wall behind; there must be a void. You have a look."

"It may be a priest hole?" said Jay as she crouched down to examine the panel in detail. "If it is, it must be easy to open as the priests had to get into them quickly. It must be hinged somewhere. You would think that you just had to push one side of the panel like this, and it would open," she pushed the left side of the panel, but nothing happened. "Perhaps the right side," suggested Will, and as his fingers pressed against the smooth oak, he detected a slight movement. "I felt something move. Not much but not a natural give in the wood."

Placing both palms on the side of the panel, he pushed harder, letting his hands spring back. There was a click, and a narrow gap appeared at the edge of the panel. "Look, it's opened a fraction." Grabbing the edge, Will eased his fingers into the gap and pulled backwards. There was no movement at first, and then the panelling flew open, and Will flew back.

They both peered into a very uninviting black opening. The air emitting from the hole smelt stale, and there was another odour, not strong but vaguely unpleasant. Will sniffed. The smell was familiar, but he couldn't quite place it.

"Wow," said Jay, "this looks interesting."

"Take the other torch, and let's have a look at what we've got here."

Will shone his torch into the abyss. Against the edge of the gap were some wooden steps that led downwards.

"Let me test these steps and see that they are safe,"

"You don't have to do all the macho work, you know. Can I remind you how many times I have saved your life?"

"Point taken, but I'm still going to test them first."

With the end of a small torch clutched between his teeth,

Will gingerly placed one foot on the first rung of the steps. Then, holding onto the top of the open panel, he gently bounced up and down to check whether the step was rotten or not. It held firm.

"I'm going down," he said. The steps were fixed into the wall at the top and felt very firm. Peering downwards, the light of the torch reflected on the ground at the foot of the steps. "Doesn't look too far down, fifteen, twenty feet, I guess." Tucking the torch in his pocket, Will descended back down the steps. The wooded rails were rough on his hands, and Will thought a quick descent would likely involve some vicious splinters. He counted the steps in his head, and as he reached twenty, his foot hit solid ground.

"I'm at the bottom," he called up to Jay, flashing his torch into the deep darkness that now surrounded him. "The steps are okay, and it looks more like a tunnel than just a priest hole."

The unidentified smell hung stronger at the foot of the steps. Will called up, "shouldn't think this has been used for decades as it smells pretty stale. See if you can wedge the panel door open, I wouldn't want to be trapped down here."

After a few seconds, Jay called out, "okay, have wedged an old snooker cue in the gap. I'm coming down now."

Will waited until Jay had reached the bottom.

Flashing his torch in a circular motion against the walls, Will said, "let's see how far the tunnel goes," then set off.

The tunnel floor was uneven, and Will scuffed his foot several times on jagged rocks. This tunnel was not meant for a quick getaway, he thought, easy to fall and damage oneself on this hard floor. As they walked, the beams from their torches created strange shadows on the walls.

"Do you think it is safe down here?" asked Jay.

The rough timber supports felt dry and firm under Will's touch, "the supports don't feel rotten, and I can't see any debris on the floor that would indicate rockfall." He shone his torch upwards, "looks as if the roof has been well lined with timbers too."

Will walked on. Turning a corner in the tunnel, he realised that Jay had stopped behind him as there was now only his torch illuminating the darkness. He was about to call out when he heard a terrible scream that turned his blood cold. It was Jay. Will stumbled back as quickly as he could on the uneven surface, grazing his hands on the rough walls as he steadied himself.

"Jay, are you okay?" he called out. Will rounded the corner and saw Jay standing still, just staring at the wall. Her torch directed at a shelf carved into the side of the tunnel, a bit like a sleeping berth. Will could see something lying on the shelf. Whatever it was had been covered in a black plastic sheet. He shone his torch up and down the length of the object to see what had made Jay scream. There was a slit in the plastic, and something had been dislodged and hung down. Will focused the beam and peered closely. "My God, it's a hand."

"It's a body," cried out Jay, "I'm not staying down here," and with that, she headed back down the tunnel towards the steps.

Transfixed to the spot, as if his legs had been cast in concrete, Will now recognised the smell that had eluded him previously; it was the odour of death. Will felt light-headed, not from horror or fear, but from a voice somewhere inside him that said, 'you have found me.' It was as if a foggy atmosphere had suddenly dissipated, and he could see clearly again. The moment lasted only a second as from up in the billiard room, Will heard Jay scream again and call out, "who the fuck are you?"

Stumbling towards the steps, Will fell, bruising and grazing his knee, "shit, shit, I'm coming, Jay," he called out. Scrambling up the steps, he launched himself head-first through the gap in the wall, rolling into the room prepared to do battle with Jay's adversary. Getting to his feet, he found Jay and Mack in a stand-off position as if they were going into a fight.

"It's okay, Jay, this is Mack, Mack the ghillie."

"Oh, I'm so sorry, Mack, I wasn't expecting to see you," said Jay.

"Mack, good to see you. Let me introduce you to my wife, Jay. We have had a bit of a shock. We have discovered this tunnel, and there's a body down there."

"A body? Oh, that is awful. Did you recognise it?" replied Mack

"No, it's all wrapped up, but apologies for that greeting Mack," Jay said, offering her hand, "I'm still a bit shaky from the discovery."

"Aye, nae problem, I was in the barn and thought I would pop in to see you both," said Mack, shaking Jay's hand.

"I think I had better phone the police and report this. I don't know the local number, so I'll dial 999," said Will pulling his phone from his pocket.

After a brief conversation with the dispatcher, Will ended the call, "they're on the way. Did you know about this tunnel, Mack?"

"Aye, my Daddy told me one existed, but I never came into the hoose much, and Dougie never mentioned it to me," replied Mack.

"Okay, I think we should leave the tunnel until the police arrive. Let's go into the kitchen and have a coffee."

Will could see that Jay was still shaky, whereas he felt somehow liberated. They all sat down at the kitchen table and awaited the police.

Trying to forget Jay's initial introduction to Mack, Will wanted to make sure he was still willing to work for them. "Mack, we see you as an important part of the team here as we re-develop and improve the estate and want you to feel that this is your home, too, for as long as you wish."

"Aye, that's kind of you," replied Mack.

Will could not believe they had found a dead body in the tunnel. Who was it? How long had it been there? If it had been a skeleton, then it might have been there for decades, even centuries, but that was not the case. The hand was still covered in skin, and the decay had not set in. Will reckoned it had not been there long. Was Dougie the killer? No wonder he had disappeared. He couldn't wait to get away. At least the police should be able to track him down.

"What a start to a new home," Will blurted out.

"Quite so," replied Jay, "death does have a habit of following you around."

"Oh?" said Mack.

"Well, I was involved in some trouble last year, no fault of my own," replied Will, "it was to do with arms being supplied to terrorist gangs. Anyway, a few people died, including a couple of my business partners. I was wounded, hit my head, but I've recovered fully. There were a lot of dodgy people involved, including some people close to me. The organisation's leader responsible for refurbishing the arms, the Boss, as everyone called him, went to jail for life."

"For life?" asked Mack.

"Yes, so did one of my closest clients, a friend really, a chap called Michael Bore, who admitted responsibility for the whole operation. Another of my partners, Sara Crombie, was sent to prison for shooting her husband. It was very difficult for me as everyone thought I was behind it, even the police. Anyway, that all got sorted out eventually and all the guilty got their just rewards. So, that was the main reason we decided to move away from London. Leave all the unpleasant memories behind us."

"Seems as if you have not been entirely successful," replied Mack.

"No, it doesn't," said Will leaning on the table resting his chin in his hands.

The doorbell rang.

"That'll be the police, I expect," and Will got up to let them in.

On the front step was a small, rugged faced man, slicked-back hair, immaculately dressed in a well-cut tweed suit and highly polished shoes. His companion was very different, burly with a round face and a uniform that looked as if it had been slept in on many occasions.

"Good morning, sir, I'm Inspector Tavish, and this is Sergeant Pearce. You are?"

"Will Slater. Yes, please come in."

"I understand you reported finding a body, Mr Slater."

"Yes, in a tunnel that runs underneath the house. Let me show you."

The three men made their way through the hall and into the billiard room. "It's down there, on the right, on a sort of shelf cut into the wall," indicated Will.

"Take a look, Sergeant."

Removing his hat and slipping on blue plastic gloves and overshoes, the Sergeant disappeared into the gap in the wall.

"So, when did you find the body, sir?" asked Tavish.

"Just a little while ago, my wife and I have just bought this house, and we were doing some exploring when we found the tunnel."

"So, you found the body. Did you touch it?"

"Well, actually, my wife found the body; I had walked a little way down the tunnel when I heard her scream, and when I rushed back, she was staring at something wrapped up in a plastic sheet. I shone my torch and saw a hand hanging down."

The Sergeant's head appeared at the entrance to the tunnel. He nodded to the Inspector and said, "we will know more when the techos get here, but it looks like a recent death to me."

"Wait here, please, Mr Slater. I'm going to have a quick look myself." Will watched as Tavish also disappeared through the billiard room wall, reappearing a couple of minutes later.

"Okay, the forensic team will be here soon, sir. Perhaps I can speak to your wife."

"Yes, we're all in the kitchen," replied Will.

As they walked back into the hall, two white-suited figures arrived through the front door.

"Through there, on the right, in the tunnel, lads," said the Sergeant to the white suits.

Will led the policemen into the kitchen.

"This is my wife Jay, and this is the estate's ghillie, Mack."

"Good morning," said the Inspector nodding to Mack and offering his hand to Jay, "I'm Inspector Tavish, and this is Sergeant Pearce. I understand you discovered the body."

"Yes, Inspector, I did."

"Must have been a wee bit of a shock."

"Well, yes, it was, with just its hand stuck out of the cover."

"Ummm, now you didn't touch anything, did you?"

"Certainly not; it was horrible."

Turning towards Will, the Inspector continued, "what about you, sir? Did you touch anything?"

"No, Inspector."

"Now, Mr Slater, I did a bit of research on you in the car on the way over. You have a colourful history."

"I don't know about that. I imagine you are referring to various difficulties last year?"

"I was, Mr Slater. Several deaths, as I recall, from the reported case, including some people quite close to you. A couple of your business partners and an old friend who was killed not that far from here in Ballachulish."

"You have been doing your homework, Inspector, since I only called less than an hour ago," Will said, looking at his watch.

"Well, I thought I recognised your name, and I find it pays to do some research on my witnesses, often speeds up the conclusion of the case."

"I hope you don't think I had anything to do with this death."

"I think I'm keeping an open mind at the moment until we have got some forensics."

Jay butted in, "that is ridiculous; I discovered the body this morning; how do you think we killed him? We only legally bought the house yesterday."

"Have you not been to the house before?"

"We came to look at it a few days ago and loved it so much that we decided to buy it on the first visit," replied Jay.

"You have not been here since?" asked Tavish.

"I popped over a couple of days ago, mainly to meet up with Mack. I called at the house to tell Dougie that I was on his land, but he wasn't there. There were a couple of strange things. The house looked as if no one was living here. The fridge was empty, and while I was in the kitchen, a man attacked me and hit me on the head. Nothing serious, just a graze."

"You, of course, reported this to the police," said Tavish.

"No, I didn't think there would be anything you could do. I wouldn't recognise the attacker, and I wasn't badly hurt."

"But this mysterious person might have been the killer, and you decided that it wasn't worth notifying us. I believe you are a solicitor, Mr Slater. I would have thought you would have treated the law with slightly less contempt."

"You are quite correct, Inspector, and I apologise; I should have reported the incident."

"A little late now. So, no idea who might have attacked you or why they were in the house?"

"We have been thinking about that," said Will looking across at Jay, "there is nothing much to steal. We agreed with Dougie that the contents, as they were, would be included in the price. He just needed to take what he wanted for his new home," Will paused, "actually, that's also strange."

"What's strange, Mr Slater?" asked Tavish.

"The TV is still here; well, it was on the day I was attacked. Dougie said he watched it a lot. I would have thought that he would have wanted to take that to his new home."

"Where is it?"

"In the snug through that door."

"Pearce take a look," said Tavish.

"It's still here, sir," said Pearce through the open door, "it's huge, maybe too heavy for him to lift out."

"Maybe," said Tavish thoughtfully. "So, Mr Slater, we have an unidentified body and an unidentified attacker. All very mysterious. I hope you haven't brought your, what did you call them, your difficulties up to this part of the country. Now, is there anything else either of you has failed to tell me?"

"Not directly, Inspector, but I think I have an idea where that person in the tunnel was killed."

Jay looked at Will with her mouth open.

"You do? Where might that be, Mr Slater?"

"Of course, I can't be sure, but I think in the bathroom in the old servants' quarters."

"Why do you think that, Mr Slater?"

"The smell. I know it sounds strange, but I have regrettably smelt death before. I smelt it in the tunnel, and I think there was a similar smell in that bathroom when we were looking around the house before we bought it."

As Tavish was busily making notes, one of the white suits appeared at the kitchen door.

"We're finished down there, Inspector. Anything you want to see before we remove the body?"

"No, but we have to look elsewhere." replied Tavish and, turning to Will, "can you show us this other bathroom, please, sir."

"Yes, follow me."

"And I'm coming too," said Jay, still looking astonished by Will's new revelation.

Will led the small party of the policemen, two white coats and Jay across the hall to the back stairs.

When they got to the top, Will pointed down the corridor to

the bathroom at the end. "That's where I think the murder took place."

"Right you are, sir; please stay here, and we will take a wee look," said Tavish, pulling another pair of blue overshoes from his pocket and indicating with his head for the two white suits to follow him down the corridor. Will looked at Jay and raised his eyebrows. "It was just something when I came up here the first time: an atmosphere, not frightening, difficult to describe, a sort of heavy feeling in the air. Some cleaning material, but it masked another smell. It wasn't until we discovered the body in the tunnel that I realised what the smell was. I call it the smell of death but think it is blood."

"No, you're correct, death does have a smell, but it is not the blood; it is all the gases that escape from the body when someone dies. They hang around for a while in the air," said Jay, "can you feel an atmosphere now?"

"No, I can't. I know it seems strange, but I feel a sense of relief as if I was meant to find that body in the tunnel. I felt the house was asking me to buy it so we could make this discovery."

"I didn't realise you were a little fey."

"I would never have thought it myself either. Not normal for a lawyer. What about you? Are you okay living here now that we have found a body?"

"You forget, you are talking to an ex-member of SO15. I still love this house. It just adds to the excitement as far as I am concerned."

Will laughed and pulled his beautiful wife towards him and hugged her. However, inside Will's head, alarm bells were ringing. Could this death be connected to his past troubles, or was it a complete coincidence? If it was the latter, the grim reaper was certainly following him about.

Inspector Tavish arrived back from the bathroom, "okay, the boys are working, but I think we need to close off the whole house as a potential crime scene. I am very sorry. I'm hoping that it won't take long as most of the rooms are empty."

"Alright, Inspector, understood. We are staying at the Lochside Inn. If you can let us know when we can come back, please."

"Aye, I will and will also get these statements written up so you can sign them."

CHAPTER ELEVEN

Sitting in their room at the inn, Will tapped away at his laptop, dealing with a myriad of new emails.

Jay lay on the bed with her iPad balanced on her lap. "You know that body gave me a real fright this morning, and I'm not one to be frightened easily."

"I know, and I thought you were going to kick the hell out of Mack on the rebound," replied Will.

"Well, he did scare me too, just standing there as I came out of that damn tunnel; however, he is huge, and I would have thought long and hard before starting a fight."

"It will be interesting to see if the police can shed any light on who the body belongs to. I imagine the police will interrogate Dougie. The body hasn't been down there that long. You would have thought Dougie must have had some involvement. He doesn't look like a murderer, although there is something strange about him that doesn't seem to fit into the 'Lord of the Manor' role," said Will.

"I agree; I think the death is recent, but because it was wrapped up in sheeting, it will make the exact time of death difficult to establish; it certainly hasn't been down there for centuries.

I didn't get the same impression about Dougie. He knew a lot about the house."

"Well, he didn't mention the tunnel."

"Hardly surprising if he had just dumped a body in it. I wonder where the tunnel leads to?"

"I intend to find out as soon as we are allowed back into the house. It was probably built for escape," replied Will.

"Depends when it was built. If it was contemporaneous to the original house, which I think Dougie said was the middle of the eighteenth century, then probably for escape. Could have been either escape from Bonnie Prince Charlie and the Rebels or escape from the British Government soldiers."

"Always supposing there is an exit at the other end."

"Well, you can check tomorrow or whenever we are allowed back in again."

"Yes, maybe there will be some clues when we take a closer look. Mack may have more information," replied Will.

"Let's hope we never have to use it."

"Mmmm," said Will.

"I think I will do more research on the house. Probably the best place to start is the local paper. Any idea what it is called?" asked Jay.

"Yes, I saw one in the bar, The Courier."

A minute or so later, Jay chirped from the bed, "listen to this, I just typed Gaur House into the search box on the paper's website, and there were two articles that immediately popped up. The first one from a few weeks ago is about Dougie's brother." Jay read out the article.

Estranged Brother in Fracas

The police were called to the Lochside Inn, Loch Tummel, on Thursday evening when a fight broke out between the elderly owner of Gaur House, Douglas Gordon and his estranged brother Walter Gordon. Both men ended up on the floor wrestling each other. Locals tried to separate them, but no sooner had they been pulled apart than they started again.

"I have never seen anything like it," said Landlord Hamish MacInnes. "Douglas is such a quiet and likeable old chap. He was sitting having a wee dram when this other younger man comes in, who I now know was his brother, sits at Dougie's table, and within minutes they are rowing, banging their fists on the table and shouting obscenities at each other. Then Dougie gets up and pushes the brother backwards onto the floor. The brother is furious and tackles Dougie to the ground. One of the other customers and I separated the pair but no sooner had we done it than they were at each other again. I was concerned that one of them would kill the other, so I called the police."

The row was allegedly over their late father's inheritance. Douglas Gordon Junior was left the whole estate on the death of Douglas Senior in 1985. At the time, Walter, the younger brother, had been estranged from his father and was living in Australia. Walter claims that he returned to Scotland to 'get what he was due.' Walter disappeared again after the incident; it is believed that he returned to Australia.

"There is obviously more to this family than outward appearances show," said Will.

"You know, there's bound to be a lot in the local paper about this body we discovered. I wonder if wc can keep our names out of the press; otherwise, our hiding place is blown."

"Yes, that is a good point; I hadn't thought about that. I will have a word with Tavish and see what he can do. He knows about our background, but whether he will be sympathetic to keeping our identity quiet, who knows?" Will sat in thought, staring into the darkness through the window.

"There's something else interesting here," said Jay, "listen to this."

Gaur House and its Secrets

Last night, local historian Billy Gaskell talked to the Pitlochry and Rannoch History Society on the part Gaur House played in the aftermath of the Jacobite rising in 1745. The main part of the house was built in 1744 and was a focal point for returning Jacobite rebels after the butchery by Government forces at Culloden in 1746. The local clan leaders hid much of their wealth to ensure it was not taken by the British. Rumour has it that these possessions were hidden in Gaur House by the then owner, James McClay, who, although a Jacobite himself, was seen as a moderate by the British and was left to his own devices. The Clan leaders would return to reclaim their possessions when a Stuart was on the throne at a future date. That never happened, and the Jacobite rebels were brought to heel by the British Government, never to be a force again. It is believed that the possessions, which in today's money would be worth many hundreds of thousands of pounds, are still hidden somewhere in Gaur House.

The current owner of the property, Douglas Gordon, says it is all wishful thinking, "it is the first I have heard about it and not sure where Mr Gaskell got his information, but it would have been better he if he had spoken to me before opening his mouth about something he clearly does not know. Had there been a stash of valuables in the house, one of the previous owners would have surely found it, which they haven't, or not to my knowledge."

"Perhaps that is what we will find at the end of the tunnel," said Will.

"Unlikely, I would think whoever left that body down there would have taken all the treasure at the same time, assuming that was where it was hidden," Jay replied.

"Mack and I will have a good look tomorrow."

"Good luck. Now on a different subject, what are we going to do about cars?" Jay asked. "We need to get rid of the hire vehicle."

"Yes, you're right. Let's go into Pitlochry first thing and see if there is a garage or dealership," said Will.

"Are you coming to bed?"

"Only if you put that iPad away," replied Will.

"Why have you got something else in mind?"

"I could have," said Will, smiling.

CHAPTER TWELVE

Will and Jay were just leaving for Pitlochry to buy the cars when Inspector Tavish phoned.

"Good morning, Mr Slater; SOCO have finished in the house, they worked most of the night, and I will let you know what we have discovered in due course. Our first task is to discover who the body belongs to."

"Thanks, Inspector, so we can go back into the house now?"

"Yes, you can."

"One further point, Inspector, I imagine the local press will be interested in the discovery of the body, and as you know, I'm trying to keep a low profile, so I wondered if we could keep our names out of print."

"I will see what I can do, but they can find out who has bought the house from other sources, so they won't need me to tell them who discovered the body."

"Yes, I suppose you are right. Well, thank you anyway, Inspector, bye."

"What did he say about the local press?" asked Jay.

"He would try to keep our name out of the paper, but he thought that they would find out who we were from other means."

"We will just have to keep vigilant."

"Yep," said Will with a sigh, "let's go and buy the cars. I'll phone Mack and tell him that we can go back into the house again."

* * *

They purchased a Land Rover Defender and a BMW X6, both late models and both because of their four-wheel drive, likely to be necessary during the winter months.

As they drove up the drive, Mack heard them and waited for them on the front steps.

"Good morning, Mack; like the new fleet?" Will asked jokingly.

"Aye, very fine, Will," replied Mack.

"Right, let's have a quick planning discussion, then you and I are going back into that tunnel while Jay does some more exploring in the house."

As they sat in the kitchen, Will broached the idea he had considered overnight. "What would you think if we converted part of the barn into a flat for you and you could move out of that caravan?"

"Aye, that would be good. It gets freezing in that van in the winter," replied Mack.

"Okay, we will see if we can get it done by this winter, but in the meantime, why don't you move in here. The water and heating will be on, and Jay and I will be staying at the inn until some of the basic renovation work is completed. It also makes some sense to have the house occupied to make sure no vandals get in."

"Aye, I will do that, thank you."

"Okay, the first project on the estate is to put in a track between here and the inn. I don't want it to be used by cars, only by bicycle or quad bike. Then the next task will be the track up from the road. We need that re-laid, or at least the potholes filled in. What do you think about the wooden bridge? Is that safe?" asked Will.

"Aye, the bridge is okay. I look at it regularly. But it could do with some railings to stop anyone falling off."

"Do we have the equipment to do all the work, or do we need to hire it?"

"Ach, no, we'll need the proper kit," replied Mack.

"Okay, make a list of what equipment we need and add what else you think needs to be done to the estate. If you can prioritise them, we can see how we should undertake the work."

"Tell me, Mack, did your father ever mention anything about Jacobite treasure buried in the house?" asked Jay.

"Aye, he did. Mentioned it to Dougie as well, but Dougie said that if there were any treasure, which he doubted, it would stay hidden as it would bring no advantage to him, just a lot of trouble."

"Strange comment. I wonder what Dougie meant?"

"I assume he meant all the press and visitors wanting to see it," replied Mack.

"Maybe," said Jay nodding her head.

"Come on, Mack, let's get into this tunnel and see where it goes."

* * *

Will tossed aside the blue police tape that still adorned the entrance to the tunnel and clambered down the steps with Mack behind him.

"Did your father tell you where this passageway went to Mack?"

"He only said there was one, and it had been built as an escape tunnel when the house was built in the seventeen hundred's, more as insurance rather than a need. The folk who built this hoose would have been very wealthy, and it would be unclear whether they supported the British King or Bonny Prince Charlie."

"Either way, it would have been a dangerous time for all Scots. After Elizabeth I died, the two countries were combined under one King, James VI of Scotland and James I of England. Jay gave me some background reading on the history."

"Aye, I remember, it was all raised again during that damned referendum thing," replied Mack.

Will went on talking over his shoulder as he started to walk down the tunnel, "as I understand it, the Parliament in London wanted to reduce the powers of the Scottish Clans well before the 1745 uprising. I suspect the appearance of Bonnie Prince Charlie claiming to want to be King of England too, was probably the last straw for the powers to be in London and was why the Clans had all their land taken away. Anyway," continued Will, "if the Jacobite treasure is true, then this might have been the exit for the clan chiefs when they left."

"Aye, it could've been," replied Mack.

The darkness encased them in their torch illuminated bubble. Nothing could be seen either in front or behind, the beams of their torches swallowed up by the darkness. The uneven floor, littered with protruding jagged rocks and pieces of flint, made anything other than slow progress hazardous. Any false step could result in a twisted ankle or a nasty fall, so Will kept his torch angled to the ground, which meant they were walking blind apart from two foot in front of them. Shadows reached out, tentacles of darkness waiting to envelop them into their eyeless world. Were any of these tunnels booby-trapped? Jay's potted history didn't mention that. If this tunnel were booby-trapped, they wouldn't spot it until it was too late.

"The air feels dry and surprisingly warm," said Will as he flashed his torch in an arc picking out the wall and ceiling timber supports. Tapping his knuckle against the rough timber, he said. "Seems firm and dry."

"No damp doon here," said Mack, "so no rotting."

"Wouldn't the rain have seeped into the ground?" Will asked.

"Aye, it could have, but the water will find its way down towards the Loch."

They moved on at a sedate pace, Mack almost touching Will's shoulder as they progressed down the tunnel. Eventually, they reached a wall that blocked their way.

"Is this the end? I can't see how anyone could get out," said Will flashing his torch around the walls and ceiling. "There's no jewels or contraband, just an old ladder."

"That must be the way out," said Mack directing his torch at the roof of the tunnel, "aye, look, there may be a hatch or something up there."

Mack picked up the ladder, tested it and climbed towards the top. He ran his massive hands along the roof, tapping here and there with his knuckles.

"Aye, there's some sort of wooded hatch here. It must be the exit to the tunnel," said Mack.

"How do we open it?" called up Will.

"I can feel something," Mack shone the torch at the relevant spot, "aye, I can see two hinges in this section of the roof. The hatch must open upwards."

"That makes sense; if the hatch opened inward, whatever lay on top would crash down onto the person standing on the ladder," replied Will.

Laying his hands flat on the roof, Mack pushed upwards, but it wouldn't budge. "Something heavy is lying on the top."

"Okay, we need to find the hatch on the outside and open it that way," said Will.

"Aye, but that won't be easy. We will need to measure the

distance carefully and try and locate roughly the spot to search," replied Mack, pulling a compass from his pocket, "I will keep taking readings, and if we count the steps back, we should get somewhere near."

Will kept a note of the directions as they progressed back through the tunnel.

Above the surface, Will and Mack started the search. They paced out the length of the tunnel in the direction of the compass readings. However, the tunnel was not straight, and the terrain outside didn't allow them to follow exactly where they believed the tunnel travelled and had to keep estimating the route.

Having reached the end of the paces, they looked around. "Well, this seems roughly the spot," Will said, indicating an area very overgrown with vegetation, dead branches and a large rock.

"Aye, it could be," said Mack looking back towards the way they had travelled, "it would be difficult for anyone escaping to be seen from the house, and there is a trail doon there that leads further away to the other side of that hillock, so out of direct sight, which would help their escape."

Turning to look in the direction Mack was pointing, Will found it difficult to spot any discernible trail. "I will take your word for it. We will need some equipment to clear the ground."

"Aye, we do," replied Mack.

"However, we don't want to make too much mess so anyone can spot the entrance."

"Why would you want to keep it hidden?" asked Mack.

It was true the tunnel had been built during times of war, and escape was often the only way to continue living. However, Will heard that voice again, telling him to keep the tunnel as it was meant to be. "I know it sounds strange, but this passageway was constructed for a purpose, and we should preserve it in case it is ever needed again."

With curiosity etched in his face, Mack nodded, "I will go and get tools and bring them back on the quad bike."

"Okay, I will start looking for the entrance."

Once Mack had disappeared, Will decided that rather than start looking for the hatch, he would try and find this trail that Mack had mentioned. If the purpose of his decision was to keep the tunnel functioning effectively, however illogical it might be, the onward trail away from the house also needed to be in play. So, he started walking in the direction that Mack had indicated into what looked like quite dense woods.

The undergrowth snapped and rasped under Will's steps. Tangled roots grabbed his feet like unseen hands, and there was an overriding smell of dampness and rotting wood. Not a breath of air moved under the dense canopy of trees, and even the birds didn't venture so far from the sky. The only sound was his breathing and the rustle of his outdoor clothes as he moved. Will stopped; he sensed someone watching him. It was the same sense that he had had several times before. Will turned full circle looking in all directions but saw nothing. Ridiculous; I will see fairies and hobgoblins next, he thought. Looking at his watch, he decided to push on a bit further along what he hoped was Mack's trail.

A branch snapped to Will's left, startling him. The wood was a tangle of thick brown tree trunks, dense rhododendron bushes and waist-high brambles, making it impossible to see anything more than a few feet. He peered in the direction of the noise. "Is there anyone there?" he called, and then a swirl of movement, branches crashing, feet thudding. Is he coming my way, Will thought? Should I fight, or should I run? He thought the latter and was just turning when he realised that the sound was moving away from him.

"Who's there?" Will called, but there was no reply, just the continuing sound of flight, and then Will saw a flash of red. The man with the red hair. My God, it's him, and suddenly he was back on the platform at Hyde Park Corner, the shove in the back, turning as he fell forward, the tube train with its headlight thundering out of the tunnel towards the platform like a one-eyed monster hungry for its prey.

Bile rose to the back of Will's throat. "Who are you? What do you want?" screamed Will as he now chased after the disappearing red flash. A branch slapped him in the face, dragging across his cheek and drawing blood; wincing with the pain, he drove on, pounding after the departing commotion.

Through rasping breaths, Will shouted, "who are you? I know you are there; I can see you." Spittle collected at the corners of his mouth, and a film of sweat encased his whole body. He could still see movement in front of him; the muscles in his legs screamed, but he raced on, jumping and skipping over the brambles and undergrowth, swerving to avoid tree stumps, but his prey seemed to be running even faster. Urging himself on, one last effort, one more spurt, one more push through the pain barrier and then, his foot caught a root, and Will catapulted into a tree trunk which drove the air out of his lungs. "Shit, shit," he mumbled, his tongue stuck to the roof of his bone dry mouth. With his last ounce of energy, doubled up in pain, lungs bursting, Will staggered on, and after a few more steps, he lunged out of the woods and could see for miles around. As his legs gave way and he plunged forward onto the grass, he caught the sight of his red-haired foe, turning to watch its fallen pursuer before skipping away into the distance - a small red deer. Will lay motionless on the damp grass, alternately sucking in mouthfuls of air and laughing at his stupidity.

His legs felt like lead, and the muscles wobbled uncontrollably, but eventually, Will managed to get up. Where was he? Where was the house? He had run a long way and was entirely off Mack's path. He had been running uphill as he could see the loch below him, and as he turned, Will caught a glimpse of the roof and chimneys of Gaur House. If he headed back towards the house, he would meet the track that led to the tunnel exit. His breathing had now calmed, and the searing pain in his legs had subdued. He took a final look across the clearing when a flash of light caught his eye from the top of a hill. He cupped his hands around his eyes and watched the hill. There it was again, just a flicker as the sun reflected off something. Will was sure that this was not a chance reflection but someone watching him through a lens.

Retracing his journey as best he could, Will eventually found his way back to the tunnel exit. Mack had already returned with various tools.

"There you are; I thought the ground had swallowed you up," said Mack and laughed. "What's happened to your face? It's all bloody."

"Just went for a scout of the land to see where we were in relation to the loch and ran into a branch in the wood. I did think I saw a flash of light as if someone were using binoculars and watching me," Will said whilst gingerly touching his painful cheek.

"Aye, could've been a bird watcher or even a deerstalker. If it was the latter, you might be lucky they didn't shoot you. Some of the landowners are running tourist destinations up here to shoot the deer. They come from all over the world. Not sure how fussy they are about the type of kill," said Mack, laughing.

"Ummm, maybe, but I can't be sure, but I think they were on my land."

Will's senses were telling him that he was the target of the watching eyes. Will felt panic rising. Had his location already been discovered? How could that be so soon? A voice cut through his thoughts.

"Aye, well, let's get cracking and find this hole before it gets dark," said Mack.

Both men donned heavy-duty gloves to protect them from the gorse and brambles and started to hack their way through to where they hoped they would find the exit to the tunnel.

Progress was slow; brambles kept catching on their shirts and trousers, causing tears and, if not extricated carefully, damage to the flesh underneath. After about thirty minutes of sweating and occasional swearing, Mack stopped and said, "I think this is about the right place."

Will looked down at the ground, but it looked like just another patch of dense low vegetation and a large rock. "I can't see anything."

"Give me a hand with this rock; it looks out of place here," said Mack pushing hard at the rock with his huge hands. Will crouched and added his weight to the process. The rock seemed immoveable.

"I have an idea," said Mack, "if you can lever the rock up a wee bit, I may be able to roll it."

Mack picked up a fallen branch. He tested it to see it was not rotten. He then wedged it under the rock and pulled it down hard until a small gap appeared between the rock and the ground. "Now you take over but don't let it drop."

Will pressed down on the branch, Mack crouched in front of the rock and inched his fingers and hands into the gap. Will was concerned; what happens if the branch snaps or I lose the grip? It will crush Mack's hands. Thin trails of sweat tumbled down Will's face, salt stinging the cut on his cheek. With ears buzzing and already tired limbs twitching, Will urged himself, "c'mon, c'mon, more, more." Will could see Mack crouched in front of the rock, his back braced straight and his knees bent in a weightlifter's stance. Mack then pushed up with his legs. Will watched the veins on Mack's neck pulsating and swelling as his face turned puce. The rock was winning, but then Mack let out a huge bellow and pumped up again on his legs. Will felt the pressure release on his branch, and the rock lifted off the ground and toppled back, closely followed by Mack, who ended up spread-eagled on its smooth surface, puffing and cursing alternately in a staccato voice as he recovered his breath.

Although every muscle in Will's body protested, he picked up a shovel and scraped the ground where the rock had been resting. Under a few centimetres of earth and debris, Will saw the outline of the wooden hatch. "This is it; this is it," he shouted.

Will cleared more ground until the wooden hatch was in full view.

"Yes, here it is, and an iron ring to pull it open." Will reached down and pulled, but it wouldn't budge.

"Let me have a go, Will," said Mack, and he again squatted in a weightlifter's stance. With his legs braced on either side of the hatch, he took the ring in both hands and, using his legs, pushed upwards. Once again, nothing moved; the only sound was the air escaping from Mack's lungs as he exerted more pressure on his legs. Then suddenly, the hatch creaked and started to move upwards until it exposed the exit to the tunnel.

Will shone his torch down the hole, and he could see the old ladder lying against the tunnel wall.

"Excellent, job well done. Thanks, Mack."

"If this is to be usable, as you seem to think it should, we need to make this hatch easier to open from both inside and outside. Perhaps lay a false screen on the outside so the exit cannae be seen. You don't want unwanted visitors at night trouping through the tunnel into the billiard room. We will need to put some lights down the length of the tunnel, too, as that floor is lethal in the dark."

"Yes, agree. I'm not planning to use it regularly, hopefully not at all, but we should make it as accessible as possible in the case of an emergency. Come on; it's getting dark now; we better get back."

CHAPTER THIRTEEN

"I'm sure someone was watching me again today when I was with Mack working on the tunnel," said Will as he lay on their bed at the Inn.

Jay stopped what she was doing and turned towards him. "Did you see them?"

"No, I saw a reflection of light caught by the sun, which I think was a pair of binoculars. Mack thought it could be a deer-stalker, but I'm sure it was on our land and therefore, whoever it was is trespassing."

"Where was this?"

"Towards the northeast, on the way to the water sports centre but further inland in the hills."

"You don't think you are getting a little paranoid about being watched? It might be a reaction to the traumas of last year."

"Maybe, I suppose so," Will was not convinced but decided not to tell Jay about the incident with the deer, "but I definitely saw something shining. That was not my imagination."

"Why don't we visit the water sports centre tomorrow and introduce ourselves to, Ummm, what was his name, Dougie mentioned him?"

"Roddy Neath. Yes, good idea as he is our next door neighbour, and he may have seen somebody. Why don't we walk from the house? It will allow us to look at the land on the way."

The following day, they headed out towards the water sports centre. They used the loch's edge as a guide; sometimes, they had to detour inland to cross small burns that fed into the loch. After about forty minutes of walking, the centre came into sight. It consisted of three buildings; one seemed to house the equipment, as Will could see various watercraft laid out at its entrance, the second changing rooms and toilets and the third was a café and what looked like living accommodation above.

Will thought the site looked neat and tidy, and an effort had been made to make a slab of concrete look as attractive as possible. There were planters scattered around with an array of colourful summer annuals, with tables and chairs outside the café. Some of the tables, laid with little pots of flowers and menu cards, were occupied by punters sipping hot drinks in the morning sunshine.

"Doesn't look too bad," said Jay.

"No, it doesn't; Dougie seemed to imply it was rather rundown. I don't think they liked each other much. His comments were probably biased. Let's see if we can find Mr Neath."

They entered the café and asked at the counter.

"He's in the office next door. Go outside and around to the far side of the building; you can't miss it," replied the girl behind the counter.

The office was the reception for the centre and had they not come via the loch they would have seen it from the car park.

The doorbell tinkled as Will pushed it open, and a man sitting behind the reception desk looked up.

"Can I help you, folks?" said the man unfolding himself from his chair. He was tall, athletic in build, with craggy features and red hair the colour of burnished copper.

It happened immediately; Will's pulse raced, sweat broke out on his forehead, his limbs wouldn't move, he couldn't talk, he couldn't even open his mouth. His brain had shut down.

"Hi, I'm Jay Slater, and this is my husband Will; we are the new owners of Gaur House, up the road.

"Aye, I know, news travels fast in these here parts. Roddy Neath," he said, shaking first Jay's hand and then Will's, who had used all his willpower to move his arm. "Please to meet you both. I hope you will be happy in this wee place. Not everyone's taste. Very remote. Aye, very remote."

"You seem to get people to your centre okay, despite it being remote," said Jay.

"Aye, word of mouth. People who like the water come back again."

"Have you been here a long time?" asked Jay?

"About five years now."

"What made you come here and start this business."

"Well, I was brought up nearby, and after I came out of the army, had to do something outdoors. Cannae sit at a desk all day. I had this idea about hiring out boats and the like. I just needed a water frontage. So, I asked Dougie Gordon at the big house, but you must know him, if I could buy a bit of his land for my business. I think he was strapped for cash, so he was happy to let me have this wee bit. Done me okay so far," said Neath, nodding to himself.

"Excellent. I hope it continues going well," replied Jay, not knowing what else to say.

Whatever had affected Will had passed, and hoping Neath hadn't seen his sudden indisposition, he said, "nice to meet a neighbour. We just thought we would call in to introduce ourselves."

"Aye, well, thanks for that."

"Good to get on with one's neighbours," Will continued, "I got the impression that, perhaps, you and Dougie Gordon didn't get on so well."

"Not sure where you heard that. Dougie and I got on okay, or he wouldn't have sold me this land. We used to have the odd chinwag and a wee dram in the inn. Not that I have seen him for a few weeks. What with running this place through the summer. I don't have much time for anything else."

"Oh, right," Will replied and continued, "as near neighbours, I thought we should look out for each other for mutual benefit."

Neath squinted his face "Aye, but what had you in mind?"

"I'm not sure, watching out for trespassers, perhaps."

"I don't have much land to worry about, and I don't have time to worry about anyone else's land."

"Just thought I saw someone over here yesterday in the hills behind you, on the edge of my land, thought he might be a deer-stalker."

"Well, if he was there, I didn't see him and as I said, don't have time to watch out, need all my time to run this business," replied Neath, "now, if you will excuse me, I'd love to chat, but I have to crack on," and he sat down and started to examine some papers on his desk.

Jay looked across at Will and signalled towards the door with her head.

"Okay, bye, nice to meet you," said Jay.

"Aye," was the reply.

They headed out.

"What happened in there?" asked Jay, "I looked at your face, and it was as if you had seen a ghost."

"I don't know. I think it was the red hair, something in my head tripped, and I think I must have had a mild panic attack. I couldn't talk for a few moments. I have never had that before. It was a little alarming."

"Don't you think you need to see a doctor? I still think it is all a reaction to last year."

"You mean a shrink."

"Well, someone who could help you."

"I don't think I need any help. I have managed pretty well. What do you expect from someone who was nearly killed three times and witnessed several murders?"

"Well, that's my point."

"Let's see how I manage before we make any decisions. Anyway, Neath seemed a bit abrupt, but I guess that is the Scots way with strangers. Perhaps a bit shy."

"I'm not so sure. There was something in Neath's eyes when you mentioned trespassers. It was as if he might be hiding something. I think we should be a little more cautious when dealing with Mr Neath," replied Jay.

"Wow, once a spook, always a spook, eh."

"Just my training, never take anything at face value, see if the facts fit the situation; otherwise, it could be fatal."

"So, you do think someone might be watching me?" said Will somewhat hopefully.

"I didn't say that, merely that I don't think Mr Neath was telling the truth. Let's face it, you will have made a few enemies last year," replied Jay.

"You think Neath is an enemy? We have only just met him."

"I'm saying anyone could know about your past, and we should trust no one."

"Very cheering. Thanks. I feel a lot better now. Not."

CHAPTER FOURTEEN

Dawkin was staring at his computer screen when Edkins knocked and entered through the open door. "Here is that list of the children in the Slater case that you asked for, Guv."

"What does it say?"

"Nothing new. Crombie had two children, Justin and Chloe. Justin went to Sandhurst like his old man. There is no trace of Chloe, which is a bit strange. I would have thought she would have shown up somewhere. Otherwise, nothing of relevance. I have included all their connections on the list."

"What about Bore?"

"No wife, no kids, didn't leave the army until he was in his forties."

"Ummm," said Dawkin leaning back in his chair and gazing at the ceiling.

"What's your thinking, Guv?"

"I'm thinking that the information is not a lot of help. Not what I was hoping for, to be honest. Okay, leave the paper on my desk, and thanks, Edkins."

Picking up the sheet of paper and stuffing it in his pocket, he tapped his fingers on the desk and continued to stare at the ceiling. He had convinced himself that the children would help to untangle the knot in the Slater case.

"Sandhurst," he said out loud, "might be worth a try", and he picked up his phone and found the number.

"Can I speak to the senior officer, please?" asked Dawkin.

"You mean the Commandant. Whom may I say is calling?" came the response.

"Inspector Dawkin of the Met Police."

"I will see if he is available; please hold."

Forced to listen to some awful canned music, Dawkin tapped a pencil with such velocity that it flew out of his hand.

"Putting you through, sir."

"Thank you," said Dawkin.

"Major General Tussock," said the cultured and baritone voice.

"Ah, Major General, my name is Dawkin, Inspector Dawkin from the Met Police. I wondered if you could answer a couple of questions regarding one of your students, if that is what they are called."

"Officer Cadets is their title, Inspector, and will try, although I don't know them all," replied Tussock.

"I appreciate that sir. The one I am interested in is Justin Crombie."

There was a slight pause, "ah, yes, unfortunately, I do know that Cadet, or should I say ex-cadet. May I ask why the Met Police are interested? His behaviour did not involve any civilians as far as I'm aware," said Tussock.

"I was the senior police officer involved in the case where his mother shot his father. I still have a few concerns over the issue and am trying to build up some background information on the family. I thought you might help. Although I heard you say, ex-cadet. "

"Yes, unfortunately, he had to leave," said Tussock.

"Can I ask why?"

In a crisp staccato military tone, Tussock replied. “Yes, I suppose so. He struck a Warrant Officer. You can’t have a cadet doing that. Authority was always his problem. Very short temper.”

“Oh, I see. Yes, unfortunate. Was he a good cadet, otherwise?” asked Dawkin.

“That is what makes it so disappointing; he would have been an excellent soldier, very driven, got that from his father, I suspect. He was here too. Before my time. Difficult too, by all accounts. Yes, he would have made a good soldier and probably the best marksman we ever had.”

“Okay,” said Dawkin, thoughtfully, not quite sure how the last fact fitted but was sure it would do, “was there anything else that seemed strange or concerned you?”

“In what way?” replied Tussock.

“Oh, I don’t know. Did he seem to have something else on his mind?”

“Well, I always thought he had the proverbial chip on his shoulder. Initially, I put that down to the circumstances surrounding his tragic family life. We get several cadets here who join where their circumstances may not have been ideal previously but who find the regime they have to follow here a cathartic process. But in the case of Crombie, he never seemed to change, and I always got the feeling that there was,” Tussock paused, “some hidden agenda, perhaps even some revenge that he might take because of his past. I know that sounds, probably, foolish,” said Tussock.

“No, not foolish, extremely interesting, extremely interesting indeed. Do you know where Crombie might have gone when he left the Academy?” asked Dawkin.

“All I know is that his postal address is his family home. Not far from here, South London. Is there anything else, as I have a meeting?”

“That has been very helpful, sir, many thanks,” replied

Dawkin, slamming down the phone and snatching a file from his desk. "Edkins, get the car. We are going to make a house call," he shouted as he marched through the outer office.

"Where are we going, Guv?"

Dawkin flicked through the file as he walked and gave Edkins the address.

"Guv," said Edkins somewhat cautiously, "is this still to do with the Slater case?"

"Yeah, it is Edkins. I have got some more information which I want to follow up."

"What info is that?" asked Edkins.

"Crombie's son was at Sandhurst, a bit of a temper by all accounts, hit an officer or something, anyway, he had to leave. The bloke running the show thought that Crombie might have had a hidden agenda to take some sort of revenge over the death of his old man."

"So, what are we going to do, Guv?"

"Thought we might give young Crombie a visit."

* * *

"Here we are, Guv, number 26," said Edkins peering through the windscreen.

"Okay, pull up outside."

Number 26 was looking tired compared to its neighbours. The front lawn needed a cut, the flowerbeds were full of weeds, paint was peeling off the windows, and the front door surrounds.

"Guess no one around to take care of the house," said Dawkin, more to himself than to Edkins.

Dawkin rang the bell. There was no reply.

"You stay here, Edkins, and I'll go around the back."

There was a tinkling of glass, and Dawkin called to Edkins, "it looks as if the back door is open, Edkins."

"Really, Guv," said Edkins noticing the broken glass pane in the back door.

"I was peering through the glass when the pane broke with the pressure of my palm," said Dawkin winking to Edkins.

Edkins didn't look amused.

"The door seems to be open, so we will just have a quick look around," said Dawkin striding into the kitchen.

"Hello," called out Edkins in case there was someone in the house who just hadn't bothered to answer their ring.

"Check upstairs, Edkins. I will check down here."

Edkins called out from the landing. "Guv, you better have a look at this."

"What you've got?" said Dawkin, as he moved towards the voice in one of the bedrooms.

Dawkin entered and looked around the room. On one wall was a huge whiteboard with writing; on another wall was a large green baise notice board with photographs stuck on with little coloured pins, and in the middle of the room was a large table with several maps spread over it.

"What have we got here, Edkins?"

"Not sure, Guv. These photos," said Edkins, his face a few inches from the notice board, "have all been taken from a distance with a long-range camera. It looks like the same house in each photo but with different people and different angles. It looks as if it is out in the wilds somewhere." He stabbed his finger at one of the pictures. "You'll never guess who's in this picture, Guv?"

Dawkin hustled across the room and was now squinting over Edkins' shoulder.

"That's bloody Will Slater."

"I reckon," said Edkins, "some distance, but reckon so."

"Well, I never. So, what is this all about, and where is that house? What's on the whiteboard?"

"Just dates and times. Perhaps a log of activity at that house?"

"Yes, maybe," said Dawkin taking a picture with his mobile phone.

"There's a number circled, 12.15; not sure what that is?"

"A time perhaps or part of a map reference, plenty of maps around, could be anything."

Both men then peered at the maps spread out on the table. Both were of Scotland; one was small scale and had a place ringed in red ink. The other was much larger in scale, and it was possible to identify individual buildings and geographical features.

"So, what do you think this is all about, Guv?"

"I guess that this is where Slater now lives, and the young Crombie has found him."

"But why?"

"I don't know, but perhaps the Commandant was correct about some sort of revenge."

"What are all these photos about, and why such a long way away?"

"The Commandant at Sandhurst said that Crombie was one of the best marksmen they have ever had. Supposing he was lining up a shot on Slater to kill him?"

"Surely, he could have done it already. It would appear he has had plenty of opportunities if the photos are anything to go by."

"Yeah, perhaps he is waiting for something to happen first?"

"Like what, Guv?"

"I don't know," said Dawkin whilst scratching his chin, "and what does 12.15 mean?"

"Should we warn him, Guv, Slater that is?"

"Let's think about this for a while. We haven't got any evidence apart from this room, where we aren't supposed to be. Besides, I'm still convinced that Slater is guilty of something even though Bore took the rap for the lot." After a pause, Dawkin added, "although, I'm getting a funny feeling about this. Take a butcher's around the rest of the rooms up here. I'll take some more photographs, and then let's scarper."

"This Crombie guy is into his cars too," said Edkins "masses of 'Do it yourself guides' on car maintenance, that sort of thing, but nothing else."

Deep in thought and staring out of a window, Dawkin didn't reply.

"You know she is out very soon," continued Edkins.

"What, who will be out?" asked Dawkin.

"The Crombie woman. The Mother, Sara Crombie. On parole."

"When?"

"Don't know exactly."

"So soon? She can't be; she's barely been in a year."

"Good behaviour, the exceptional circumstances of her case and all that, on parole," replied Edkins.

"There's something about that woman. I can't quite put my finger on it. Very smart. Much smarter than her hubby by all accounts."

"Yeah, but however much you hate someone, to kill them, particular your husband, well, that is something else, eh?" replied Edkins.

"Unless you were guilty of something that only he knew about."

"Something that would get you a longer sentence than manslaughter, you mean Guv."

Dawkin's face crunched with a frown as he headed downstairs, deeply disturbed, but he wasn't sure why.

CHAPTER FIFTEEN

Marius Vassily and Christophe Wesinivic stared out into the gloom. The rain cascaded down the windscreen in thick rivulets. The temperature was several degrees colder than in London; the clouds were low and grey to match the atmosphere inside the car.

"It's not even mid-afternoon, but it feels like nighttime," said Christophe clearing the condensation from the side window with his sleeve. "Who would want to live in a place like this? It always seems to rain."

"Well, this is the area where that journalist thought Slater was living, so this is where we have to look," replied Marius.

They had hired a car at Glasgow airport using false ID, then driven to Pitlochry without any real plan to find Slater.

"How do we find this little bastard?" said Christophe. "I thought Scotland was small with few people. There are so many people and so much land, even here in this unpronounceable place - shops, people, cars. I can't understand what anyone is saying with their funny accents. We will never find him."

"If he's in this area, there must be someone who knows him."

"Yes, but who, and we don't want to be advertising ourselves if we are going to kill him."

"We need to stay somewhere tonight. I saw a hotel back there. Let's see if they have any rooms."

They turned around and pulled into the car park of the Fishers Hotel.

"This looks okay."

Having booked in and paid in advance with cash, both men entered the bar.

"Why don't we ask here, no one will remember us, and we booked in under false names," suggested Marius.

"Okay, worth a try, I suppose."

Marius walked up to the bar. "Two pints of lager, please."

"Certainly, sir. Are you staying? Shall I put it on your bill?"

"No, I'll pay cash, thanks."

While the barman pulled the drinks, Marius asked, "a friend of ours has recently moved up here, and as we are in the area, we thought we would call in on him, but we don't have the exact address. His name is Will Slater. He is a solicitor and moved up from London a few weeks ago. Do you know him at all?"

"No, I'm afraid not, pal, although the name is vaguely familiar."

Marius and Christophe took their drinks to a table at the far end of the bar and slumped down into their chairs.

After a few minutes, the barman came over to them, waving a newspaper in the air. "I thought I recognised the name," he said, "look, it's in the local paper. They found a body in the house that he and his wife had just bought. Only one mention of his name, but I knew I had seen it."

"Thanks, that is excellent," said Marius reading the article, "but where is Gaur House?"

"Kinloch Rannoch way," replied the barman, "don't rightly know the house myself, but someone will be able to direct you."

* * *

Marius and Christophe decided that they would time their visit to Gaur House for later in the evening. The Boss had taught them that everything was more threatening when it was dark. They switched off their phones to avoid tracking and followed the satnav directions to Kinloch Rannoch.

"We should have checked the exact location of the house on our phones," said Marius.

"Yes, but don't switch them on now. Look, there's a pub; someone in there will know where Gaur House is," said Christophe.

"Do you think that is a good idea? Do we want anyone to know who we are?"

"Look, we will be back in London tomorrow, and we have hired this car under a false name. There is no connection between Slater and us, and we can get the train back instead of the plane, so we won't need to give any names."

"Okay, you go and ask," replied Marius.

Marius pulled into the Inn's car park while Christophe went inside to ask for directions.

Hamish MacInnes was behind the bar.

"Excuse me, sir, can you direct me to Gaur House?" asked Christophe.

"Aye, could do. What would you want there at this time of night?" asked Hamish.

"I and my friend," said Christophe pointing in the general direction of the car park, "are old business partners of Will Slater, who owns the house, and as we are in the area, we thought we would visit."

Christophe watched Hamish as he moved his head from side

to side, lips tight, presumably assessing whether he should give him the information requested. Hamish replied, "okay, follow the road up the lochside for about a couple of miles. Then take a sharp wee turn to the left into the drive that leads up to the house. You need to drive slowly, or you will miss the turn in the dark."

"Thank you," said Christophe, who hurried out of the inn towards his waiting friend in the car park.

"Okay, let's get going; I'm sure the man in the pub is going to phone Slater immediately."

CHAPTER SIXTEEN

Looking forward to a large malt whisky, Will propped his bike against his new fence and walked across to the inn.

As Will walked into the bar, Hamish called out, "Will! I was going to phone; a couple of strange-looking men were asking for you. Eastern European, I think. I gave them the directions to the house."

Without replying, Will turned, ran across the road, vaulted onto his bike and pedalled as if a gold medal was in sight. How long would the car take to reach the house? The road was windy and dark, and the turn was sharp, and Mack had purposely taken down the sign to the house so as not to advertise its whereabouts to passing traffic. He thought, perhaps eight minutes to get to the turnoff? Then, maybe, three minutes up the drive in the dark, so a minimum of ten, perhaps twelve minutes? Hunched over the handlebars, his legs driving into the pedals, he counted down the seconds. His breaths came in short sharp rasps as the cold air refilled his lungs and his thighs now throbbed from the build-up of lactic acid. He had to get back to protect Jay.

There was no time to warn her on the phone; Will just had to concentrate on peddling. Jay would put up a fight, and they would probably kill her as they were after him. As he got nearer to the house, he could see its lights flickering through the trees, and this urged him to pedal even faster. Every second counted. These men would be armed. He had left by the front door; had he picked up the key? He pictured Jay sitting at the kitchen table sipping a glass of wine. They would kill her on the spot. He removed one hand from the handlebars and felt his trouser pocket.

Yes, thank God, the key was there. The blood pressure hummed in his ears as he strained to hear the noise of the approaching car. He exited the woods like a charging animal, the wheels on the bike slewing over the gravel. No car, no car, his brain registered. He could now hear it behind him, slower and tentative on the dark approach track. Finally, he reached the front of the house and with the last effort from his rubber legs and aching lungs, leapt from the still moving bike onto the front step; he almost fell over but regained his balance and fumbled in his pocket for the key. The headlights from the approaching car lit up the front door like the Berlin Wall.

Hands shaking from exertion, he dragged the key from his pocket; the key slipped in his hands as he tried to enter it into the lock. The light from the car headlights illuminating its target, any moment a bullet in the back, so concentrate, he thought, get the key in the lock and turn it. The key slid in, and he turned and pushed at the same time. He fell through the open door, and as he rolled forward, he slammed it closed with his foot, the noise resounding through the house. He tried to call out, but there was no sound from his breathless lungs. He scrabbled on all fours until his legs managed to take his weight; doubled up and hobbling, he reached the kitchen, where Jay looked up in alarm.

"What's happened?" as she stood up and rushed towards Will.

"Men, men coming," he said through gulps, "men coming, outside, kill us. Lock door, door," pointing to the kitchen door.

Jay turned the key in the lock and grabbed hold of Will's arm, dragging him from the kitchen into the area under the stairs, where she stopped for a second, flicking a switch and sending the house into darkness. "Come on, quick, upstairs," she whispered, "I have to get something."

Will felt Jay leave his side and move up the staircase as he started to navigate his way in the darkness. His breath was coming back, but his legs felt as if they belonged to someone else. In the dark, the stairs had become a dangerous passageway with builders' kit cluttering the steps. "Bugger," he cursed as his foot and a large paint pot tried to share the same tread of the stair. He almost lost his balance but clutched onto the bannister rail as two torch lights appeared at the top of the stairs. "Come on, up here," called out Jay quietly, take this torch, "if they break-in, we will wait here and let them search. They won't know how to turn on the lights. If they come up the main staircase, we go down the other one and vice versa."

Good plan, Will thought, unless they split up and come up different stairs. He couldn't voice his concern as he was still trying to get his breathing into some natural rhythm.

In the stillness, Will heard breaking glass then a door opened. Will looked across at Jay, but it was difficult to see her face in the darkness. Then the silence was cut open by a voice thick with accent.

"We know you are here, Mr Slater. Our Boss wants you to remember him. He is the one you owe all that money to. We can do a deal; you let us have what you owe the Boss, and we all walk away and all forgotten. What do you say, Mr Slater?"

Will heard a chair being knocked over in the kitchen, and another voice said, "shit, where is the torch on my fucking phone." Will's eyes were becoming used to the darkness, and he turned to Jay, who put a finger against her lips.

"Don't make us do something nasty, Mr Slater. Be reasonable, and then we can all leave alive."

Two beams of light danced up and down in the hall as the two men made their way out of the kitchen. “We know you are here, and we will find you, Slater.”

Beam number one headed towards the lounge and beam number two towards the stairs. Will felt Jay give his arm a little tug and saw her shadow move away from the landing balustrades towards the rear stairs. He could see beam number two start to climb the staircase as the light rose and steadied as it took each step upwards. Will sensed Jay moving and as he turned towards her, reflected from the intruder’s torch was a glint of metal.

She whispered, “time, I think,” and then a bright light burst open the hall, followed by a crack of a pistol in Jay’s hands that reverberated through the empty landing. Jay pulled Will back further towards the rear stairs. The running of feet broke a brief silence, and beam number one arrived in the hall. “If that’s how you want to play it, Slater,” and then another flash and bang from beam number one.

“Come on,” whispered Jay, “let’s get to the back stairs.” Ears still echoing from the noise of the shots and his heart jumping around in his chest, Will scuttled across the landing after Jay. He could hear steps approaching up the main staircase, so as quickly and quietly as they could, they descended the back stairs and edged into the passageway that led to the hall. The hall was now dark, as both beams had gone up the main stairs.

“The front door?” Will whispered to Jay. “Yes,” was the reply. It wasn’t easy to see anything. In London, there would be some illumination from outside. Here there was just darkness and more darkness. Will could feel Jay close to him, and he sensed she was urging him forward. He didn’t think he could risk the torch, so he tried to picture the route to the front door and what obstacles might be in the way. There were building materials everywhere. What was in the hall? Will couldn’t remember exactly. Keeping his back to the wall, he slid along using his leading leg to feel for any obstacles. There was the sound of doors being thrown open from upstairs and then footsteps proceeding along the landing. It wouldn't be long before the beams find the other flight of stairs. Will hustled towards the front door. At the corner of the hall, his feet caught the edge of a metal ladder that fell flat, its metallic ringing indicating their location.

"They're down there," came a voice from the landing as one of the beams made it's way back to the top of the main stairs. " They are trying to escape," as a shot crashed into the front door.

Will saw Jay aim her pistol at the torch on the stairs and pull the trigger. The torch didn't fall just seemed to jump to one side.

Will whispered to Jay, "come on, can't go through the front door. It has to be the tunnel," as he manoeuvred Jay through the door to the billiard room.

Behind him, Will heard a crash and then a series of thumps down the stairs followed by raised voices. It sounded like the builders' materials had successfully booby-trapped the stairs, and at least one of the torches had fallen. Risking his own torch, Will and Jay made their way around the billiard table to the panel in the wall. Will wasted precious seconds as he tried to locate the switch mechanism; he could sense the beams were getting nearer all the time.

"Get in," he mouthed to Jay as the panel door sprung open, and Jay disappeared into the darkness. Will was just trying to pull the panel door closed behind them when one of the beams appeared at the billiard room door. "He's over there," the beam shouted. Will left the panel door open and chased after Jay. Will could see the shadowy movement of Jay's torch in front of him and called out, "behind you, keep moving." He thought about turning on the lights to illuminate the tunnel but decided against it. They had a slight advantage over the pursuers as they knew where they were heading. The uneven floor made progress hazardous, even with torches. As Will rounded a bend in the tunnel, he saw Jay stumble to the ground but was up as quickly as she had fallen and was away again. The rough wall acted like sandpaper on Will's hand as he used his outstretched arm to keep balance, his feet twisting and turning on the uneven floor. He could now see lights behind him. The beams were in the tunnel. He tried to estimate how much further it was to the end. At the end of a longish straight stretch of the tunnel, something whistled past Will's head, followed by a loud bang and debris bouncing off the wall. Ears ringing, Will ducked, almost losing his footing before he rounded another bend and refuge for a while. He tried to increase his speed, but he couldn't afford to trip and fall. The soles of his feet and toes ached from the bruising on the floor. Ragged breaths emerged from his raw and rasping lungs. His legs were shaking as every muscle and sinew cried out for rest. His chest tightened as panic crept through him like an invisible enemy. Around another bend and then up ahead, he saw Jay placing the ladder against the end wall. Behind him, he heard a clattering followed by several expletives, as one or both of the beams must have fallen. He could see Jay gliding up the ladder, torch in her mouth and hand outstretched as she reached the top to push open the hatch. Will hoped she had enough strength as otherwise, they were both dead. He could hear Jay straining with the effort as he trundled on in his ungainly gait towards the end wall as fast as he could. The blood pressure hammered in his ears, making every noise sound as if it were in a bubble in his head. A loud wrenching sound echoed through the darkness, and a release of air, like a cork, pulled from a bottle. Jay had opened the hatch. All he had to do was get there and up the ladder. Will flashed his torch up to the roof of the tunnel, and where the exit hatch had been was now just a dark patch with Jay's legs propelling herself upwards and out into the darkness. Head down, he moved forward, every step a battle of mind over body. He was almost there. Almost in touching distance of the ladder. In his mind, he could already feel the coarse wood of the ladder sides in his palms. He heard Jay call from above, and as he reached for the ladder, he tripped, dropping the torch on the ground. Trousers torn and knees grazed, he reached up to grab hold of a lower rung. The gravelly sound of footsteps and laborious breathing were closing in behind him. Concentrate, he thought, a dozen upward steps, and he would be safe. His foot found the lower rung as his sweaty palms grasped the gnarled and coarse-grained wood of the ladder sides. Up he pushed, muscles taught and tearing with pain. Each aged rung creaked, sagging under his weight. Concentrate on the next rung; he urged himself, just a few more to freedom. He couldn't hear Jay anymore, but he could hear voices below him. Cool air from the open hatch rustled his hair. A couple more steps, and he would be out. The voices were louder and the tunnel lighter. As his foot pushed down on the next rung, the wood moaned under the pressure. A cracking sound, and Will's foot moved downwards, not upwards. His chin bounced off a rung, and splinters of wood embedded themselves into his palms as he slipped down the ladder. He thrust down a leg to reach the next rung, but the added downward force cracked that rung too. He was now hanging by his arms, his feet swinging in the air, unable to find a foothold. Will's momentum had changed, and so had his balance. He threw an arm upwards to reach the rung above his head, but the movement made the ladder swing out from the wall. Shoulder muscles screeched with pain as Will swung on his arms, trying to move the ladder back against the wall. He looked up. The ladder was almost vertical and toppling backwards in slow motion. Panic rose in his throat; falling to the ground would likely cause serious injury or even death. He thrashed around like a fish in a net, trying to lean forward to halt the ladder's relentless progress. The voices below had stopped; presumably, Will thought, watching how this drama would unfold. The ladder had picked up speed and was now leaning backwards on its downward trajectory. Will heard a piercing scream and realised it had come from his mouth. A scream of desperation and fear as he looked down. Everything was moving backwards until he felt a pull on the shoulders of his jacket that momentarily halted the seemingly inevitable fall. What had his jacket caught on? There was nothing but space all around. The ladder had slipped away from under him, and he heard it crash to the ground. Yet, he was suspended in mid-air, his legs dangling beneath him, and then he felt himself moving upwards through the dark space. The edge of the hatch was now level with his eyes, but still, he climbed until he felt himself swing round in the dark, and then there was solid ground beneath the soles of his feet. Will looked up, and still attached to the shoulders of his coat were the two massive hands of Mack. Will felt sick; he wanted to collapse on the ground and just lie there.

"Don't just stand there, Pal," said Mack, "help me get this rock in place."

Jay had already slammed the hatch closed, and Mack had his large back pressed against the rock that they had removed not so long ago. Although still shaking and feeling nauseous from his near-death experience, Will crouched next to Mack and pushed against the rock, and very slowly, he felt it roll onto the top of the hatch. Voices could be heard below them. A bullet ricocheted through the hatch onto the underside of the rock, and the three of them jumped back.

Will looked at Mack shaking his head, lips pursed, eyebrows questioning.

"I was out on the estate by the loch, just keeping a watch out for any trespassers, when I saw you cycle back and run inside. Then all the lights went out just as I saw two men by the kitchen door. I knew there was trouble. I thought I would surprise whoever they were by using the tunnel to enter the house," said Mack.

"How did you get here so quickly?" asked Will.

Mack looked across at the quad bike sitting on the path beside the hatch.

"Come on, we must catch them at the front," said Jay.

“This is only made for two,” said Mack indicating the quad bike.

“We’ll manage,” said Jay pulling Will towards the bike.

CHAPTER SEVENTEEN

Will clambered on the bike behind Jay and Mack, who drove. The distance back to the house by the track was further than through the tunnel, but Will hoped that the extra speed of the bike would enable them to cut off the intruders. His head squeezed tight against Jay's back, limited his vision to only the side. Mack gunned the bike, and the engine roared and pulsated between Will's legs as they tore through the darkness like some demented nocturnal animal in search of its prey. Mack swung the bike one way and then the other to avoid tree roots and burrows. Sometimes the obstacles came too quickly, and the bike hit them head-on. Twice, Will was flung upwards, arms locked around Jay's waist, only to crash down painfully onto a poorly padded seat. Strange shadows with arm-like tentacles reached out towards him as the bike flew through the woods.

Above the shrieking of the bike's engine, Will heard a car start. "Come on, they are getting away," he shouted as the bike neared the end of the track.

The quad bike sped around the side of the house and onto the front drive. In the distance, the red taillights of the intruders' car bumped up and down on its way to the road.

"The shortcut to the inn," shouted Will pointing in the direction of the path that he had cycled up not that long before.

Mack twisted the throttle, and the bike raced down the path. Stomach still complaining from the rough treatment, fingers numb from holding onto Jay and his cheek rubbed sore from chaffing against her coarse jumper, Will peered around her. He could see Mack hunched over the handlebars with his head protruding forward like some character out of a child's cartoon film. As they took the first bend on the path, the light from the bike caught the outline of a figure standing very still at the edge of the wood. Will looked back over his shoulder, but whoever it was had been swallowed up into the mouth of darkness. Will was sure it had been a figure and thought he even vaguely recognised the person. Another bend in the path, more gritting of teeth, and Will forgot about the sighting and concentrated on holding onto Jay as the bike roared like an angry lion as it accelerated down a straight stretch of path. The intruders would drive much quicker away from the house, and even though the quad bike would be faster than his cycling, it would be touch and go as to who got to the road by the inn first. Will hadn't planned on what to do when they reached the end of the path. How would they stop the car? Could they stop the car? As they neared the road, a flash of lights and metal hurtled past the inn.

"He's going too fast," said Mack, "he needs to brake now to take the bend," as he brought the bike to a halt.

A stabbing pain shot up through Will's groin from the buffeting as he leapt from the back of the bike. He could see the intruders' car brake lights flash repeatedly, but the car didn't slow down. The wheels on the passenger side of the vehicle lost contact with the road. The car crabbed sideways to the right on two wheels, like some stunt trick, until the vehicle's front hit the low wall that separated the road from the loch. The car flipped up into the air. Its boot forced open from the impact, flapping up and down as if waving to a departing friend. The car twisted and somersaulted as if performing some gross gymnastic routine before it crashed down on its roof into the loch. Will just stood there as the horrific tableau unfolded. Jay started towards the car as the headlights dimmed as it sank, but Will grabbed her arm. "There is nothing we can do; the water is freezing and murky with peat," as the surface of the water bubbled, with the air forced out. A moment later, the headlights were gone.

CHAPTER EIGHTEEN

Noise from the crash had attracted people out of the inn, and Hamish rushed over. "Are you okay? What happened? Was it anything to do with those two men asking for you? Was that them in the car?" he said, turning towards the spot where the car had left the road.

Will was unsure why Hamish should associate the crash with the two men but let the thought drift away. "Yes, it was them. We chased them off. They were up to no good, so they must have decided to make a quick exit and misjudged the bend in the road."

The crowd outside the inn had grown, and one or two locals had stopped their cars to enquire. Most were transfixed to the spot where the car had disappeared into the loch, now only marked by the gap in the wall. Even the ripples had faded. Time seemed to stand still, and Will took off his coat and put it over Jay's shoulders. In the distance, Will could see blue lights reflecting in the dark sky as the emergency services sped towards the incident. A police car stopped in the road in front of the crowd.

Inspector Tavish got out of the passenger side. "What

happened?" he asked one of the onlookers, who recounted a story as if they had seen it. Not convinced, Tavish asked again, "did anyone see what happened?"

"We did, Inspector," said Will.

"Ah, Mr and Mrs Slater, we meet again so soon."

"Two men broke into our house, and we chased them off and, in their rush to escape, crashed through the wall and straight into the loch."

Tavish walked over to the gap and flashed his torch into the water.

"The loch is deep here; I fear they're for the fishes now. Sergeant Pearce and the constables will take statements while I get someone to pull the car out of the water."

Will watched Tavish walk back towards his car; his phone stuck to his ear.

The watchers still milled around in the road. Some with drinks in their hands as they talked in animated voices.

Hamish had brought out whiskies for Will, Jay and Mack. Will could hardly get the glass to his mouth as his hands shook so much.

"Are you okay, darling?" enquired Jay.

"No, I feel awful. I can't stop shaking; my body feels as if someone has punched me all over. Those men were going to kill us. That, that man in prison, the Boss, he sent them to kill us."

"We don't know they would have if we had paid them the money that was owed."

"Yes, they would; we would be the only ones who knew they had the money. They weren't going to pay back the Boss. Why should they?"

"Yes, you may be correct."

Sergeant Pearce walked across to them, "I'm taking statements in the front bar. If you could come in, please, Mr and Mrs Slater."

After Pearce had finished, Will watched through the window

as another larger police vehicle arrived together with a tow-away truck. The occupants from the first vehicle changed into wet suits and breathing apparatus and manoeuvred a small rubber dingy into the water.

Tavish entered the bar, and Pearce murmured to him.

Approaching Will and Jay, Tavish said, "I understand from the Sergeant that there was some shooting at the house."

"Yes, Inspector, the intruders were armed, and I think they would have killed us if we had not escaped," replied Will.

"Very lucky if you ask me. Two armed men and you both escaped." Tavish paused. "Oh, of course, Mrs Slater, you are ex-police, SO15; that must have helped."

"Well, I was probably a little less frightened than, perhaps, a civilian. You are well informed, Inspector."

"As I said before, I make it my business to check up on the people on my patch. You are an interesting couple for this neck of the woods. But tell me, the two men seemed to be escaping from you, not the other way around."

Will replied, "they chased us through the house, and we made our escape through the tunnel, you know, the one with the body."

"Yes, I do remember, Mr Slater."

"Well, thanks to Mack here, we got out and blocked their exit. Then, we raced here to see if we could cut them off by the inn."

"Rather unfortunate that you didn't cut them off, Mr Slater. Now tell me, has this anything to do with the gang you had a run-in with last year?"

"Yes, I believe it does. The men specifically mentioned their boss, who is in prison. So I think they were here to take revenge."

"Why would they want to do that, Mr Slater? What possible good would that do? My experience of criminals is that they rarely take revenge against non-criminals."

"I think they thought they could extort some money from me. Money that their boss thinks is owed to him."

"Why did they start shooting then? Killing you would have

finished their plan."

"Perhaps because we hid and then escaped."

"Mmmm, I still think it's strange that they should start shooting without any provocation. You don't own a gun, do you, Mr Slater?"

"Only shotguns for use on the land."

"What about you, Mrs Slater, gave them all back when you left the force?"

"Most certainly, Inspector."

"What about him?" said Tavish nodding in Mack's direction,

"Mack has a shotgun licence, too," cut in Will.

"Mmmm, we will have to get SOCO over to the house again. Suggest you stay here tonight as I don't want anyone else traipsing around."

"I turned all the lights off, Inspector. Tell your boys the switch is under the stairs," said Jay.

"Okay," said Tavish with a slight nod of thanks, "I will let you know when you can go back in."

"Inspector, we are the victims here; I feel that you are treating us like criminals."

"That's as maybe, Mr Slater, but I don't like shooting on my patch, and until I find out what has happened, I'm keeping an open mind on everything."

Will watched Tavish march out of the door.

"Bloody man, who does he think he is?" said Will under his breath.

Taking Will's arm, Jay replied, "you can see his point of view, we are strangers in his area, and since we have arrived, there has been one thing after the other. He is suspicious, that's all."

"Well, I don't see his point at all, everyone is innocent until proven guilty, and he seems to think we are guilty of something," then, after a pause, Will added, "I suppose we had better see if Hamish has got rooms for us tonight."

Mack took the quad bike back to the barn and his new home,

and Will and Jay sidled into the bar. Most of the regulars had left, no doubt, to recount their evening's excitement to loved ones at home.

"Lydia has rustled up a few sandwiches; you must be hungry," said Hamish.

"That's very kind of her," replied Jay.

"Another wee dram with them?" asked Hamish.

"That would be great."

"Could you rustle us up a room too?" asked Will.

"Of course, I suspected you would need one. Your old one is free."

"Like old times," said Jay.

"The renovations to the house must be progressing well," said Hamish.

"Yes, they are and can't wait until we get rid of the builders."

"Must be a big place to run and keep clean," suggested Hamish.

"Tell me about it," replied Jay, "as soon as I have cleaned the dust off one surface, the builders have sanded another wall, and the dust is back."

"Sounds as if you need some help."

"Actually, Hamish, I could do with some help. Perhaps someone local could come in and help me clean a few days a week. Do you know anyone?"

"Funny you should ask, but there is a lassie in the village, said she was looking for some work, cleaning, cooking, generally anything. I have got her details somewhere here," said Hamish rummaging on a shelf behind the bar. "Here, here we are, Lena Swift, and her number's there too."

"Do you know her?"

"Not really, came up from London to look after a relative, but she seems like a nice lassie, and I think she would get on with you both. So why don't I get her to give you a call, Jay? Get things started."

"Okay, suppose it can't help to meet her and then make a decision."

"Excellent will speak to her in the morning."

"Time for bed now," said Will," and thanks for everything, Hamish."

"Ach, no problem."

* * *

As soon as Will and Jay were inside their room, Will asked, "how did you get that gun?"

"Harry Allan called me; you remember him?"

"Of course, the black Range Rover, I knew I recognised the driver. It was him in it, wasn't it?"

"Yes, it was, but, at the time, I didn't know it was him," replied Jay.

"How could I forget your old boss at SO15, who for a long time thought that I was the brains behind the terrorist arms dealings."

"Yes, well, he contacted me to say that he had heard something on the rumour tree."

"You mean GCHQ."

"Whatever. The rumour is that a contract has been placed on your life."

"My God. So, they didn't want the money, just to kill me. Why didn't you tell me? When were you going to tell me?"

"It was only a rumour, and I thought you were anxious enough as it was. Harry said he would let me know if he heard anymore, but in the meantime, he issued me with a gun for our protection."

"I could have been more prepared if you had told me."

"I doubt that, on this occasion. We seem to have repelled the first invaders, but we had better shore up our defences. Harry wanted to warn me as he thought that if they could catch who was trying to kill you, then it might lead further up the chain."

"That was big of him. So, you let me become another target as before. For goodness sake, you don't work for SO15 anymore."

"I realise I should have told you, but I was doing it for the best. Harry didn't think anything would happen so quickly, if at all. I thought that I would protect you, and apart from becoming a hermit, we have to face our enemies. We must see who they are and defeat them, or we will forever be fearful of our shadows. The police or SO15 can't protect us for the rest of our lives. Wherever we go, someone will find us eventually if they want to. So, we have to face it head on."

"It's all very well you saying that, but it's my life that has got a contract on it."

"I know, but I will likely get caught in the crossfire, perhaps literally."

"Yep, I get that too. So, apart from the contract on my life, another chain of people is trying to kill me. I thought that had all ended."

"We all thought that, but Harry thinks that the article has brought others out of the woodwork. Those who think that the money you have is rightly theirs."

"I knew it. I told you that article was going to be dangerous for me. Bloody journalist."

"However, if you are dead, they won't be able to obtain any money. So, my guess is there are two different people or groups of people."

"Very reassuring. One group wants me dead, and the other wants me alive until I pay them and then what? This whole scenario is awful. I might as well have a target painted on my back."

"Look, we're going to have to do this together. We did it before. No one is going to help us, certainly not forever. I'm sorry that I didn't tell you about the contract; I realise now it was a mistake. Okay? Right, I'm going to have a shower before bed."

Sitting on the bed, listening to the shower running in the bathroom, Will went through in his mind the events of the last few hours. He had thought the traumas of the previous year and his several near-death experiences were over. They appeared not to be. He looked down at his hands and noticed they were shaking, and suddenly he felt tired. His body ached from head to foot. He lay back on the bed and tried to sleep, but the adrenaline that still coursed through his veins wouldn't give up its grip. He tried to process the sequence of events in order, but something else was vital that he couldn't quite recall. Something he had seen. He willed it back into his brain. What was it? Something he had seen that was out of place. No someone. Sitting bolt upright on the bed, Will shouted, "Jay."

Jay rushed in, her hair dripping and a towel draped around her, "what is it?"

"Roddy Neath, I saw him at the house."

"What do you mean you saw him at the house."

"As we were driving along the path towards the inn, I caught sight of someone standing in the shadows of the wood. Just watching. Just a glimpse, momentarily, and then he disappeared into the darkness."

"Are you sure it was Roddy Neath? Why would he be there?"

"Well, I only saw him for a second in the reflection of the bike's light, but it certainly looked like his build, and I don't know, the way he stood. It just reminded me of him. I don't know why he would be there? I have had this feeling that someone has been watching me, so perhaps it's him."

"Well, he did behave quite strangely when we met, but why would he be watching you? Perhaps you should tell Tavish."

"Yeah, I will first thing in the morning."

CHAPTER NINETEEN

The water trickled over the Boss's head from the partially blocked showerhead. He looked around. No privacy, showers only three times a week and godawful soap. He thought of the opulent bathroom he had at his house, a massive walk-in shower, showerheads the size of dinner plates, fluffy white towels and underfloor heating. It had even been better in the services, except when they were on tour. Some of those locations had been a bit primitive. Strange, he thought, from peacekeeper to rabble-rouser. He knew which he preferred. As he tried to get a lather from the soap, he watched another inmate enter thc washroom. The Boss had always tried to look smart and keep himself fit and trim. He used to watch what he ate and drank and used the gym in his house every day. He metaphorically turned his nose up at the newcomer. A big man, great rolls of blubber congregated around his midriff, sweat dripping down between his man breasts towards a tiny penis. The Boss turned his back and concentrated on his ablutions. Much to his annoyance, the newcomer came up right behind him and spoke so quietly that it was barely audible above the running water.

"We hear that you have put out a contract."

Turning around, the Boss replied, “maybe, but what has it got to do with you. That is my business and not yours.”

“You are being asked to withdraw the contract.”

“Why?”

“Because he is wanted alive for now, as he is valuable.”

“Fuck that, he owes me a shedload of money, and I ain’t going to be able to use it now, so I want my revenge. I don’t care a fuck whose asking; the job is being done as we speak, and now fuck off so I can finish my shower.” The Boss turned away from the newcomer to rinse the soap off his shoulders.

“That’s a pity,” said the newcomer.

The Boss felt a sharp pain in his side and looked down. Nothing to see, perhaps a slight red mark. The newcomer had gone. The Boss felt light-headed as he stepped out of the shower and reached for his threadbare towel, but he never got to it as he was dead before he hit the grubby tiled floor.

CHAPTER TWENTY

Will stood in the doorway to the inn and watched a couple of police officers looking closely at the road. He assumed they were checking skid marks or whatever they do in these circumstances. Apart from that, all other human activity around the loch edge had ceased. A group of seagulls, calling noisily, were busily prancing up and down the foreshore. The police tape marked the gap in the low wall, but otherwise, all looked the same across the loch.

A police car approached from the direction of Gaur House. It stopped, and Inspector Tavish got out and approached the inn.

"Good morning Mr Slater. Have you got a few moments as I would like to speak to you and Mrs Slater?"

"Yes, of course, I was going to call you this morning as I've remembered something that may be useful. Let me get my wife first. Why don't we talk in the bar? It should be empty at this time of day."

The three assembled in the bar, and Tavish asked, "what was it you wanted to tell me. Mr Slater? Why don't you go first."

"I remembered it last night. When I was on the back of the quad bike chasing the intruders, I thought I saw someone standing on the edge of the woods. It was only a fleeting glance, but I think it was Roddy Neath. He owns the water sports centre on the other side of the loch.

"Fascinating, Mr Slater. Do you know Mr Neath well?"

"No, I have only met him once."

"I see, but you still feel it was him watching you, in the dark, in the woods, as you sped past."

"As I said, I can't be sure, but there was definitely someone, and my impression was that it was him."

"Okay," said Tavish nodding his head, "I will pay Mr Neath a visit." He then opened his notebook and scribbled something down. "Did you see him too, Mrs Slater?"

"No, I didn't see anyone, Inspector."

"Okay, that's all, nothing else that you can remember? Nothing you want to add or admit about the break-in at all?"

"Not sure what you mean about admit, but no, there is nothing that we want to add," replied Will, taking a surreptitious look across at Jay.

"Mrs Slater?"

"No, nothing to add, Inspector."

"Good, but I have some questions for you. We have finished at the house, but my techo boys tell me that two different guns were fired in the house. I thought you said only one," said Tavish looking across to Jay.

"I don't recall saying that, Inspector. There were two intruders, so they presumably both had guns."

"Couldn't you tell the difference between the sounds? An automatic makes a different sound to, say, a revolver," challenged Tavish.

"You know as well as me that a revolver makes a deafening sound. It certainly wasn't that."

"As we said, Inspector, why would that surprise you, two intruders and two guns? Makes sense to me," chipped in Will.

"Possibly," but Tavish persevered with this line of enquiry.

"Two shots were fired down the stairs from two different guns. We recovered one slug from the ceiling and one from the back of the front door. Two shots were fired upstairs, again from different guns."

"That would be correct, Inspector," replied Will, "they fired two shots from the hall, I think to frighten us, not to kill us, and then they both fired when they heard us escaping into the billiard room."

"Mmmm," mused Tavish with his head slightly to one side, "pretty bad shots, if they were aiming for the billiard room, one in the ceiling and one in the front door?"

"As I said, Inspector, warning shots. It was dark; all the lights were off."

"My boys tell me there were two different bullet casing sizes found- a nine by 18mm case, probably from a Makarov and a nine by 19mm, probably from a Glock or something similar. You would know all about Glocks, Mrs Slater, as they are issued to plainclothes officers, secret service sort of thing. I imagine something you would have had in your day."

"Spot on, Inspector, glued to my hip," said Jay patting her jeans.

Tavish paused. "Now the funny thing is that we only recovered one gun from the car, the Makarov; you would have thought that we would have found two."

"Perhaps they dropped one, or it got washed out of the car window when it went under," said Will.

Tavish stared long and hard, first at Will and then at Jay and snapped his notebook closed. "Would you like me to assign a car to watch the house tonight?"

"No, I don't think that will be necessary, thank you, Inspector," replied Will.

"Okay, I'm sure I will have further questions, but that will do for now. I will call on Mr Neath and see what he was doing last night." Tavish turned and left the bar.

"Not sure we convinced him about the guns," said Will.

"No, definitely not, but he has no evidence, so we will just stick to our story," replied Jay.

"Let's go back to the house. I'll get Mack to sort out the security, CCTV cameras and alarm trips in the grounds."

CHAPTER TWENTY-ONE

Later that night, back in their bed in Gaur House, a voice invaded Will's dream. He tried to see who was speaking, but the face was in a shadow. The voice was quiet but very urgent and would not go away. He tried to call back and ask who was there, but as hard as he tried, nothing came out of his mouth. His shoulder was now vigorously shaken.

"Wake up, Will, there's someone in the house," Jay whispered into Will's ear.

Eyes now open, he turned to Jay and asked why she was whispering.

"So, whoever it is can't hear us."

"Don't we want to frighten them off? I'll put on the light." Will flicked the switch of the bedside lamp. Nothing. "Try yours," he said. Jay tried her lamp. Nothing.

"The lights are fused," said Will.

"No, they have been turned off. That's my trick; whoever it is knows this house and where the fuse box is," said Jay.

"Who is it? Do you think someone else is coming to kill me? I don't think I can take much more of this."

"How should I know who it is? But I intend to find out, come on. There's a torch in your drawer. You take the back stairs. I'm going to take the main staircase."

Will watched Jay slip on a pair of jeans and tuck her pistol into the belt. "Shouldn't we call the police, supposing they are armed like yesterday?"

"If we wait for the police, whoever it is will be gone, and I want to know who it is."

In the darkness, Will's mouth turned down at the thought of a different set of intruders in the house. He was also unsure about not calling the police. He would have preferred to push a wardrobe up against the bedroom door and await the boys in blue. "I can't hear anything. Perhaps they've gone," said Will, not relishing prowling around in the dark.

"Maybe," replied Jay.

They both listened in the darkness. Was that a creak? They listened. Yes, a door creaked, not much, but they both heard it. Will switched on his torch and nodded at Jay. They left their bedroom. Will watched Jay edge towards the main stairs. He turned, and keeping his back to the wall, sidestepped along the landing towards the back stairs. Flashing the beam of his torch in an arc, Will saw what he needed on the floor, a heavy screwdriver left by the ever-present hoard of builders. Picking it up by its metal shaft, Will now had a handy blunt instrument should he need it. Out of the corner of his eye, he could see the light of Jay's torch bobbing around as she made her way down the stairs. Will reached the back stairs, turned off his torch and listened. Every house had its particular noises, like a living creature breathing in the darkness. It usually was the distant hum from the electrics, the wind through a gap in the old wooden framed windows, or the creak from ageing floorboards as they expanded and contracted. Will was only just learning the natural aches and groans from this elderly house. He could now see the beam from Jay's torch moving around in the hall like an agitated spectre looking for its peace.

Will stood very still, holding his breath so as not to disturb the stillness. What was that? He thought he heard a noise from the servants' quarters above him. The noise was not loud but discordant with the rest of the house's murmurings. He listened, all his senses alert. This time he heard a scraping sound. Will couldn't work out what the noise was. The hairs on his neck stood up. There it was again; it sounded like something was being pushed. A piece of furniture being moved, but there was nothing up there. All the rooms were empty; there was nothing to move. The hairs on Will's neck were doing double time, as was his pulse. He had a vision from a film he had once seen of a creaking rocking chair gently moving by itself in an empty room. He shook his head to chase away the ludicrous thought.

Should he call Jay? But that would warn who or whatever was upstairs. Like a recurring nightmare when you know opening the door is a mistake, but you still go and do it, Will stepped onto the first tread. His slippers made no noise as he climbed. Holding his screwdriver in one hand, Will used the other to feel the wall as he took each step sideways, every moment expecting that something would charge out of the darkness towards him. He could switch on his torch but decided not to. Reaching the top, he realised he had been holding his breath and breathed out.

Will peered along the corridor. The bathroom door was closed. A faint light from inside outlined the entrance. The brightness of the light fluctuated. It must be a torch moving around the room. Still the scrapping noise. Shuffling in his slippers down the dark corridor, he edged his way towards the dim light. As he got closer to the bathroom door, he could see that it was not fully shut, and he would be able to peer through the open crack. One more step and he would be able to see.

Through the small gap, Will caught a glimpse of someone squatting on all fours by the bath. He inched forward to get a better look, but this last shuffle left him standing on a loose floorboard that shrieked in the silence and echoed throughout the corridor. Then total darkness, the torch in the bathroom turned off. As Will fumbled with his torch, it was knocked out of his hand as someone pushed past him. A slight peppermint smell lingered in the air for a moment. Will swung his screwdriver, connecting with more air. As he sensed the quick movement of escape, Will lunged at the shadow, just a denser patch of darkness as it moved away; his hands felt the shiny plastic of a rain jacket. He couldn't get any grip as the shadow continued to move away from him and his hands slipped down the coat, forcing him into a rugby-style tackle as he fell forward. Will's momentum was now downwards, his nails dragging on the intruder's course trousers, his fingertips trying to grip onto the flapping material. Will's hands slipped down and reached a boot, and he clung on. The shadow stopped, and the boot kicked backwards, catching Will squarely in the face.

"Ahh," he cried and let go, and the shadow disappeared down the corridor. Clutching his nose, Will staggered to his feet and called out, "Jay, he's on the back stairs," as Will heard the scampering of the shadow's footsteps down the wooded treads. Will scrabbled on the ground for his torch and flicked it on, and relocating his slippers, he started after the shadow. The house was lighter now; Jay must have turned on the lights. He met her coming towards him at the next landing.

"Are you okay?" she asked.

"Yes, fine, he must have gone across the landing and down the main staircase. Come on."

Jay was quicker than Will in his slippers and overtook him descending the stairs two at a time. She disappeared through the hall towards the kitchen. As Will reached the kitchen, he saw Jay standing at the back door, peering out into the night.

"He got out here. I can't see anything. No point in blundering around out there; he will be well gone. Did you get a look at him?"

"No, but I think it was Dougie Gordon."

"Why?"

"Well, he was about the right size, and as he passed me, there was a faint smell of peppermint. I noticed it on him when we first met."

"But why would he break-in? He owned the house for years. But whoever it was, did know where the main lights switch was. And unless you forgot to lock the kitchen door last night, he also had a key."

"But we haven't got anything to steal, and what was he doing in the old servants' rooms?"

"I think we should take a look. Lock the back door, leave all the lights on," replied Jay, tucking her pistol back again into the waistband of her jeans.

Switching on all the lights, they made their way up to the bathroom on the top floor. Will walked around the bath while Jay stood at the door and examined the room. "It's empty. I can't see why anyone would want to be in here," said Jay.

"Before he turned out his torch, I caught a glimpse of him on the floor about here," said Will crouching down. "I also heard a scraping sound, a bit like moving furniture."

Jay peered over Will's shoulder. "Look, there are scratches on the floor as if the bath has been moved."

"Yes, I can see them now." Will pushed against the bath, and it moved the few inches of the scratch marks and stopped. "That was the sound I heard. I can't move it any further."

"So, Dougie, or whoever was up here moved the bath a few inches and then back again. It makes no sense."

Will peered under the bath with his torch, but there was nothing to see but a thick layer of undisturbed dust. "He couldn't move the bath too far, in any case, as all the pipes were joined to the wall, and if he pulled those off, presumably there would be water everywhere."

"Agree, another mystery in this house. It's quite exciting," said Jay.

Will looked at her and raised his eyebrows. “Perhaps we should have taken up Tavish’s offer of a police presence outside. Anyway, I think we should tell Tavish in the morning; otherwise, he will be berating us again for hiding something from him.”

“Okay, let’s get back to bed for what’s left of the night. Think we will keep all the lights on.”

CHAPTER TWENTY-TWO

"Thanks for coming, Inspector Tavish," said Will opening the door to the dour-faced policeman.

"I was coming over in any case."

"Oh, oh good," replied Will wondering what Tavish wanted from them now. "Come into the kitchen, Jay's in there."

Entering the kitchen, Tavish asked, "so, what did you want to see me about?"

Jay answered, "we had another strange intruder last night, nothing stolen, and we're okay, but thought we should inform you."

"Perhaps you should have accepted my offer to keep someone outside. Did you get a look at this person? I assume it was a man?"

"Yes, a man and no, we didn't get a good look, but he must have known the house as he knew where to turn off the main switch for the lights," replied Jay.

"And we think he had a key as there was no obvious sign of any break-in," chipped in Will.

"What was he doing in the house, then?"

"Well, that's the strange thing. I caught him in the old

servant's bathroom upstairs. I think he was trying to move the bath."

"Why would he want to do that, Mr Slater?"

"Very good question, Inspector. I wish I knew. Anyway, it's impossible to move it because of the pipework. However, there is something else. I think last night's intruder was Dougie Gordon."

"Why do you say that?"

"When we first met him, I noticed a smell of peppermint, as if he were chewing gum or sucking sweets. I smelt the same thing last night."

Tavish raised his chin and looked down his nose at Will, "I'll make a note but assume you don't want to make a formal statement."

"No, we don't," said Will glancing over to the nodding Jay.

"Why did you want to see us?" asked Jay.

"Right, the first reason is that I have some news. I'm afraid not very comforting. I have had the report back from the garage where the intruders, or should I say the first lot of intruders' vehicle was taken for examination. The reason that they missed that bend in the road was that the car brakes had been tampered with."

"My God, that is awful," said Will.

"It is and puts a different complexion on this case. What was an RTA, a Road Traffic Accident, is now a murder inquiry. Are you sure you didn't know these men, Mr Slater?"

"You don't think I had anything to do with their deaths, do you?"

"I don't think anything, Mr Slater. As I have said before, I only deal in facts, and they are that two men broke into this house, threatened you, then several firearms were discharged, and the next thing, the two men are dead."

"How far could they have driven with the brakes as they were?" asked Jay thoughtfully.

"Not far, I am told," replied Tavish.

"So, the brakes must have been tampered with when their car was parked in our drive," said Will.

"Increasingly, that looks like the case Mr Slater, and the only people in this house, at the time, were you and Mrs Slater," said Tavish looking across at Jay, "and your Ghillie, Angus Mack. So, I have a limited choice of suspects."

"What about the man I saw at the edge of the woods? Possibly Roddy Neath?"

"I only have your word for that, Mr Slater; neither your wife nor the Ghillie saw anyone. I have spoken to Neath, and he says he was at his centre all evening."

"Does he have an alibi?"

"No, but alibi or not, I'm struggling to grasp why Neath would want to kill two men that we assume he had never met and had only just arrived in the area. You, on the other hand, Mr Slater or even you, Mrs Slater, had every reason to kill them."

"But we wouldn't have had the opportunity. We spent all our time trying to get away from them until they left, and then we chased them. What about Mack, is he under suspicion too?"

"Do you think he tempered with the brakes?" asked Tavish.

"No, of course not."

"As I say, I'm not discounting anything, but I can't see why the Ghillie would want to kill these men any more than Neath. Besides, his story ties in with yours."

"So, you haven't got any evidence against us, Inspector, have you?" said Jay.

"No, all circumstantial, and that is why I'm not arresting either of you at the moment."

"If the brakes were not working, wouldn't there have been a warning light on the dashboard?" asked Will.

"I would assume so, but why they didn't heed it is anyone's guess. It was dark, and the intruders were concentrating on getting away from you both, so perhaps they missed it or thought the risk was the lesser of two evils," replied Tavish menacingly.

"This is ridiculous. I can hardly believe what I'm hearing. We are the victims. Yet again, you're treating us like criminals," retorted Will.

"As I said, I'm keeping an open mind, which leads me to the second reason for my visit. I have now heard back from forensics as to the identity of the body in your tunnel." Tavish paused, perhaps for effect, "the body belongs to Dougie Gordon."

"Really?" said Will and Jay in unison.

"Aye, it's Dougie Gordon, alright, no doubt."

Will's face was full of confusion as he looked across at Jay. "But, but it can't be, we bought the house from Dougie, and that body has been in the tunnel far longer."

"All I can tell you is that whoever you bought the house from wasn't Dougie Gordon. Perhaps we should call this other man Mr Peppermint," said Tavish with a wry smile.

"How did Dougie die, Inspector?" asked Jay.

"Technically, it is an ongoing enquiry, so I'm not supposed to tell you, but he had been shot."

"Oh, that's awful, another murder," said Will.

"Quite so, Mr Slater, as he didn't put himself in that tunnel."

"What about Dougie's brother. Do you know where he is?"

"How do you know about him?" asked Tavish.

"I did some research from articles in the local paper and saw the one where the brothers had a barny at the inn."

"We are, of course, looking into all possible avenues of enquiry."

"Do you have a description of the brother? We could see if it matched the Dougie that we knew?" asked Will.

"I will check what we have on record."

"Also, Inspector, as a matter of interest, did your techy boys think that the upstairs bathroom had anything to do with Dougie's death? Perhaps last night's intruder was trying to cover his tracks or something?"

"You were correct; we did find blood in that bathroom, and

it is a match to the real Dougie Gordon. So, there is every possibility that he was injured or killed in that room. As to what your intruder was doing up, there is anyone's guess. He could hardly be covering up something that we have already established."

"Yes, I can see that, but it is still strange that he was up there, trying to move the bath."

"Well, we need to find this chap. I take it you'll not be going anywhere, either of you, as I'm sure I will want to speak to you again."

"No, we are not planning any trips, Inspector."

"Good, I will be off now. By the way, I would suggest you get the locks changed."

"We will," replied Jay.

After Tavish had left, Will slid down into a kitchen chair, feeling bewildered by the news.

"Does that mean that we may not own this house?" asked Jay.

"Only if whoever sold it to us didn't have ownership. I'm sure George McCorkney would have checked that correctly. Wait a minute, George said that it was a company that owned the house, and all the shareholders registered in tax havens. I thought that strange as I didn't think Dougie would be the type to embark on tax avoidance. But that all makes sense if Dougie wasn't the owner but his brother."

"Assuming you are right, and we don't know it was the brother, how did he or the company get their hands on the ownership of the house?"

"If the brother were ruthless enough to kill Dougie, he would be capable of forging Dougie's signature in a blink of an eye."

"Yes, that makes sense, but why sell the house to us if he had unfinished business inside. Why not wait to sell rather than break in later?"

"Maybe there was another reason why the house had to be sold to us at that time," said Will.

"You mean someone wanted us to buy this house?"

"Yes," said Will, "exactly, and it had to be now."

"It fits in with your feeling that we are being watched. Someone wants to know where you are and keep tabs on you."

"I thought you didn't believe me about being watched?"

"I wasn't sure and thought you might be a bit paranoid, but there are too many unexplained events that are, maybe, coincidental, but I'm beginning to feel they are all linked together somehow."

The doorbell rang.

"I'll go; perhaps Tavish has changed his mind and has come back to arrest us," said Will.

A minute later, Will was back, "look who's here," as Harry Allan, Jay's former boss at SO15, sloped into the kitchen.

"Harry, what brings you here?" said Jay.

"I bring you some tidings, mostly good but not all."

Will slipped back into his chair again and indicated for Allan to sit opposite.

"Tell all," said Jay.

Turning to Jay, Allan asked, "you told Will about our meeting?"

"Of course."

"Okay, I heard you had to use the gun too. Effective by all accounts."

Will fidgeted in his chair, making imaginary circles on the table with his index finger. He was annoyed by Allan's presence. He wasn't sure why. Perhaps some jealousy around Jay's former close working colleague, or just because Allan was a very arrogant individual. "It wasn't the gun that killed the intruders; their car brakes were cut," interjected Will.

"I hadn't heard that. Do the police know who cut the brakes?"

"No, they don't yet. Jay and I are the only suspects. It seems nothing changes. So, what did you want to tell us?" said Will, sharply enough to make Allan sit back in his seat.

"Two nights ago, the leader of the terrorist gang that you had the bust-up with in Surrey was murdered in prison. Our sources say that he was the one who put out the contract for your death."

"Gosh, I suppose that is good news for us, although not great for him," said Jay looking across to Will, who was still looking angry over Allan's presence.

"Yes, I suppose it is. Not that I knew there was a contract until I was almost killed. But I assume with the Boss's death it goes away," said Will somewhat grudgingly.

"Almost definitely," replied Allan. "However, the grey cloud is that we don't know why the Boss, as he liked to be known, was killed. He might have upset someone in prison, or it could have been to make sure the contract was made null and void."

"But who would want to do that?" asked Will.

"That's what we don't know. We will keep listening, but if this is low level, it may not be picked up. We assume whoever it is, wants you alive."

"Well, that's comforting, I suppose, but only up to a point."

"Yep, think you need to keep being alert, but think the immediate danger has passed, which means, Jay, I need to take the gun back, please."

"Of course," and Jay left to reclaim the gun from the bedside table.

"I will be going now, but if I hear anything, I will let you both know."

Feeling slightly warmer to Allan, Will said, "okay, thanks and thanks for letting us both know."

Allan nodded, pocketed the gun and left.

CHAPTER TWENTY-THREE

Will sat on the patio, steam rising from the mug of tea that he grasped in his hands. His heels bounced up and down and rocked a loose paving stone under his feet. He closed his eyes; the afternoon was peaceful, just a whisper of a breeze rustling the leaves and some seagulls arguing over their supper. Winter was around the corner, and the last rays of late autumn sunshine highlighted the trees. The leaves, with their subtle russets and oranges interspersed with the hot and fiery reds, reflected against the deep blue of the loch, but there was no tranquillity within him. Even his favourite tree, the vast larch, with bright yellow leaves that looked like a flaming torch against the cloudless sky, brought no respite to his inner torment. There were too many unanswered questions for him to feel at ease.

Will stood up and tossed the remains of his tea into a flowerbed. Tomorrow the security equipment would be installed, which would give them all some added protection. However, he felt restless and uneasy as he glared around his domain.

Suddenly a glint of light from a hill in the distance caught his eye. There it was again. He raced to the barn where Mack was tinkering with a tractor.

"Get the bikes started. There's someone on that hill that I mentioned to you. Watching me. I want to see if we can catch them."

"If we approach from behind, he might not see us until it is too late," said Mack, "follow me." The two men edged their quad bikes out of the barn and headed in the opposite direction to the hill, planning to make a long sweep and approach it inland.

The route that Mack chose was very rough, and Will saw Mack standing up on the footplates of the bike to ease the constant jolting up and down as the bikes traversed an ocean of grass hummocks. Will had tried standing too but had almost lost his footing, so his bottom would have to suffer the buffeting. After about ten minutes of more pain, Mack stopped his bike, and Will pulled in beside him. He estimated that they were on the other side of the hill now.

"We should go the rest of the way on foot; otherwise, whoever is up there will hear the bikes," said Mack.

"Agree," Will replied, noting that Mack had brought a shotgun with him.

"Just in case," said Mack, seeing Will eyeing the gun.

The summit lay in a line of hills between the loch and the mountains further south of their position. The land was all Will's, so they walked confidently towards where they thought they saw the light. As they got near the top, the click of Mack's shotgun breach being closed resonated in the still air. Suddenly Will was frightened. What if there was someone up there and they had a gun?

The approach they had taken meant that the summit remained hidden from view until the last few steps.

There was no one there.

The top of the hill was a flat plateau with vantage points looking all over Will's land and house.

"I reckon there was someone here," said Mack, "look, the grass has been flattened from someone standing or lying down."

"Well, whoever it is, they are trespassing, and I'm sure they have been watching us. At least it proves me correct, although I don't understand why or what intention they have for doing so?"

Mack was examining the ground closely, "everything is dry, so no footprints, but you see the way the bracken is snapped over there," he said, pointing away from the hill. "I think they have come from the east. I reckon from the direction of the water sports centre. It would be easy for someone to slip up the back of the centre and keep walking up to here."

Will shivered as an outline of Roddy Neath with flowing red hair passed through his mind.

* * *

As Will pushed through the kitchen door, a young woman was seated at the table talking to Jay. She was pleasant-looking; very fair hair with freckles covering her pale complexion. Well suited to this climate, Will thought.

"Oh, hello, I'm Will, and you are?"

Standing, the woman thrust out a hand. "Lena, Lena Swift."

"Will, this is the woman who was looking for work and gave her details to Hamish, remember?"

"Of course, I do; nice to meet you. I understand that you live in the village but were originally from London?"

Lena looked slightly taken aback by the comment, "yes, I rent a flat in the village and, yes, originally from London."

"What made you come up to this quiet place?"

"I had an aunt who was not very well, living in Pitlochry, and as I hadn't got a job in London, I suggested that I could come up to help her. Unfortunately, she died a little while ago. However, I liked it up here so much that I decided to stay. My aunt left me some money, but I need a job to help pay the rent and don't want to go back to London. This job sounded ideal. I don't have any formal qualifications but can turn my hand to pretty much anything."

"To save Lena money, I suggested she live in; we have plenty of space," said Jay.

"Yes, if you are happy, darling, then that's fine with me. Lena, we will be redoing all the old servants' quarters soon, so I was planning to put in a couple of apartment type suites up there so you could have one of those in due course."

"Thank you, that sounds fabulous."

"Lena is happy to start tomorrow if that's okay?"

"Fine by me," replied Will, shrugging his shoulders.

"Great, thank you. I'll see you both tomorrow morning."

Jay showed Lena out and returned to the kitchen.

"She seemed very pleasant but quite young. Will she want to do all the cleaning and chores?" asked Will.

"It's not just cleaning, a bit of cooking, and she can help with some decorating as well, rather a housekeeper than a cleaner."

"Have you taken references?"

"Not yet; she gave me a couple of names which I will follow up on."

"It's funny, but she reminded me of someone. Can't quite put my finger on who? It was some mannerism. I'm sure I have seen it before but can't quite remember," said Will screwing up his face as if he was in pain. An uneasy memory lurked in the shadows.

Leaving that thought unanswered, Will continued, "Mack hopes the new security systems will be arriving tomorrow."

"What are they going to consist of?"

"There will be infra-red cameras and alarms positioned on both the main drive and the path to the inn, as well as at various strategic points on the estate. One is covering the outbuildings and Mack's new dwelling and at various spots in a half-mile radius of the house."

"So, what happens if someone trips one of the infra-red cameras?" asked Jay.

"There is an alarm in the study and Mack's flat. Screens monitoring the cameras will be in both places, and we will be able to tell which camera is tripped and watch the film. In addition, there will be an intercom set up between here and Mack. The 'trips' are set so that small animals, foxes or small deer won't set them off."

"What happens if we're not in the study or asleep at night when an alarm goes off?"

"That's the brilliant idea; we will have apps on our smartwatches that will give us the warnings."

"Oh no, I don't have to have one of those hideous smartwatches, do I?"

"You don't, but I advise it. I suppose we could programme the alarms to your phone instead."

"That's okay, my phone goes most places with me, and if I'm alone, I'll just make sure it's always in my pocket," replied Jay. "Oh, don't forget Lucy is back for the weekend."

"Are you going to pick her up?"

"No, a friend lives out this way, and I'll pick her up in Pitlochry. I'll have to take her back on Monday morning. It will be an early start, but apparently, she has a free period first thing."

"You'll need to watch the weather as it is forecast to turn very icy, even with some snow."

"But, we aren't even into proper winter yet."

"Ah, but this is Scotland, not the South of England."

Will made himself a cup of coffee and stepped outside the kitchen door. His mood was dark, like the clouds scudding across the sky. A sense of apprehension overwhelmed him. Something ticked away at the back of his brain. Not even the new security system could eradicate his feeling of helplessness. Events seemed to be out of his hands, he was blundering around from one disaster to the next, and he felt that the next one would be bad, very bad indeed. He had persuaded Mack to let him keep one of the shotguns in his wardrobe.

Will watched the clouds rolling up from the east. A noticeable chill had crept up like an unwanted guest. Will shivered, but not entirely from the cold.

CHAPTER TWENTY-FOUR

Will looked out at the falling snow. "I said the weather was going to get colder. You'll have to be careful when you run Lucy back to school tomorrow morning."

"It may have all cleared by then; who knows. You're just a worrier," replied Jay.

"Maybe, always good to plan. I think I might pop up to the inn and have a test of the infra-red cameras now the security is set up."

"You mean you want to pop up for a couple of drinks and a chat before dinner," replied Jay.

Will laughed, "well, I might have a quick one while I'm up there. Be unsociable not to. Be back by seven-thirty, don't worry if the alarm is tripped, it will be me," he laughed again.

He decided he would walk, rather than cycle, as being a London boy, there was always excitement when it snowed, and everything appeared magical even to a grown adult. He suspected after a couple of years in Scotland, some of the magic would wear off.

He pulled on a thick coat and his walking boots. He also tucked a torch into his pocket.

The snow was now falling heavily, and he pulled his beanie over his ears. The wind had picked up too, and snowflakes blew into his face, momentarily clinging to his eyebrows and eyelashes. Winter had come early this year. He hoped it would not be like this until spring as it would delay some of the work on the house and estate. The snow had deadened the natural sounds of the woods apart from the crunch under Will's feet. The new path was level and constructed of compacted gravel rather than asphalt or concrete, but the tree and rhododendron roots would invade the path again in time.

Will had erected a new wooden gate at the end of the path and a sign that said "Private Property" to persuade the adventuresome hikers that this was not a footpath.

The inn was relatively quiet as Will entered.

"Good evening, Will," called out Hamish from behind the bar, "your usual?"

"Yes, please, and good evening to you, too. The snow's coming down pretty heavily now," replied Will.

"Aye, I think the ploughs will be out tonight, but it's not good for business. No one wants to come out in this weather,"

"How is business?" asked Will.

"Well, not too bad, could always do with more custom."

"Have you always run an inn?"

Hamish flicked his tea towel over his shoulder and rested his forearms on the bar, "good lord, no, I was in the services before. Did my ten years and decided to do something else before I got too old or got killed."

"Saw a bit of action then?"

"Aye. All in the Middle East, Iraq, Afghanistan, but I was lucky, no damage, although I saw a lot of deaths and serious injuries."

"So why this?" said Will looking around the bar.

"I met Lydia on a home visit. Her parents ran a Chinese restaurant, and they wanted her to take over. But she had better ideas and trained as a qualified chef. She got a job in Edinburgh as a sous chef in one of those smart places. When I came out, we got married and looked around for a place to run. You know, me behind the bar and her cooking. This place came up for sale, and here we are. Fancy another for the road?"

"Sounds good to me. Then I'm going back to test the new security equipment that we have put in place."

"Because of those two men?" asked Hamish.

"Partly, but we are off the beaten track, and anyone could wander around. In fact, for some time, I have had the feeling that someone was watching us or me in particular."

"How strange. Have you spotted anyone?"

"No. I know it does sound strange, but I just have that sense of a pair of eyes on my back."

"So, this security equipment will stop anyone approaching without you knowing?"

"In principle, yes, but we can only have the cameras and alarms on the main access routes and a few strategically placed on the estate but close to the house. So, if anyone knew the land well, they could get to the house without hitting a sensor. For example, along the edge of the Loch and up to the back door. Anyway, I have done the best I can and hope it will never be used in anger, so to speak."

"I hope not too," replied Hamish.

Will finished his drink, said goodnight and left. He crossed the road and stopped at the gate, looking around him. There was no one around. The lights from the inn reflected for a short way, but then they were gobbled up by the darkness. He switched on his torch and started to retrace his steps back to the house. Will trudged along the path towards his home. Rustling from the undergrowth made him stop and shine his torch in the direction of the noise. He could see nothing, probably a fox, he thought, but again, he felt that someone was watching him. The wood was less dense here, and Will's earlier footprints had been covered by snow, but as he flashed his torch a little further up the path, he noticed new footprints that led into the dark edge of the wood. There had been someone else out here. Perhaps still out here?

"Is there anyone there?" called Will? There was no reply.

Pointing his torch at the ground and concentrating on the line of the path, Will hustled on and broke into a trot, the snow crunching under his walking shoes. He felt very vulnerable; the fallen snow muted everything; he started to panic. This would be an ideal place for an attack. How stupid to walk back from the inn in the dark. What had he been thinking about? In the distance, he could see the lights of the house through the trees; he started to run faster, slithering and slipping where ice had begun to form. Head down, charging for the lights and safety. Will barely saw the figure that stepped out onto the path in front of him. He tried to stop, but his momentum and lack of traction from his feet meant that he ploughed straight into the figure with such force that he bounced back onto the path.

"What the hell…." Will didn't finish his sentence.

"Will, are you okay?" said the voice from the figure towering above him.

"Yes, yes, fine, Mack, you frightened the life out of me. What are you doing hiding in the woods?"

"I wasnae hiding. You said you had seen someone snooping about and thought I would take a wee look myself. I thought I heard someone or something, and I heard you call out and then nothing until I saw this man running with a torch and stepped onto the path."

"There was another set of footprints in the snow. I'm sure there is someone out there. Did you see or hear anyone?" asked Will.

"I can't tell; you made so much noise it would've covered anyone moving away."

* * *

With slightly rubbery legs, Will walked into the kitchen where Jay was getting supper ready.

"Hi, Hon, been having fun and games in the snow?"

"What do you mean?"

"Well, you said that the alarm would go off as you tripped the devices and the app on my phone, and the alarm in the study has gone off several times."

"Mine hasn't," said Will tapping the face of his watch.

"Must be out of range. Perhaps you need to be nearer the house."

"That makes sense. Where's Lucy and Lena?" asked Will.

"Lena's got a night off, and Lucy is in her room. Why?" asked Jay.

"I thought someone was watching me whilst I walked home from the inn. I met Mack, but he didn't see anyone. Just wondered if the girls had been out, that was all."

"Perhaps we can spot something on the cameras," suggested Jay.

Will and Jay moved into the study.

"This screen is divided up into different images," explained Will, "each representing a live stream from each camera. A small light will flash in the corner of the image if a camera has been tripped. This is the camera that we need to look at."

Will enlarged the image to cover the whole screen. The path to the inn clearly seen via the infra-red camera.

"Nothing on the live stream," said Will, "let's look back," and fiddling with the mouse, he rewound the film watching the clock at the bottom of the screen. "This is about an hour and a half ago; that should be about enough."

Jay looking over Will's shoulder, said, "look, that's you going to the inn. That would be the first alarm soon after you left."

"When did you hear it again?"

"I don't know, perhaps about thirty minutes later. I thought it was you coming back and was surprised when you didn't appear. Then I sort of forgot about it until it went off again."

Using the digital clock at the bottom of the screen, Will ran the film forward.

"Okay, let's look at thirty minutes later."

They both watched the screen, which remained unchanged even though the clock quickly flicked over at the bottom.

"There, look, stop," said Jay.

Will rewound the film, and both watched it in real-time. There was just an empty path for a few moments, and then a figure emerged from the edge of the woods.

"Yes, there he is. That's where the footprints were in the snow. I knew there was someone out there. I'm not going completely gaga."

They both peered at the screen as the shadowy figure walked up the path towards the inn and then darted off into the woods.

"Why would he do that? Why not continue on the path?"

"Don't know," replied Jay, "perhaps he heard Mack?"

"What was he going to do, attack me?"

"Don't know the answer to that question either. Unless whoever it is, is just trying to frighten you."

"Well, he's certainly doing that, but why, for what purpose?"

"The figure walks like a man. Do you recognise him? I think he looks youngish by his movements."

"I don't think it is the same person that I saw the night we chased the intruders. He's too tall to be the bathroom intruder but could be the man that attacked me in the kitchen, right sort of build, perhaps. Oh, I don't know, could be anyone," said Will.

"Let's run it forward and pick you up coming back." Will fast-forwarded the film for about fifteen minutes, and then they both watched in real-time until the form of Will entered the screen.

"Look, I'm already moving quite quickly, so I'm already spooked. I must have already heard him and called out." They both watched as Will ran towards the camera and then out of the picture. They continued to watch, and about five minutes later, the figure emerged again from the woods and just stood on the path and stared towards the house.

"You see why the alarms kept tripping. First, you are going to the inn, then the figure, then you returning, and then the figure again," said Jay.

"I suppose if he had wanted to do me harm, he could have. It's almost as if he knew where the cameras were and wanted to tell us of his presence."

"Exactly," said Jay, more to herself than Will.

Jay hugged Will. "Don't worry, you still have your personal bodyguard here, and I can still remember the odd trick or two."

"Do you think we should tell Tavish?"

"What is he going to say or do? He can't post someone to watch the house indefinitely, and we don't know this person will do us any harm. Might be a disaffected local who has taken umbrage at a southerner living up here."

"Hmmm, maybe. I think I'm going to put another gun cabinet in the house, so we have one here legally," said Will.

"Whoa, hold on, we can't start shooting people on suspicion; we would need to call the police," replied Jay.

"I know, but if it is someone else from the old days, they won't wait for the police to pitch up. So, I need some protection before I make the call."

CHAPTER TWENTY-FIVE

Later that evening, Will peered out of the window at the white wilderness. Snow was falling again, and drifts had formed strange white sculptures as the wind had whipped the snow into a frenzy.

"Which car will you take tomorrow - I would suggest the Land Rover?" asked Will.

"No, I hate that thing; it's so hard on the bum. I'll take the Beemer," replied Jay.

"Do you think you will be okay on the roads with that?"

"Yes, the ploughs are out, just our drive could be the problem, but Mack said that the trees had sheltered it from most of the snow."

"Okay, if you are sure."

* * *

That night, a swarm of bees buzzed in Will's ears. In his sleep, his hand flicked around his head, but the buzzing continued. Slowly, the dream dissipated, but the buzzing continued. His wrist tingled and vibrated - his watch. The alarm had been activated. Sliding out from under the warm duvet and wrapping his dressing gown tightly, he raced to the study to look at the screens to assess any imminent danger.

The flashing screen lit up the dark study as Will flicked on the light switch. The focus of the relevant camera was somewhere on the estate. Blinking to clear all the sleep out of his eyes, Will peered at the live stream, but there was nothing, just tree trunks, branches and patches of snow that had escaped the clutches of the tree canopy. He couldn't recognise where it was in the dark, and nothing was moving on the screen now. Will rewound the film until he saw something flash in and out of the camera's view. Then, turning the recording to real-time, Will watched what had triggered the alarm. Crossing the screen was an enormous stag, probably the size of two men. Will sat back in his chair and laughed out aloud. The intercom rang on the desk.

"Have ye seen the pictures, just a daddy deer?" said Mack.

"Yes, just sitting here watching it now. A bloody big thing, what is it doing so close to the house?" replied Will.

"Cannae do anything about it really, probably got lost in the snow or saw a hind that he was following. Turn off all your alarms as I'm going out to chase it away; otherwise, it could keep crossing the trips all night. See you in the morning."

Will switched off the alarm on his watch and was just going back to bed when Jay arrived in the study.

"What is it?" she said in an alarmed voice.

"Nothing, thankfully, just a huge deer. Mack will chase it out of the security ring and says we should turn off our alarms tonight. Let's get back to bed as you have a longish drive tomorrow," said Will.

"Is it sensible to switch off the alarms?"

"We will be up in a few hours, and no one is going to be out tonight in this weather," replied Will.

Jay frowned as she switched off her phone.

* * *

The following morning, Jay and Lucy set off to make the journey back to Lucy's school in Edinburgh. The grey, leaden and foreboding skies had disappeared, and as dawn peeked above the horizon, it promised to be a much better day. Whitish grey walls, created by the snowploughs, lined the roads.

Jay manoeuvred the car carefully through Kinloch Rannoch and Tummel Bridge, peering through the windscreen and using the automatic gears to control the vehicle's speed.

Having left Pitlochry behind them with Lucy busy texting on her phone, Jay felt the worst of the road conditions were over. Relaxing a little, she accelerated to catch up on time as little traffic was on the road.

Up ahead, the lights from the village of Dunkeld twinkled in the dawn light. As she approached the village, Jay applied pressure to the brake pedal, but the car didn't respond, and it started to drift to the right across the road. Jay could sense Lucy now looking at her. Black-ice, don't use the brakes, she thought. Jay flicked on the four-wheel drive to get more traction and turned the wheel into the skid, but the car didn't slow down. She pumped the brakes several times in panic, but still, the car glided across the road.

The car was now on the westbound side of the road heading towards the embankment and the trees. 'Shit, shit,' we are going to crash.

"Mum, Mum," she heard Lucy scream beside her. The tyres growled as the car hit the gravel at the edge of the road, and then there was no road, just air beneath the vehicle as it flew over the embankment. It bounced nose-first into the grass, suspension thumping on the hard ground. The seat belt tore against Jay's shoulder as the airbag swallowed her up, and blackness released her from the hell.

CHAPTER TWENTY-SIX

Will heard his watch buzz, and from the study window, saw a police car come up the drive. "Come in, Sergeant, makes a change to see you rather than Inspector Tavish. Has he given up on me?"

"No, another matter, Mr Slater. Look, I have some bad news. There has been an accident involving your wife and daughter."

"Oh, my God, are they alright?"

"Well, they are both alive; your daughter just has cuts and bruises, but your wife is much worse, and they think it could be touch and go. They have taken them both to Perth Royal Infirmary. Can I drive you there?" asked Pearce.

Will thought for a moment. "Thanks, Sergeant; I'll drive myself as I'll need a car to get back. Where did the accident happen?" asked Will.

"On the A9 between Dalguise and Dunkeld. There was no other vehicle involved. However, a witness in a car following Mrs Slater said it looked as if she had started to brake at the bend just before Dunkeld, and the car just seemed to lose control, and it went straight across the road and hit a tree. I'm so sorry, Mr

Slater; what with everything else, this seems like the last straw," said Pearce.

"It does, it does. I'd better get off."

"Okay, let me know if there is anything that I can do."

"I will, Sergeant, and thanks."

Will picked up his coat and phone and started for the hospital. Could this be an accident, or was this a deliberate attempt on Jay's life? Plugging his mobile into the hands-free system in the car, he called Mack and Lena to let them know what had happened. He then phoned Jay's parents and promised to call them when he had further news from the hospital.

He travelled the same route as Jay would have done a little earlier. The road passed along the northern edge of Loch Rannoch and then turned right onto the A9 through Pitlochry towards Perth. When he reached the spot where the accident had happened, he slowed down. A police vehicle stood at the side of the road. Below the embankment, the BMW's bonnet concertinaed into a tree. Will's stomach heaved, and he couldn't get the image of the crushed car out of his head.

* * *

"I have come to see Jay Slater and her daughter Lucy; they were involved in a car accident a couple of hours ago," Will said to the receptionist.

Directed to the ward, he asked the ward sister how they both were.

The Ward Sister looked down at her screen. "Well, Mr Slater, Lucy is in that bay just across from you there, and she's badly bruised, some abrasions, possible concussion and generally very shaken up. We have sedated her because she needs to rest and keeps asking after her mother. Your wife is currently in theatre with a broken pelvis, broken arm and a head injury. She is quite poorly. I will have more information when she comes out of theatre."

"When do you think that will be?" asked Will.

"Hard to tell," said the Sister looking at her watch, "she went down about forty-five minutes ago, so I would think within the next hour."

"Okay, thank you. I'll sit with Lucy, but please come and tell me as soon as there is any news."

"I will, Mr Slater, I surely will."

Will phoned Jay's parents again to give them the news and said he would call them as soon as Jay was out of theatre. He pulled up a chair and sat by the side of Lucy's bed. There were livid red bruises on Lucy's face, a large plaster under her chin, and bandages on her left hand and arm. Will lent across and kissed Lucy on the forehead.

"I'm here, Lucy; it's Will," he said.

Settling back in a chair, Will wondered whether the accident was too much of a coincidence, considering what had already happened. Was this a deliberate attempt on his family's life? Will involuntary shivered as the thought crossed his mind. It was all a nightmare from which he never seemed to wake up.

The warmth of the hospital and tiredness from the stress sent Will into a shallow slumber. He awoke with a start, his shoulder shaken. Will looked up and saw a kindly looking man staring down at him.

"Mr Slater, my name is Simon Rislip. I have just finished operating on your wife."

Will jumped up, "how is she, doctor?"

"She is as well as can be expected. She has been in a very nasty crash and has suffered some severe injuries. The broken pelvis and arm will all mend perfectly in time, although it will be painful for a while. However, we are much more concerned about her head injury. There is a blood clot on her brain, which we have operated on and relieved the pressure as best we can. We will keep a very careful watch over her for the next twenty-four, thirty-six hours," the doctor paused.

"Is she going to be okay?"

"It's too early to tell Mr Slater. She is physically strong, but only time will tell. I will let you know as soon as there are any developments. As I said, the next twenty-four, thirty-six hours are going to be crucial."

"Okay, thank you, doctor," replied Will.

"I understand this is your daughter?" said Rislip.

"Yes, my stepdaughter, my wife's daughter," replied Will.

"Well, she's in much better shape. A few cuts and bruises, the cut under the chin might need some work in the future to remove the scar, but otherwise, there should be no lasting physical effects from the accident. We have sedated her for a few hours, but she should be coming around soon. I will look in on you both and, of course, your wife before I finish tonight."

"Thank you, doctor; I will be here when you come back later."

Rislip smiled and left the ward.

Will phoned Jay's parents with the current news and said they were coming up and had booked themselves on the night sleeper train to Perth.

* * *

Will settled himself back in his chair and watched Lucy sleeping. A thought flashed through his mind. If the accident had been deliberate, might someone come back and finish the job? Was he being too dramatic, especially for the highlands of Scotland? Even so, he positioned his chair facing towards the opening to the bay of beds. Will dozed again. Something startled him, and he jumped in his chair. It was a nurse that Will didn't recognise, and immediately, his senses were on alarm mode.

"Sorry to startle you, but your wife is out of recovery and is conscious, and you can pop in to see her for a couple of minutes."

The nurse ushered Will to a smaller room, where he saw Jay lying in bed surrounded by equipment and attached to various drips. As he approached, he could see Jay smiling weakly. His relief was so profound that his emotions took control, and as Will bent over and kissed Jay's forehead, tears poured down his cheeks, splashing onto Jay's pillow. He crouched down beside her bed and held her hand gently.

"I thought I had lost you," he said.

Will could see that Jay was trying to say something. Words were forming on her lips; he bent down. "Car, accident, be careful," Jay whispered in a croaking voice.

Will was not sure what Jay meant, so he replied, "don't worry, I will sort it all out, and I will be careful."

Will watched Jay's eyes close and fall back to sleep.

What had Jay meant? What had she wanted to say? It must have been significant, and as he thought about it, Dr Rislip walked in.

"Ah, you have seen your wife, excellent," as he scrutinised the clipboard he had taken from the bottom of the bed.

"How is she?" asked Will.

"She seems to be doing okay, and as well as we could have hoped. We're going to monitor her head injury closely. She will be in hospital for a little while longer. However, she does need a lot of rest, so we need to restrict visitors to a minimum and a very short period each visit."

"Will she make a full recovery?" asked Will.

"Yes, I think there's a reasonable chance that she will make a full recovery, Mr Slater," replied Rislip.

"Okay, thank you very much, Doctor."

"I think Mrs Slater needs to rest now, and you should probably get some too; there is nothing you can do for a few hours, and we will contact you if there is any change."

Will phoned Jay's parents and headed home.

* * *

He drove back past the accident location. The BMW had been towed away, and the only visible signs were large scars on the tree's brown trunk.

Lena was waiting for him when he got home and made him dinner. Flopping into a chair in the kitchen, drained of any emotion, tiredness creeping through every sinew and muscle, he watched, almost in a daze, as Lena moved around the kitchen. Even in Will's soporific state, something stirred at the back of his mind. The actions, the way Lena moved, reminded him of someone; he concentrated, willing his memory to recover the image from its overloaded database, but it would not comply, and Will gave up.

CHAPTER TWENTY-SEVEN

The Daily Telegraph was spread out on the kitchen table, covering the breakfast plates, mugs, marmalade jar and milk jug as Jim Dawkin flicked over the pages.

"Jim, please fold up your paper," asked Hazell, Jim's wife, who was busy trying to tidy up so she could go out to work, "Sergeant Edkins' late this morning?"

"No, he had an errand to do first thing. He'll be here shortly," came the reply without Dawkin's eyes leaving the paper.

Jim heard his wife talking, but her voice was distant, somewhere else, as he concentrated on a small paragraph that had caught his eye about a car crash in Scotland.

"Jim, please move the paper," the voice was louder this time as Dawkin's brain synchronised to his surroundings. Folding the paper around the article, he jumped up, grabbed his jacket off the back of the chair, and with the newspaper tucked under his arm, shouted to no one in particular, "that's it. That's it. There has to be a connection. Too much of a coincidence. Where the fuck is that idiot Edkins?"

"Language, Jim, language, you are not in the station now."

Dawkin strode out of the kitchen and straight out of the front door bellowing down his phone to find out where Edkins was. Fortunately for Edkins, he was just pulling up to the kerb outside Dawkin's house.

"Look at that," said Dawkin thrusting the page of the paper with the relevant article into Edkins' lap. "Read it and tell me what you think."

Edkins, confronted with a whole page of the morning paper, was unsure which article he was supposed to read. "Which one, Guv?"

"That one, that one," replied Dawkin, poking the page with a chubby finger.

"The one about the car crash?"

"Yes, yes, of course, that one. Read it out loud."

"Okay," replied Edkins.

Woman seriously injured in car crash.

The wife of Will Slater, the solicitor involved in a terrorist gang trial last year, is fighting for her life as the car she was driving veered off the road and crashed into a tree yesterday. The accident happened on the A9 in a remote part of Scotland, between Pitlochry and Edinburgh. A passenger, thought to be the driver's daughter, was also injured in the car. There were no other vehicles involved. Slater has remained hidden following a series of events last year that left a trail of deaths and a number of convictions for terrorism. Many millions of pounds also disappeared with him.

"Bloody hell, he is sure unlucky," said Edkins.

"What do you mean unlucky? Slater is guilty as hell. Who wrote that article?"

"A bloke named Fringell."

"Yeah, he did a big exposé in the paper a few weeks back. He's got his teeth into Slater. Good job, if you ask me."

"I don't know, could be a coincidence, Guv."

"No, that's not a coincidence. I feel it in my water. Slater was guilty, alright, and someone else knows it too."

"But we couldn't prove anything."

"I arrested him twice, Edkins."

"Yep, Guv, but we had to let him go on both occasions, and we were close to a charge of wrongful arrest at least once."

"Bloody legal profession makes us look like fools."

"Where to Guv?" said Edkins starting the car.

"Station, as quick as you can; I need to see Stint about this."

"Really?"

"Yes, really, Edkins, I need to do some more digging but will need Stint's permission."

* * *

Dawkin knocked on his boss's door.

"Ah, good morning, Jim. What can I do for you?" said Chief Inspector Stint.

"Good morning, sir. Sorry to interrupt you, but do you remember the Slater case a year ago and that gang of arms dealers?" asked Dawkin.

"Yes, a feather in your cap sorting that all out. Thought you might be sitting at this desk on the strength of it," joked Stint.

"Well, sir, I don't think the case is closed, and I would like to re-open it."

"Why, as I recall, all the loose ends were tied up nicely?"

"Quite so, sir, too nicely. Do you remember that banker in the Virgin Islands who had two numbers to phone in case of a withdrawal of funds? One telephone number couldn't be traced. Pay as you go, probably. Well, the chap from the Financial Services Commission on the Islands called me a while back to tell me that he redialled the second number as an off chance and his call was answered."

"Who was it?" asked Stint.

"They never spoke, but we now know the phone is or was

then at any rate, still live, and the only person not in prison or dead is Slater," replied Dawkin.

"And…? asked Stint.

"Well, I have always thought that he was behind the whole operation all the time. He played us all. He controlled all his partners and Bore, his client, and when it got too hot, he betrayed them all and got away with a lot of money. Apart from that, he was also a smarmy bastard."

"So, what has brought all this to the fore again, Jim? It can't be just the telephone call. We are talking about a case of over a year ago?" asked Stint.

"Well, his wife and stepdaughter were badly injured in a car accident in Scotland yesterday, and I think it is all connected," replied Dawkin. For the time being, he decided to omit his unauthorised break-in of the Crombie house.

"So, let me get this straight, Jim. You want to re-open a case that was resolved on the strength of an answered telephone call by someone unknown and a car accident hundreds of miles away?"

"That's about it, sir. I want your permission to fly to Scotland and do some more investigations. I know I can nail Slater this time."

Dawkin watched as Stint slowly leant back in his chair, pushed himself away from his desk, crossed his leg and peered at him through squinting eyes.

"Jim, I know you're a good copper and have a nose for crime, but this is really too far off the wall. Have you spoken to the Scottish police? Was there anything odd about the crash?"

"Yeah, I did give them a bell, but they haven't even examined the car yet. I got the impression that they weren't going to bother. Their view was that Slater's wife lost control on a patch of ice and wham," said Dawkin clapping his hands together for effect.

"Hmmm, I'm afraid I don't think there is enough evidence to warrant any more time spent on this, Jim."

"I thought you might say that, sir. What would your view be if I took some holiday and just happened to take it in Scotland?" asked Dawkin.

"Well, where you take your holiday is entirely up to you and, I imagine, Mrs Dawkin. Can you spare the time?"

"Yes, sir, I will brief Edkins and will only be away a couple of days. You won't know I wasn't here, sir."

"Okay, but you make sure that everyone knows this is your holiday, and if I get any bad vibes from anyone, including the Scottish force, then you'll be for the high jump," said Stint.

"Gotcha, sir and thank you," replied Dawkin.

"Don't thank me, it's your holiday," said Stint pulling himself back to his desk towards a file that lay open before him.

Dawkin packed an overnight bag and explained to his wife that he had to travel to Scotland for a couple of days. He didn't mention that it was coming out of his holiday entitlement. If he could tie something up, then Stint might allow him to rescind the holiday request.

"Don't forget to pack plenty of underwear and thick socks, love," said Mrs Dawkin, "it will be cold up there, so take your warm pyjamas and that thick pully Auntie Mabel gave you for Christmas."

"I can't take that; it has a reindeer on the front," replied Dawkin.

"Well, they have reindeer in Scotland, don't they?" said Mrs Dawkin, sounding unsure whether she was correct.

"That's not the point, dear," replied Dawkin, "I can't walk around wearing a pullover with a deer wearing a Santa Clause hat; in fact, I can't walk around in a pullover with any deer on the front." With that, he snapped close his bag, kissed her goodbye, and headed out to his waiting taxi.

* * *

"Inspector Dawkin," said Pearce offering his hand, "Sergeant William Pearce, although everyone calls me Bill, welcome to Scotland and Pitlochry. Now, what brings the Met up to this remote part of the country?"

"As I said on the phone, I'm interested in the RTA involving Mrs Jay Slater."

"Why would that be Inspector? Not sure there is much to add; it appears that Mrs Slater hit a patch of ice and came off the road."

"Slater, and to a degree, his wife were involved in a big terrorist case last year, and I thought this might have something to do with it. Were there any other vehicles involved?"

"Fortunately, no other vehicles, and I can't see how this can have anything to do with a case in London last year."

"I think that is for me to decide, Sergeant."

"Well, with all due respect Inspector, I don't think my Inspector Tavish will be amused by the Met arriving on his patch."

"Have there been any other incidents involving the Slaters since they have been up here, Sergeant?"

Pearce paused for a moment before answering, "well, fortunately, we don't get many serious RTAs and to get two in a few weeks involving the same family is a little strange."

"What did you say, Sergeant, two RTAs involving the Slaters?"

"Aye, two men broke into the Slaters' house, but the Slaters chased them off. Quite a tough couple, those Slaters."

"Yes, quite so; what happened, Sergeant?"

"Someone, we don't know who, cut the brakes of the intruders' car, and as they drove away at speed, they crashed, and both men were killed."

"Had their brakes cut, two men killed," repeated Dawkin to

himself. "I would like to speak to the senior officer investigating Mrs Slater's accident, please?" asked Dawkin.

"There is no investigating officer, sir. It was an RTA, and the constable who attended the scene wrote up his report. There was no one else involved, and as far as we are concerned, the incident is closed."

"Well, I want it re-opened as I think this is all connected with my case."

"I can't do that without permission, sir," replied Pearce.

"Well, let's get permission, shall we, Sergeant. Whom do I speak to?" asked Dawkin.

"Inspector Tavish is the senior officer in the station, sir."

"Okay, let's go see him."

"Sergeant?" said Tavish, as Pearce knocked and entered his office with Dawkin in tow.

"This is Inspector Dawkin up from London, and he wants to open the Slater RTA case Guv," said Pearce.

Tavish looked Dawkin up and down with a look that he might have given to his cat for bringing in a partly chewed mouse.

"Jim Dawkin," said Dawkin offering his hand.

"Dawkin," said Tavish, not bothering to rise from his chair as he shook the other's hand, "you better sit down and tell me what this is all about,"

"A while ago, I investigated a case involving Will Slater; Mrs Slater, the woman in the accident, is his wife."

"I know who Mrs Slater is."

"Yeah, sorry, of course, you do, well, it was a complicated case, and although most aspects were tied up, there were a few loose ends." Dawkin decided not to mention that he thought Slater was still involved somehow, as he suspected the local bobbies were probably well acquainted with Slater. "When I read the report about her crash, I thought there might be some connection," said Dawkin.

"Well, Dawkin, what makes you think that there is any connection? Or do you think of us as humble plod, in some out of the way place, who don't know what we are doing and need the Met to show us how it's done?"

Dawkin could see that this was not going the way he wanted. "Of course, I don't, nor the Met think that, but we thought you might have been unaware of Slater's connections previously, and that information might be helpful in this case."

"Dawkin, I make it my business to know who and what is going on in my patch. I know full well about all the Slaters' history, but as far as I can see, they were victims rather than criminals, and indeed Mrs Slater used to be one of us. As regards helping in this case, as you put it, it seems fairly straightforward to me, Mrs Slater hit a patch of ice on the bend, and regrettably, the car left the road and hit a tree. Nasty business, although I gather Mrs Slater is a little better."

"I apologise if I seem to be questioning you, Inspector Tavish; that was certainly not the intention. I just wondered if anyone had checked the car to see if there were any, say, malfunctions, particularly as I understand another car connected to the Slaters had its brakes cut recently?"

"How did you hear about that? asked Tavish, flashing a snarl across at Pearce.

"Well, I mentioned it, sir," said Pearce, "as it seemed somewhat strange that there had been two car accidents involving the Slaters in short order."

"The two incidents don't seem to be related. Where is the Slater car now? Have the engineers had a look at it?" Tavish asked Pearce.

"No, sir, they are snowed under; I thought we could do it locally."

"Not that idiot Brown?"

"Yes, sir, he picked it up from the accident site a couple of days ago."

"Has he reported back?"

"Not yet, sir."

"Okay, Pearce, go and rattle his cage and take Inspector Dawkin with you."

"Thank you, Inspector," said Dawkin.

"I don't expect to see you again, Dawkin, this is my patch, and you should stick to yours," said Tavish waving his hand.

"Understood, and thanks."

Dawkin and Pearce exited Tavish's office with some haste.

"Shall we go in my car as I know the way?"

"Thanks, Sergeant. Is the garage near?" asked Dawkin.

"Aye, it's in Pitlochry, a few minutes down the way," said Pearce.

Pearce drove Dawkin the half-mile down the road to what appeared to be a rather run-down garage on the edge of the town.

"Are these people okay? Tavish didn't seem to think much of them, and it doesn't look very high tech?" asked Dawkin.

"Aye, they're good mechanics. The owner knows what he's doing, although a bit laid back at times. He'll tell us if anything was wrong with the car. Tavish and Finn Brown fell out about something entirely different."

* * *

"Finn, how are you?" asked Pearce to a large, red-faced man in oily overalls who was leaning into an engine of a car. He turned to wipe his hands on a rag that looked even more greasy.

"Aye, okay, Jim, what can I do for you?" replied the mechanic.

"This is Inspector Dawkin up from London. Have you had a look at the BMW that crashed a couple of days ago?"

"Aye, have had a wee look."

"Nothing to report?" asked Pearce.

"Not at the moment."

"Have you looked at the brakes?" asked Pearce.

"No, not yet."

Dawkin was beginning to see how this man would have annoyed Tavish, "is it possible for you to have a look now?" asked Dawkin.

Brown stared at Dawkin with an expression of such incredulity; it was as if Dawkin had asked him to do a double somersault on his forecourt.

Pearce stepped in, "do you think you could put it up on the ramp and have a look now, Finn? Got a bit of a rush on."

"Aye, I suppose so, as it's you asking," replied Brown giving Dawkin another stare as he walked past him into the yard at the front of the garage. "The Beemer's out here; I'll just get a cable tied to it and get it onto a ramp."

Finn called out to someone in the garage, and a younger man appeared and attached a hook on the end of a thick metal cable to the front of the BMW and disappeared back into the garage. Dawkin heard a winch motor start, and the BMW shuddered and then began to move towards the inside of the garage. With some manoeuvring from Finn, he positioned the BMW onto the ramp. Finn raised the ramp, picked up a bulb wrapped inside a metal cage, hooked it onto the underside of the BMW and peered up into the engine bay.

Dawkin walked around the vehicle. The windscreen was completely shattered but still in place, and the front of the car had concertinaed but not into the passengers' compartment. The deflated airbags hung loosely over the two front seats as if resting, having completed their assignment.

"This is strange," called out Brown.

"What is it?" asked Dawkin and Pearce together.

"Look at this," said Brown waving a piece of hose that both Pearce and Dawkin peered at, but without knowing why they were looking at it.

"This could be the cause of the accident; brake fluid pipe has a small nick in it," said Brown.

"Could this have happened in the accident?" asked Dawkin.

"Aye, possibly," said Finn and held the end of the pipe closer to the light, "could have happened in the crash."

"It didn't hit another vehicle; it just ploughed across the grass and hit a tree," said Pearce.

"Let me have a look at the other three brakes," said Brown.

Brown ducked down again under the car. After a few more minutes, he reappeared.

"This is really strange because there are nicks in all four brake hoses. That is too much of a coincidence."

"You mean the brakes were tampered with?" asked Dawkin.

"Aye, I reckon so."

Pearce chipped in, "surely, if there is any deterioration in the performance of the brakes, a warning light flashes up on the dashboard."

"Yes," replied Brown, that's correct, but these are only minor nicks. It would have taken a wee while for the brake level to go down to set off the warning lights."

"So, Mrs Slater could have driven a distance before the lights went on?" asked Dawkin.

"Yep, a few miles. It was snowy, wasn't it," said Brown rubbing his chin, "so perhaps she was driving slowly and using the automatic gears to slow down, but when she got on the main road, she would start using the brakes and drain the fluid."

"But this looks like a skilled job; someone that knows what to do and how much to cut," said Pearce.

"Aye, this has been done by someone who knows quite a lot about cars," replied Brown.

"I assume it wouldn't take long to do it? asked Dawkin.

"No, as long as you knew what you were doing, a couple of minutes with a sharp knife. The hoses are lined with a metal braid."

Turning to Pearce, Dawkin asked, "did the other car that had its brakes cut come here too?"

"The Eastern Europeans' car, yes, it would have," replied Pearce.

"Were the brakes tampered with in the same way, Mr Brown?" asked Dawkin.

"No, I would have spotted that; on their car, it was just a cut through the brake fluid line. Simple."

"Wouldn't there have been a warning light on that car too?"

"Yeah, it was a new model, so would have," replied Brown.

"Because it was hired and they were not used to all the dashboard signs, maybe they just missed it. They were driving away at speed, probably concentrating on the road," said Pearce.

"Perhaps," said Dawkin, "but if a proper fix can be done so quickly, why not do the same on the Eastern Europeans' car too?" After a pause, he added, "unless a different person did it."

Dawkin stood there trying to piece together what he had learnt and then said, "well, Sergeant, this looks like an attempted murder on Mrs Slater, not an accident. You might want to let Inspector Tavish know. I'm sure he will want to be informed of what's happening on his patch. Now, why don't we make a house call on Mr Slater and let him know what we have found."

"I'm not sure Inspector Tavish would like that, sir."

"Rubbish, Sergeant, Slater and I are old friends."

Pearce looked confused but nodded slowly.

CHAPTER TWENTY-EIGHT

Will phoned the hospital to check there was no worsening of Jay's condition. She was still stable, and it was now just time. Her parents were there and promised to call should there be any change.

He poured himself a large scotch, which he hoped would calm down his anxiety. His watch buzzed, indicating something had triggered an alarm. He moved quickly to the study to examine the monitors and saw a police car coming up to the front door. Peering at the image, he recognised Sergeant Pearce getting out of the car, but he put his face close to the screen to make sure he was not mistaken as to the identity of the other occupant. He would know that walk anywhere, head pushed back, chest thrust out and the arrogant strutting short strides, rather like a cockerel inspecting its hens. What on earth is he doing here, he thought?

"Good evening, gentlemen," said Will as he opened the door.

"Good evening Mr Slater," said Pearce, "this is Inspector Dawkin, although I believe you know each other."

"We sure do," said Will.

"Good evening, Mr Slater," said Dawkin.

"You had better come in. Let's go into the lounge," said Will leading the way. "I've just poured myself a drink. Can I get either of you anything before you explain the reason for this visit?"

"I'm on duty, thanks, sir," said Pearce.

"I don't mind if I do, Mr Slater, as technically I'm on holiday, this not being my patch," replied Dawkin.

"Whisky, okay?" asked Will.

"Perfect."

Lena had made up the fire before going out for the night, and a huge log was burning in the hearth. Both policemen stood in front of the blaze warming their hands while Will poured Dawkin's drink.

"Please, sit down," said Will indicating to the settee as he sat in an armchair facing them both. "So, what's this all about?"

"As you know, Mr Slater,' said Pearce, "we thought that Mrs Slater's accident was due to adverse road conditions, as we found nothing immediately obvious to show otherwise. The car had not been fully inspected before today."

Will sat forward, a frown creasing his face.

"Get to the point, Sergeant," interrupted Dawkin, "Slater, I read in the paper about the accident and thought it was a bit of a coincidence and that it might be connected to the events of last year."

Pearce continued at his own pace, "anyway, Mr Slater, Inspector Dawkin thought it might be worth taking a closer look at the car whilst he was up here, rather than waiting a wee bit longer."

"And?" said Will louder than he meant.

"Come on," said Dawkin clicking his fingers in an attempt to get Pearce to hurry up.

Pearce glared at Dawkin, "so, this afternoon, we had a wee look at the car your wife was driving…."

Dawkin interjected, "and the brakes had been cut intentionally, which would have caused the car to crash."

Will looked at both men and then said, "you are saying that

someone deliberately tried to kill my wife and stepdaughter?" He sat back in his chair.

"Yes, that's what the evidence shows," said Dawkin in his usual forceful manner. "Do you know anyone who would want to kill your wife, Mr Slater?"

Pearce looked horrified, "now hold on a moment, Inspector, this is not your case, and I will be asking the questions, not you."

"I'll answer his question," said Will. "I would have said no, but like you, Inspector, I was concerned about the coincidence, bearing in mind the other events lately."

"What other events, Mr Slater?"

Will felt disinclined to provide Dawkin with any more information but thought it would probably be the only way to get rid of him. "We have had a couple of uninvited visits to the house. The first was from a pair of Eastern European gangsters who tried to kill Jay and me. The second was from someone, and we have yet to discover whom."

"I see, and you believe the accident was connected?"

"How would I know? However, it is very worrying if someone who has a grudge against me would try and kill my wife and daughter," replied Will.

"Quite so, quite so," said Dawkin.

"We are continuing to do further tests on the car, Mr Slater, and will, of course, let you know if we find anything else," said Pearce.

"Do you know much about cars, Mr Slater?" asked Dawkin.

"If you mean, do I know where and how to cut the brakes, the answer, emphatically, is no. I now know why you are here, Inspector. You read about the accident and thought, Slater is up to it again. Trying to get rid of his wife this time. It is despicable to think I could do such a thing."

"Well, it would appear there is someone out there who is."

"Whoever tampered with your car had quite a lot of mechanical knowledge," said Pearce. "And it would have taken quite a few minutes to undertake. Have you noticed anyone hanging around?"

"Well, not specifically, but for a while now, I have had this feeling that we are being watched. I mentioned it to Inspector Tavish, and Mack, my ghillie, has put in security cameras and alarms around the estate, and we spotted someone on a camera last Friday, but it was impossible to make out who it was, although I'm sure it was a man," replied Will.

"Did you report it?" asked Dawkin.

"Well, no, what could we say, or the police do. Just someone watching in the woods. We thought they were just trying to spook us."

"They did more than that," retorted Dawkin.

"We don't know there is any connection," said Pearce. "What about immediately before your wife's accident? Any trips on the alarms?"

"No," replied Will, "except a large stag did set off the alarm the night before the accident. Mack turned off the system until he could get the stag out of the alarmed zone."

"Very convenient, so anyone could have prowled around without being seen or heard after the system was turned off. Someone could have deliberately chased the stag into the alarm zone to cover their movements. They wouldn't know that you had turned off the alarms but could assume that you would think it was the stag again as this person moved around." said Dawkin.

"I guess that is correct." Will put down his glass. "But it was just the alarms that were turned off. The cameras were still working, and we might be able to see something."

Will led the party into the study and fiddled with the keyboard rewinding the tape until the relevant date. "Look, Lucy and Jay, getting into the car. That must have been the morning. I'll go back."

The three of them peered at the screen.

"Stop, look," exclaimed Dawkin, "there's a person by the car. Go back."

Will rewound the tape further.

"Right, now play it forward," said Dawkin.

They watched and saw a hooded figure approach the BMW. The figure lay down on the ground and shone a torch under the car near the front wheel. The figure took something from his pocket, reached under the car, and repeated his action at each corner of the vehicle.

"There's your man or woman, Sergeant. Do either of you recognise this person?" said Dawkin.

"Impossible to tell from this image," replied Pearce, "what about you, Mr Slater?"

"I can't be sure but think it could be the person who was in the woods that same night. The one I mentioned. Looks similar on the screen, same sort of build, tallish and slim."

"And you have no idea who he might be?" asked Dawkin.

"No, Inspector, not at all."

"Well, he has taken a dislike to you and your family."

There was a pause; no one was sure what to say next.

Dawkin shuffled his feet and said, "to be perfectly honest, Mr Slater, I still have my suspicions about you. Death and destruction seem to follow you. I am sorry about your wife, but I think I have proved my point, and there is more to this accident than meets the eye."

"That's up to us to deal with, Inspector, not you," said Pearce.

Nodding in agreement, Dawkin added, "yes, quite so, but I will be keeping a close watch from down south."

"I think it is time we left, Inspector," said Pearce, "thank you for the help, Mr Slater, and if I hear any further news, I will let you know."

As Dawkin started to walk down the front steps, he turned. "One way or the other, someone is out to get you, Slater."

* * *

Will was tired after his jousting with Dawkin, so he poured himself another large whisky and flopped into the settee to consider the information he had just received. Fidgeting with his glass on the arm of the chair, he tried to make sense of everything. Dawkin still seemed to think that he was guilty of something and no doubt had passed those thoughts on to Pearce and Tavish. Will doubted that the police would be any help and what could a few bobbies do to protect him. No, he was going to have to sort this out himself. There was some evil person or persons who wanted to harm him. He needed to take some positive action. But what? Where to start? What about the bathroom intruder? Who was that, and why there? There appears to be nothing in the room.

Checking that all the doors on the ground floor were locked, Will clambered the creaking back stairs, flicking on lights as he passed the switches. Even with the light switched on, the top floor corridor seemed dark and somehow menacing as he made his way into the bathroom. He looked around, but there was nothing. Just the bath that didn't move more than a few inches. Will walked over to the window and peered out into the darkness. He could just make out the lights from the inn on the other side of the loch. Why was this important? Forehead creased in thought, he made his way down to the floor below and flung open the door at the end of the corridor. It was empty. A bedroom still to be refurbished. He looked across the room to where he should be able to see the light from the inn. But there was no window, just a bare wall. The window was on a different wall and had a different view. He recalled the lack of symmetry in the placement of the windows on the outside. He didn't think anything of it at the time but now wondered if there was a reason. Will closed the open bedroom door and paced out the length of the corridor up to the back stairs. He then did the same on the third floor corridor right up to the bathroom door.

There was a discrepancy. There were ten more paces on the upstairs corridor. Will re-did the pacing; there was no error. The top floor corridor was longer. Then it all made sense, the bathroom intruder and the shifting of the bath. It was likely that the bathroom would have been put in during the late nineteenth century, whereas the room that housed the bath would be part of the original building. There was something hidden under the bathroom floor - another room accessed from under the bath. Getting down on his hands and knees, he examined the scratch marks he had seen earlier. He pushed the bath, and it moved the same distance as the scratch marks. Without rupturing the pipes attached to the bath, it would not move any further.

Will turned one of the bath taps. A puff of air escaped, followed by a gurgle from the ceiling, and then a trickle appeared that turned into a steady stream of rusty brown water. Will assumed that this water must be coming from a tank separate from the rest of the house. There was a hatch in the ceiling that Will hoped would house the tank and the stopcock for the water. A trip downstairs, and Will returned with a pair of decorating ladders, a wrench, and a metal scaffolding pole. The hatch in the ceiling was tight shut. Grabbing the scaffolding pole, Will drove the flat top into the hatch cover. As the hatch cover flew up into the loft space, many decades of dust, unrecognisable detritus and a mummified rat showered Will.

Dust blew up his nose and collected at the back of his throat, and grit particles got in his eyes. Coughing hard, he staggered down to his bathroom, where he stuck his head under the shower, then took a drink from a bottle of water on his bedside table and hoped he had not just experienced an Earl of Carnarvon moment. Picking up a torch, he set about his task again. At the top of the ladder, stale and musty air greeted him as he leant through the gap in the ceiling. Pulling himself up into the void and crouching down on one of the ceiling rafters, he flashed his torch around the loft space. It was empty apart from a sizeable water tank. Large enough to contain anything! Heart beating quickly and not just from the exertion of clambering over the rafters; rust flaked under his fingers as Will peered over the edge of the tank.

Just water. Brackish brown water. His heartbeat eased, and he looked for the stopcock. It was old and rusted, and he hoped that it would turn and not snap off. Bracing himself with knees pressed against the side of the tank, he twisted the metal valve. It moved, but he wasn't sure if it was turning or just the metal fatiguing under the grip of the wrench. He twisted again, and a sound like the scratching of a fingernail down a blackboard echoed through the space as the valve slowly gave up its fight and started to turn. Will hurried down the ladder and turned the tap. For a few minutes, a tank full of brown and suspiciously smelling water poured out of the tap until it turned into a trickle and then just a drip. Tank empty; it was time to disengage the water pipes. Wedging the scaffolding pole between the wall and the pipes, he pulled hard. The pipes were made of lead and bent without fracturing. He had to reposition the pole a couple of times before the pipes broke away. He could now, finally, move the bath. Pressing his back against its side, he pushed. The bath screeched as it crabbed its way across the old wooden floorboards until it rested against the far wall. The newly exposed floor offered no explanations, merely a layer of dust. No ring on the floor or anything remotely looked like an entry point to what might lie underneath.

Another trip downstairs for more drinking water and a rummage through the builders' tools. Picking up a claw hammer and a chisel, Will returned and started to remove the floorboards. The boards rasped as the long nails were prized away from their host joists. Having released three boards, Will shone his torch through the black hole. More dust and debris. He thought he saw a movement; he recoiled away. He peered through the gap. The joists didn't seem to run the length of the room. Two joints had been cut and strengthened by another running at a right angle, leaving a rectangle space in the middle, about a metre square.

There was another floor beneath the joists. Will shone his torch. More dust. Leaning over the edge of the newly formed gap in the bathroom floor, he pushed his hand into the opening, it touched something soft, and Will recoiled again in a panic and jumped up. What was that? He stood looking down into the hole. He breathed slowly to try and control his fear. He shone his torch down and saw a piece of old material. He smiled to himself. Another trip downstairs, this time, for more water, a pair of gloves and a small brush. He also found a mask that the builders used for sanding. With his nose and mouth covered, the torch in one hand and the brush in the other, he leant over the gap to uncover what lay beneath. The dirt was thick but dry and swept away easily. Lying flush on the secondary floor was a large metal ring. More dusting revealed the outline of a door or hatch in the floor. Will pulled on the ring, but the passing years had sealed the edges. There wasn't enough room to get into the hole and get nearer to the ring.

Sitting back on his haunches, he considered his next move. Then from the depth of the house, he heard a noise. Someone was moving downstairs and not very quietly, perhaps, more than one. The blood drained from his face, and his hand shook as it reached down for the claw hammer. He stepped out of the bathroom towards the stairs.

CHAPTER TWENTY-NINE

Will reached the first floor landing. The house was still. Perhaps he had imagined it. Was there someone in the house? Then he heard a voice, and his heart missed a beat.

"Will, it's Mack. Are you okay?"

"Yes, yes, fine, upstairs, come up."

The large and comforting figure of Mack climbed the stairs. "The alarm went off, all the lights are on, the backdoor is unlocked, and it's very late, so I thought I should come in," said Mack.

"I was at the top of the house doing some work, but I was sure that I had locked the back door." He looked down at his wrist, "ah, I took my watch off in the bathroom to wash my face an hour or so ago."

"Perhaps we should check the house? suggested Mack.

"Yes, we should, but perhaps, you can help me with something first I could do with your strength."

"Okay, I'm awake now."

"Of course, I got a bit carried away. What time is it?"

"After eleven."

"Sorry, Mack, this shouldn't take long. I'm in the bathroom at the top of the house."

Both men climbed the stairs and looked down into the hole in the floorboards. "There's an iron ring pull for the hatch, but it's sealed tight. However, you might be able to pull it up."

Mack lent over the hole. "I think I'll need something to slot into the ring for leverage."

"The scaffolding pole is too long. I'll pop downstairs; there has got to be something else amongst the builders' kit," said Will.

He hurried down the stairs to the ground floor hall, where a pile of builders' materials were under a dust sheet. Kneeling on the floor and rummaging through one of the builders' toolboxes, Will heard Mack behind him. "Look," said Will, "this should do," pointing to a short, stout metal rod. There was no response, and Will turned to see why Mack had not replied.

Dougie Gordon lowered a shotgun towards Will. "Sounds as if you have done all my work for me, Will. Let's go up and take a look, shall we?"

Will could see Mack still crouched over the hole when the pair reached the bathroom.

"We have a visitor, Mack, Dougie Gordon."

The visitor waved the barrel of his gun in greeting.

"That's not Dougie Gordon."

"I know," replied Will, "because Dougie Gordon was murdered and left in the tunnel to rot. So, who are you?"

"I'm Walter Gordon, Dougie's brother."

"So, you killed Dougie," said Will.

"I didn't do it, and you can't prove I did. Anyway, I'm the one with the gun, so you do what I say, understand?"

Mack and Will nodded.

"I know what you've found. I have been looking for this ever since I arrived back in the UK. I worked out where it must be, like you, I guess. Have you opened it yet?"

"The hatch, you mean?"

"Yes, the hatch or whatever it is under the bath."

"We were just about to."

Walter lifted his gun. "Well, get on with it."

Will passed Mack the metal rod, and bending over the hole, he inserted it into the ring and pulled upwards using a joist as leverage. There was a pop as air escaped from under the hatch as it eased open. Will shone his torch, and all three men peered into the new void. The darkness swallowed up the beam.

"There has to be something down there, the treasure left by the clansmen all those years ago. Look, what is that shining?" said Walter.

The three men peered in again, and there was a glint far down in the hole.

"Get in," said Walter, waving his gun at Mack.

"There's no ladder," said Will.

"Use that one," said Walter waving to the ladder by the loft hatch.

Will helped Mack lower the ladder into the hole.

"So, it was true, and I've found it. All the 'old wives' tales' were true," said Walter beaming from ear to ear.

"A slight problem, Walter, you didn't find it, I did, and as you don't own the house anymore, if you ever did, this all belongs to me."

"Oh, I don't think so; you would never have found it if you hadn't disturbed me in here."

"You haven't thought this through, Walter. How are you going to get whatever is down there, out of the hole and away?"

"Shut up, or I might kill you both, as you seem to think I killed my brother. Right. Kneel down, Slater, with your hands behind your back." Walter used cable ties to secure Will's wrists. "Now you," indicating to Mack, "get down that hole and start bringing up all the goodies."

"Be careful, Mack. You don't know how safe it is down there," said Will.

"Aye, I'll take care."

Will watched Mack disappear into the hole. It was a tight fit. Mack's clothes rasped against the side of the hole as he descended.

"Are you at the bottom yet? What have you found?" shouted Walter down the hole.

"The only thing here is a small gold trinket. Must be what we could see shining."

"Look around; there has to be more down there."

"There isn't, and I'm coming up."

Slowly Mack's head appeared above the lip of the hole; sweat poured down his face. Mack tossed a gold object at Walter's feet, "there you are. That's all that remains of the old treasure."

"There's got to be more down there; you're lying," said Walter.

Will watched as Walter's face turned puce. He waved his gun and stamped his feet. "Walter, why would Mack lie? You have the gun."

"Because you want to keep the treasure for yourself. I know your type."

"Walter, logic dictates that it is very likely that someone else had found the treasure over the last three hundred years, probably when the bathroom was put in during the nineteenth century," suggested Will.

"No, there is nothing in the old records that shows that. One of my ancestors would have recorded it."

"Not so sure, Walter; I guess that someone did find it and sold the pieces secretly, not to cause any suspicion. Of course, assuming there was anything down there at all."

"No, you're tricking me; there is something down there."

Will was now sure Walter was unstable as he made tiny jerky movements with his body. "Why don't you go down and look yourself."

"Ha, and then you close the hatch and bam," as he demonstrated this action, he raised the shotgun towards the ceiling and pulled one of the triggers. The noise in such a confined space was deafening. The disorientation from the noise caused Will to topple over from his kneeling position onto the floor. Will could see Walter still wielding his gun.

"Now, kneel next to your boss, Mack." With one hand on the shotgun pressed against Mack's head, Walter used his other hand to tighten a plastic tie.

A manic laugh echoed around the empty bathroom.

"I lied earlier, I did kill my brother, and I'm going to kill you both too. Regrettably, I cannot see another way."

Curled into a foetal position, with breaths now shallow and ragged as fear and panic rose through his entire body, not again, thought Will. What had he done to deserve this? Having managed to survive repeated attempts on his life, now some deranged throwback wants to have another go. Lying on his side, he had a good view of the bathroom door, and momentarily his attention was drawn by a flicker of movement in the corridor. What was that? Is there someone else out there? He had to keep Walter talking.

"Tell me, Walter, why go to all the bother of selling me the house? You could have kept it after killing your brother and looked for the treasure yourself."

"I don't have to tell you anything."

"No, but what's the harm if you're going to kill us? I would like to know."

Will noticed that Walter looked calm for the first time since surprising them; he had stopped rocking on his feet, and his face folded into a frown.

"Well, as you say, it won't matter now. I was told I had to sell this house to you via some offshore trust or something. I had to sign lots of papers. I would keep the sale proceeds if I agreed, but I had to kill my brother first. That wasn't difficult; I hated him anyway, and he cheated me out of my inheritance, so he deserved to die. I was instructed to leave the house immediately after I had shown you around. So, I didn't have time to look for the treasure. I had worked out where it was. I still had a set of keys, so I thought I could sneak in and see if I could find it, but the bath was stuck to the piping so that I couldn't move it."

Sudden interest replaced Will's panic, "who made you sell the house to me and why, Walter?"

"I don't know, anyway; why should I tell you?"

"It would be good to know, Walter, before I die."

"Huh, a man approached me and said that I could make a lot of money, but there were some conditions, and as I said, one was that I had to sell this house to you and nobody else."

"Who was he, Walter? Did you know him? What did he look like, this man?"

"Well, it was…." Then there was a sound, not loud, but Will knew what it was, he curled up even tighter, but he couldn't take his eyes off Walter, who just stood there for a few seconds, his mouth open and a look of puzzlement on his face and then almost in slow motion he fell forward, thudding onto the bathroom floor. A shadow appeared in the doorway.

"Get down, Mack," Will screamed.

Another muted sound, and the shadow was gone.

Will just stared at the empty doorway and then at the prone figure of Walter. Another death. Would it never end?

"Are you okay, Mack?"

"Yes, think so; what happened?"

"Don't know but think our lives have just been saved. We need to get free and call the police."

"Kick me that chisel, Will."

A couple of minutes later, Will rubbed his wrists where Mack had removed the ties.

As soon as they both got downstairs, Will dialled 999. He poured Mack and himself large whiskies and sat down to await the police.

They did not have to wait long as the wailing arrival was pre-announced by alarms on Mack's watch. Something flashed through Will's mind, something that needed an answer, about the alarms, but it faded with the thought of the more imminent and difficult conversation that was just about to take place. Will thought that this was not going to be easy to explain.

"Good evening, or should I say good morning, Mr Slater."

"Probably good morning, Inspector," said Will to a tired and dishevelled looking Tavish.

"So, what has been going on here?"

"I think I have discovered who killed Dougie Gordon and who was our bathroom intruder and why."

"That's very interesting, Mr Slater, and who is this mysterious person?"

"It's Walter Gordon, Dougie's brother."

"I see, and you know that for a fact?"

"Well, it's what he told Mack and me. I believed him as it made perfect sense."

"We will, of course, check up on his identity. Where is he?"

"He is in the upstairs bathroom. Dead," replied Will.

"Dead?"

"Yes, he had us tied up. I think he was going to kill us both when someone appeared at the bathroom door and shot him."

"So, we have an elderly self-confessed murderer threatening to kill you both, when out of nowhere a mystery gunman suddenly appears at the door of the bathroom and kills this, Walter Gordon, just before he was going to shoot you and Mr Mack?"

"That's about the long and short of it, Inspector," said Will nodding in agreement but realising how improbable it all sounded.

"Ha," grunted Tavish, "and this Walter Gordon confessed to the murder of his brother."

"Yes, he did," replied Will.

"But he is not here to confirm it. Very convenient, if I may say so, Mr Slater."

"For us, perhaps not for Walter Gordon."

"Quite so, quite so. But Walter Gordon was the only one, apart from Mr Mack, here, who could substantiate your story. Did he say why he killed his brother?" asked Tavish.

"Yes, he did. He was offered money to kill Dougie and then impersonate him and sell the house to Jay and me."

"Why on earth would anyone want to do that?" asked Tavish.

"I haven't quite worked that out yet, but I think it is all part of a wider plot against me and the need for someone to know exactly where I am."

"For what purpose, Mr Slater?"

"Well, I had originally thought it was to get some money from me, but now I wonder if it is just to kill me."

"Well, it seemed as if they had a good opportunity tonight but passed. You know, Mr Slater, I didn't like that Dawkin man from London, but I'm beginning to wonder..." Tavish paused and rubbed his chin.

"What are you beginning to wonder, Inspector?"

"Why I have so many dead bodies on my patch, all since you arrived. It can't be just bad luck or a long line of coincidences," Tavish peered at Will through coal-black eyes. "I wonder if Dawkin might be correct, and there is something we need to find out about you, Mr Slater, something not very pleasant."

"I have nothing to hide, Inspector, but agree it would appear all very inconvenient for you."

"Inconvenient, it most certainly is. I will arrange for statements to be taken from you both tomorrow. I will send Sergeant Pearce. SOCO will finish upstairs, remove the body, and let me have their report. I'm now going to look at the scene, but I'm sure I will be speaking to both of you again soon. Good morning."

CHAPTER THIRTY

It was 7 am before the police entourage finally left Gaur House, and Will hadn't slept for twenty-four hours. He phoned the hospital to check on Jay and to say he would be over in the afternoon. Checking that all the windows and doors were locked, he went to bed and slept fitfully for five hours.

After giving formal statements to Pearce, Will drove to the hospital. He was still feeling rough, but his spirits rose when he saw Jay, looking much better, although still attached to wires and tubes.

Will leant across and kissed her. "How are you feeling today, darling?"

"Bored and wanting to get home. The doctor says that providing I take it easy and stay off my feet for a week or so, I can go home tomorrow."

"That's great news."

"Will, you look awful. What on earth has happened?"

"Not sure where to start, so much has occurred. Soon after I got home last night, I had two visitors. Sergeant Pearce and that awful Inspector Dawkin."

"Inspector Dawkin, what on earth did he want?"

"Well, to be honest, I'm not clear what he was doing in Scotland anyway. He said he had read about your accident in the papers and thought it was connected to the old case. He still thinks I was the mastermind behind that whole operation. Anyway, he and Pearce brought some alarming news. The brakes on your BMW had been tampered with."

"I tried to tell you that the brakes weren't working and to be careful."

"Yes, I remember; I wasn't sure what you were trying to tell me."

"So, the brakes were cut deliberately. Someone tried to kill us, and we have no idea who is behind it."

"I suspect Dawkin thinks that I cut the brakes. He asked whether I knew anything about cars."

"That man is ridiculous."

"I can't agree enough, but he seems to be still interested in me. Anyway, let me go on, as the evening goes from bad to worse. I felt pretty depressed after that news and by everything else that has happened recently. I realised that I had to sort this out myself. With you in here, I had no one I could trust. I had to try and unravel some of the unknowns. So, I thought I would start in the upstairs bathroom. Whilst I was up there, I realised by the dimensions of the house that there was a space under the bathroom floor. Mack and I…."

"How did Mack get into this story?" asked Jay.

"It's a bit complicated, but the alarm went off, and I didn't hear it. I had taken off my watch in our bathroom and was a long way from the study. Mack heard it and came in to investigate. At the time, I didn't think too much about it but realised it was Walter Gordon who had entered the house and set off the alarm."

Jay shook her head, "so Walter Gordon is now in the house too?"

"Yes, I said it was complicated. You remember you read me that article about the Clans' treasure being hidden in the house?"

"Yes, I remember."

"Well, that was what, I think, was hidden under the bathroom. Because none of the house's previous owners admitted to finding it, Walter thought it must be still there. During his brief occupancy of the house, he had worked out where the hiding place was but never had enough time to look properly. He admitted that he broke in that night to see if he could access the space under the bath."

"Wow, I suppose that clears up one mystery."

"Well, more than one, I think. When we discovered that none of the treasure remained, Walter went crazy and said he would have to kill Mack and me. He said he had killed his brother, so killing us would be simple."

"My God, so what happened? Did you overpower Walter?"

"No, someone shot him."

"What do you mean, shot him, how? When?"

"Walter had tied Mack and me up, and I really thought it was curtains for us both. Walter was completely unstable, shaking, sweating and waving his gun around. Then I saw a shadow at the bathroom door, and the next thing, Walter had been shot. The person came right into the bathroom and made sure Walter was dead by shooting him again."

Will could see that Jay was shocked by the story and hoped it would not worsen her condition. "But they didn't shoot Mack or me, and whoever it was just disappeared silently into the night. Mack and I managed to get free and phoned the police."

"So much to take in," said Jay, shaking her head, "so Walter did kill his brother, and he admitted it."

"Yes, but bloody Tavish won't necessarily accept it because there is no corroboration apart from Mack and me."

"That's okay; there are two of you."

"Yeah, but I get the impression that he thinks Mack will agree with anything I say."

"Okay, but he can't deny that there was someone else in the house, the person who killed Walter?"

"We haven't had that discussion yet, but if you take his logic of not believing me about Walter killing his brother, then Mack and I could have killed Walter to hide who killed Dougie."

"But he knows we didn't kill Dougie; the timescale is all wrong."

"Yes, but I suppose we could have arranged it. Tavish is just very suspicious of us both, mainly because of our record."

"There are so many questions buzzing around in my head. But the most immediate ones are, who killed Walter, why, and how did he get in the house?"

"That's a good point; I knew there was something that I couldn't quite work out. The alarms went off when Walter got in; I just didn't hear them. But nothing happened when the killer entered. Mack had his watch on, and there was no alarm. They must have had some knowledge of the area to know that we could not alarm every access point onto our land. For example, along the shore of the loch," Will paused, "that, of course, means we might know who shot Walter."

"Quite possibly, but that's not the issue; how did anyone know that Walter was in the house in the first place?"

"I don't know, but I think Walter had to be killed because he knew the person who is behind all that is happening to us, and quite probably the person who shot him," replied Will.

"Do we have any idea why Walter killed Dougie? Did he say anything before he died?"

"Well, that's the last part of the story and possibly the most worrying."

"Really?"

"Yes, the reason why Walter killed Dougie was so he could impersonate him and sell us the house. If Walter did what he was told, he could keep the proceeds from the sale. As you read in that article, there was no love lost between the two brothers."

"Okay, Walter was shot for fear of him telling you who made him sell the house."

"Yes, that would appear to be the situation. But that only raises the question of why did someone want to sell us this particular house? How could they have known we would buy it. You saw it on the internet."

"You know, thinking back, it was an email from an agent. We had tried so many I just assumed that they had picked up the information from another agent and sent it directly."

"Do you still have the email?"

"Yes, probably on my phone, over there," said Jay pointing to the table next to the bed.

Will scrolled back through the emails. "Fortunately, you seem to keep all your old ones. Here we are, and the website." Will pressed onto the link. "It says, 'This page is no longer available'."

"We must have been hacked. I remember the Wi-Fi was slow immediately before the advert popped up. A perfect sting by all accounts," replied Jay.

"My God, yes, clever and calculating. This is not just one individual. This whole scenario has been put together like a military manoeuvre. It is so shocking that either of us could have been killed, and they are still out there. But who the hell are they?"

CHAPTER THIRTY-ONE

Will arranged for a private ambulance to bring Jay back to Gaur House. Will, Mack and Lena were waiting for her as the ambulance pulled up in front of the house.

The ambulance crew lowered Jay down in a wheelchair.

"Going to be a bit bumpy getting up those steps, luv," said the driver to Jay as he looked across to the front door.

"We can go through the kitchen door, which is flat," replied Jay.

"Don't worry, we can manage from here, thank you," said Will to the two crew.

Jay was delighted to be home, and Will and Lena fussed over her whilst she made a trip around the ground floor in her wheelchair as if reminding herself of the house.

Sitting back in the lounge drinking a mug of tea, Jay said, "after your visit yesterday, I had some thoughts. Pass me that pad of paper, hon." Jay scribbled something down and passed it to Will.

The note read, '*I think we are being listened to. Don't say anything.*' Will nodded.

"It is still nice out; why don't you push me down to the bench by the loch? We can take our tea with us."

"Okay, sounds like a good idea."

Now both sitting and looking down the long expanse of the loch, Jay said, "I've spent the last twenty-four hours trying to piece this all together and can't pretend that I have all the answers, but one thing I'm certain about is that the house must be bugged in some way."

"Why do you think that?" asked Will.

Jay went on, "every time you are in danger, someone pops up to keep you alive. First, the East Europeans and then their boss is murdered. Then Walter threatens to kill you, and he is killed."

Will interrupted, "are you sure SO15 is not still involved, your old mate Harry Allen? It sort of feels like their kind of undercover work."

"No, not as far as I'm aware. I think Harry would have told me if they were. No, this is someone else, and it must be to do with the money," replied Jay.

"Yeah, I got there some time ago about that. Then I wondered if it was just some sort of revenge. But it feels so complex. Why not just turn up and ask for the money?"

"That's naïve; they can't do that as, firstly, the money is not theirs, and you are not willingly going to give it away; and secondly, it would just indicate who was behind this operation. Everything to date points to whoever they are, wanting to keep you alive."

"Okay, so far, but what about the BMW? I could have been driving that car, not you."

"The point is, you weren't driving the car, and someone knew you weren't going to drive it."

Will slowly nodded his head, "because someone heard us discuss the journey and which car you were going to take."

"Exactly. It all fits in with Walter too. There could only be one way that whoever this is, knew that Walter was in the house and would kill you and Mack. It is not as if the killer was passing, saw the lights on, popped in and low and behold, there was Walter about to kill you. They had to know what was going on and stop Walter from 'spilling the beans'."

Will nodded slowly, "they have been listening."

"Possibly watching too. Yes, that is the only rational explanation. It also fits in with the wider picture. If there were someone that had something that you wanted, you would like the targets to stay somewhere where you could get to them."

"You mean not moving around, travelling, going abroad. Just staying in one place."

"Exactly, cooped up somewhere that can be watched and listened to."

"This house. We were led here. The fake estate agents web site, Walter selling us the house, so they knew where we would be and could watch and listen to us."

"Sounds a bit farfetched, I know, but it is starting to make sense."

"I don't know," said Will, "hell of a lot of planning. We might not have liked the house, and then what would have happened? Supposing we had decided to go to one of the Scottish islands? They need people in this plan; how would they manage that?"

"They would have had to adapt their plan. I have got this feeling that we are up against quite a sophisticated network that probably could pop up anywhere we were going."

"That would have to be huge."

"Or loosely formed only brought into action when needed."

"What, like the lifeboat service?" said Will.

"Not quite, but, yes, people with different roles who can act if requested. Sleepers, of some description.

"Can the money be worth all this effort?"

"Twenty million pounds or whatever you have got left. It is a big incentive. More worryingly is the fact that they have a grudge against you too."

"Because they were happy to kill you and Lucy in the car. But you had nothing to do with the money."

"Not directly but, I guess, by association. Someone hates you, not enough to kill you, yet, because they need you, but they have no compunction in ruining your life by killing me."

"My God, that is awful," Will shook his head, trying to assimilate the information. "I don't know; it sounds like something out of a thriller, not real life."

"There's one way to check my theory and see if we can find a bug. If you were going to bug this house, where would you put it, Will?"

"I would probably start in the study. Where I make business calls."

"Okay, let's take a look; we can't be obvious as they may be watching or listening. So, let's pretend we are going there for a purpose. Put on some music to dull our voices."

Will pushed Jay into the study, chose a piece of music on his phone and put it into the dock on his desk and waited until the opening chords of King Crimson blasted through the room.

"Pass some papers for me to look at, and then pretend you are looking for something that you have mislaid."

Will opened each drawer and peered in as if looking for something. The wood was smooth as he ran his fingers along all the exposed surfaces of each drawer. Outside the long middle drawer under the lip between the drawer and the top of the desk, Will's finger felt a small circular object protruding from the wood. He nodded across to Jay and then pulled a paper from the drawer. Jay pretended to read the document and mouthed a response as if in agreement with its contents. Then they both left the study as 'The Court of the Crimson King' reached a crescendo in the background.

"There will be others," Jay whispered, "we need to do a sweep. I'll make a call outside. Can you push me?"

Sitting outside the back door, Jay called one of her old colleagues in SO15 and agreed that someone would come from Glasgow as soon as possible.

CHAPTER THIRTY-TWO

Early the following morning, a small man arrived in a small nondescript white van; he carried a small black suitcase.

"Good morning; I think you are having some problem with your electrics."

Will was a little confused for a minute.

"Your wife called last night and asked me to take a look."

"Of course, I am sorry; yes, please come in."

"I will check the whole house to make sure everything is complying and in good working order. Anywhere you would like me to start?" asked the small man.

"Why don't you start in the study," said Will and showed him the way.

"Leave it to me. Will see you a bit later." The small man opened his black bag to reveal a plethora of kit.

Conversation with Jay had to be perfunctory, so Will thought he would take a walk while they waited for the small man to report back. After an hour, he strolled back to the house. The small man was in the kitchen having a cup of coffee with Jay.

"You're back," said Jay, "why don't we take our coffee outside as it is such a nice day?"

The three of them went out to the bench by the edge of the loch.

"Well," said the small man, "you were correct - quite a sophisticated operation. I have found four listening devices, bugs in four different rooms, the study, the kitchen, the main bedroom, which I assume is yours and the lounge. But," said the small man raising a finger, "they have been watching you too, on three different fibre-optic cameras. One in the study overlooking your desk, one in the kitchen and one on the first landing. None in the bedrooms."

"How does it work? Will they be nearby watching and listening?" asked Will turning his head as if he were looking for someone in a nearby tree.

"Can't tell," said the small man, "the devices will be feeding a transponder somewhere, yes, perhaps in one of the trees, and it will communicate by satellite phone to the internet. So, whoever it is could be anywhere."

"They must be near," said Jay.

"Why?" asked the small man.

"A couple of days ago, they saw or heard something that concerned them, and they were here within the hour to deal with it," replied Will.

"Well, sort of narrows the area, I suppose."

"Can't we track them? I thought everything like that is possible now?" asked Will.

"I have done a quick trace, but as I would have expected, there are a series of IP addresses all linked. It would take a long time to trace, and there would be an in-built warning somewhere along the way. Then the link would break."

"That all sounds very complicated."

The small man shook his head, "not that difficult on the dark web if you know where to look. There are plenty of people offering their services for just this kind of thing."

"So, should we leave them or remove them?" asked Will.

"If you remove the devices, they will know you are on to them and may hasten whatever action they are going to take. If you leave the devices, you can at least plan around it."

"Won't they have seen you looking for them?"

"I was careful to try and hide my purpose. They may be suspicious, but if the devices remain in place, they won't be sure."

"They may have heard us last night, although we were careful," said Jay.

"Yes, but they won't necessarily listen live, and once again, if the devices are left untouched, they can't be sure."

"Okay," said Will, "if we want to talk about anything, then it has to be in the dining room, library or bathroom."

"That's it, in a nutshell."

"Thank you very much," said Jay.

"A pleasure, and if you want me to remove them in due course, let me know through your normal channel." The small man picked up his bag and walked around to his white van, and drove off.

"Who are these people? They have certainly gone to a huge amount of trouble," said Will.

"I agree, so let's think this through. The house was not bugged so that they could stop others from killing you. When they set this up, I guess they wouldn't have any idea that your life would be in danger from anyone else, let alone Walter Gordon. So why bug us in the first place?"

"They wanted information," chipped in Will.

"Yes, but why the cameras too. Listening would have been enough to get information. No, they wanted to see something, something they needed. Something to do with the money."

"Passwords and codes for the banks. The chap said that there was a camera pointed towards the desk and therefore the computer screen."

"Have you transferred any money since we have been here?" asked Jay.

"Yes, several times to maximise rates."

"So why have they not transferred it all out by now?"

"Because any external transfers to an account that is not mine need my fingerprint as an extra protection."

"Bingo, if we are correct and this is all about the money, then they do need you alive, or at least until the transfer is made."

"Thanks, very reassuring," replied Will. "But there is something else that we should consider. It appears that whoever is behind this whole operation is probably local and known to us."

With a deep furrow on her brow, Jay nodded, "yes, I had already got to that conclusion."

CHAPTER THIRTY-THREE

The pages of the morning newspaper crackled as they were turned at speed. Dawkin read the words, but they were not entering his brain, as he was too busy trying to catch something else in its shadowy corner but too dark to see. Dawkin flicked over the pages with even more gusto.

"Sergeant Edkins has arrived, love," said Mrs Dawkin, peering out of the kitchen window.

"Makes a bloody change, early for once," replied Dawkin.

Mrs Dawkin said, "Eileen and Jack have invited us over for dinner on Saturday evening."

"That will be nice," said Dawkin, still in another place.

"Well, at least sound a bit enthusiastic," said Mrs Dawkin, "you know you always get on with Jack, talking about sport, and Eileen is an excellent cook."

"Yep," said Dawkin as another page crackled. The Slater case was still uppermost in his mind, convinced that there was something he already knew that would provide an answer, but he couldn't find it. Something he had heard, or something he had read, or something he had been given.

"They have asked us over for seven-thirty. Will that be alright for you, love?" asked Mrs Dawkin.

There was no reply. Dawkin sat staring at the open page of the paper; then, in a shadowy recess of his mind, a light flicked on. 'Where the fuck is that list," he said more to himself as he pulled a wad of papers from the inside of his jacket pocket. His hands shook as he fumbled through the documents that spread out on top of the newspaper. Flattening the piece of paper on the table, he traced down it with a stubby finger until he got to the relevant line, "that's it," he said, slapping his hand on the table, "the army, the bloody army." He scooped up the rest of the papers and stuffed them back into his jacket pocket. I have to travel to Scotland again, he thought. There was no choice; I might already be too late. He knew he wouldn't be able to convince his boss, so Dawkin decided he wouldn't tell him, or at least not immediately and from a distance.

Standing, scuffing back the chair, Dawkin headed for the front door.

"Love, please don't leave the newspaper," called Mrs Dawkin, as the front door closed, "spread out over the table."

* * *

"Edkins, drive me to City Airport; I'm in a hurry."

"Where are we going, Guv?"

"We're, as in us, are not going anywhere. However, I'm going to Scotland."

"Not the Slater case again, Guv?"

"Yes, Edkins, the Slater case. Tell me, Edkins, that paper you gave me on the children and siblings, was there anything on it that might have had some connection to the main characters in this case?"

"Well, not sure there was Guv."

"That's why you're a sergeant, Edkins. The fucking army.

That's the fucking connection. They have all been in the fucking army. Crombie, Bore, Crombie's son and God knows who else. It's like some secret society, even that evil terrorist Boss. That's got to be the connection. They look after each other in combat and look after each other when they come out. I can guarantee that there are people in Scotland who served with one of these buggers in the army. That's who I have to find pronto." Dawkin was quiet for a moment staring straight ahead; then, another thought came to mind. "Who told you about Sara Crombie getting out of the clink, Edkins?"

"One of the liaison team, Guv."

"Have you got their number?"

"'Expect so."

"Call them please, and find out when she will be out."

Edkins pulled the car over and flicked through his phone, then dialled a number. There was a short exchange of conversation, and Edkins closed the call.

"Yesterday Guv, she got out yesterday, December fourteenth, nice just in time for Christmas."

"What date, yesterday, December fourteenth, shit, shit, shit. The number, Edkins, on the board in Crombie's house, 12.15. It wasn't a time or place. It was the date, but the way the Americans say, December fifteenth. Today. It's going to happen today, Edkins."

"What is going to happen today, Guv?"

"I think Slater is going to be killed today. Get the 'blues and twos' on, as quick as you can."

"Why don't you call the Scottish police and tell them?"

"I will call from the airport when I know what flight I am getting. But they won't believe me. I have to get there myself."

"Anyway, I thought you said Slater was guilty and behind this whole thing?"

"Even I can make mistakes, Edkins, even me."

CHAPTER THIRTY-FOUR

The alarm signified that something was moving towards the house. Will peered at the screen and watched a taxi navigate through the final few potholes and onto the main drive. A delay before anyone got out of the car; presumably, the passenger paying the fare assumed Will. Then the passenger door swung open, and a woman emerged. Will blinked several times to make sure that his eyes were registering the correct image on the screen. It can't be, he thought as he got up to open the front door.

"Sara?" said Will in surprise as he greeted her on the front step," I thought you were..."

"In prison?" said Sara Crombie. "Just released on parole for good behaviour."

Will just stood there with his hand still attached to the door, "I'm sorry, I just recalled that awful day when your husband pulled a gun from his pocket and waved it in my face. You know, I can still almost feel the pain when he hit me because I told him I hadn't got what he wanted."

"Well, he was a vicious bastard," replied Sara.

"I knew he was going to kill me once he had all the bank

details for the money. I could see the hatred and contempt in his eyes. I remember thinking, I knew I had to shoot him before he shot me."

"Just a shame you didn't finish him off rather than let me do it for you."

"I still don't understand why you had to kill him; he was immobilised; we just had to wait for the police."

"I don't quite know myself. I have had plenty of time in prison to think it through. All I could come up with was that something snapped inside. I can barely remember that day at all now. I suppose it was the years of mental oppression, his obsession with an army-style life and the general arrogance and aggression of the man. Suddenly all I wanted to do was hurt him. Hurt him badly. I looked down, and the gun was in my hand, and I just pulled the trigger."

Will tilted his head to one side as he considered the efficacy of her answer. He was not convinced.

Whatever the reason for Sara killing her husband, he was sure that it was no off chance that she should pitch up at his front door as soon as she was out of prison. It had to do with the money. There could be no other explanation. A nervous twitch caught at the corner of Will's eye. He rubbed it. There was something else that sent out a warning. The way she stood, no, a mannerism; he had seen the same one recently.

"Will you ask me in?"

"Ummm, yes, of course, yes, just was shocked to see you, hadn't realised you would be out so soon. Come in, but I want to know why you are here?" said Will. "Jay," called Will.

"Yes, Will," said Jay wheeling herself into the hall.

"It's Sara Crombie."

"Oh, hello," said Jay.

"Hi, gosh, what's happened to you?"

"I was in a car accident; I'm getting better, just waiting for the pelvis to strengthen, then will be fully weight-bearing again. So, what brings you here? I assume you weren't just passing."

Just as Sara was about to reply, the alarm went off in the study. "Jay, show Sara into the lounge; I'm just going to see who this is," said Will.

On edge, Will went into the study to see who was approaching. More trouble, he thought. Will felt a wave of relief as he watched the solid figure of Sergeant Pearce walk up to the front door.

"Hello, Sergeant," said Will as he let in the policeman.

"Good afternoon, Mr Slater," replied Pearce; "how's your wife?"

"Much better, thank you, she's back home."

"That is excellent news, sir," replied Pearce.

"What brings you here? You are our second surprise visitor of the day."

"Well, it's a wee bit strange," said Pearce in a confidential manner, "I got a call from Inspector Dawkin earlier today, he was phoning from London City Airport, and he tells me he's on his way to this house and that I needed to get a team over here too. I told him I couldn't do that without a reason but would pop over myself if that would help. So here I am."

"Didn't he say what it was all about?"

"No, but he sounded very agitated and said that he had some important news, and then his flight was called, and he rushed off. He did add that you should be extremely careful as you were in danger."

"I should be careful and in danger? What did he mean by that?"

"I don't know, but I imagine it will not be long before we find out. Dawkin was catching the 11.40 flight to Dundee and said he would get a taxi from the airport. That's going to cost him a pretty penny," said Pearce looking at his watch. "If he took off on time and not too much traffic, he should be here by, I reckon, 2.30."

Will wondered if it was anything to do with the sudden appearance of Sara Crombie. "Okay, not long now, and then we will see what made this emergency dash so important. Sergeant, come through and meet our first surprise guest of the day."

* * *

Will noticed that Sara had moved through the lounge onto the terrace and followed her out.

"Sara, this is Sergeant Bill Pearce. Sara was a Partner of mine when I had a practice in London."

"Pleased to meet you, Mrs Crombie. Your name rings a bell."

"Quite likely, Sergeant," and turning to Will, "what a magnificent view. This place must have cost a fortune."

"You still haven't told us why you are here, Sara?" asked Will.

"Perhaps, we can have a chat in private," said Sara nodding towards Pearce.

"I'll go inside and wait for the Inspector there," volunteered Pearce.

"Wait, Sergeant," said Will as a loud crunching of gravel towards the front of the house indicated a car approaching at some speed, "that must be Dawkin; let's see what he has to say." Before the gravel had finished scrunching under the car tyres, a shrill warning voice filled the air.

"Slater!"

Will turned towards the voice and the footsteps pounding on the terrace paving stones. Dawkin rounded the corner of the house charging towards them, coat flapping, arms waving like some strange prehistoric bird.

"Get inside, get inside," he screamed. As he flapped towards the group, he tried to hurdle a low flower planter on the terrace. Dawkin miss-judged the height, his toe flicked the top, and he part dived and part flapped into Sergeant Pearce with such force that both men crashed backwards into Will and Sara as a gunshot echoed off the hills.

CHAPTER THIRTY-FIVE

"Get inside. Quick, help me get this man inside. He's hit his head; it's bleeding," said Dawkin trying to haul Pearce to his feet. Sara moved inside first, followed by Will and Dawkin, with Pearce resting on their shoulders. "Keep down and away from the windows. Dial 999 and get an ambulance; tell them we need an armed response," Dawkin shouted as he came through the door from the terrace.

"I'll call," said Sara pulling a phone out of her bag.

"What's happened?" asked Jay, "who's shooting at us?"

"I don't know, but I'm going to find out," said Will rushing out of the room.

Lena arrived in the lounge trailed by Mack carrying a shotgun.

"What's happening?" asked Mack.

"Someone is shooting at us," replied Jay and then hurriedly, "Lena, can you find some bandages from the first aid kit in the kitchen?"

"How is the head?" asked Dawkin.

"Okay, must have hit the corner of the door sill as you knocked me down," replied Pearce.

"Yep, sorry about that, Sergeant, but at least we are all still alive."

"It hurts but don't think it's too serious."

"Who is shooting at us?" asked Jay again, to which no one replied.

Will arrived back in the lounge carrying a shotgun retrieved from his bedroom.

"What are you going to do with that?" asked Jay.

"I'm going to find out who is trying to kill us."

"That is madness," said Jay, "wait until the police arrive."

"No, whoever it is will have gone by then and just come back at another time."

"I think I know who it is out there, and your life is in danger, Mr Slater, seriously in danger. I think the cutting of your car brakes was meant for you and not for your wife," stated Dawkin.

"Well, who is it?" asked Will.

"Justin Crombie."

"No, surely not, it can't be him, I told him..." Sara paused, "he's at Sandhurst."

"Nice to meet you again, Mrs Crombie," said Dawkin.

"I can't say the feelings are mutual."

"You told him what?"

"Nothing, it doesn't matter," replied Sara.

"When did you get here?"

"About an hour ago, and what has it got to do with you?" asked Sara.

"I have no doubt that's your son out there."

"Why are you so sure, Inspector?" asked Will.

"We paid a visit to the Crombie house," said Dawkin nodding in Sara's direction, "and we found maps and long-range photographs of this house. I also discovered he is an exceptional shot. So putting two and two together, I think he means to kill you, Slater. Perhaps revenge, who knows? But, until we catch him, we can't be sure."

"Right, we're wasting time and even more reason to catch him now," said Will, "I'm going to leave via the tunnel. I think I know where he was shooting from and should be able to get close without him seeing me."

"You should stay here, Will, no point in exposing yourself outside," said Mack, "I will go; I can move quicker, and he won't be expecting me."

"No, this is my battle, and I can't expose anyone else to injury because of my actions. You stay here, Mack, and protect Jay," said Will.

"Will. this is madness! You will be killed; we must wait for the armed response team," pleaded Jay.

"I agree, you should stay Slater, but if you insist, then I'm coming with you," said Dawkin.

"I'm going; if you want to come with me, that's up to you," said Will.

"Right, you, give me your gun." Dawkin said, holding out his hand towards Mack, "what type is this?"

"Benelli 828 shotgun, latest model, costly, so please take care of it," replied Mack.

"Come on," said Will, "let's get going before we lose him," and picked up Mack's bag containing spare cartridges.

"So, where is this tunnel?" asked Dawkin.

"It leads onto the estate about a quarter of a mile from the house. The exit is in the woods, so Crombie won't see us coming."

"Okay, let's get this over with," said Dawkin.

Dawkin followed Will through the tunnel and out onto the track.

"We are heading over in that direction," said Will pointing to a range of hills south of their position, "it overlooks the house, a perfect vantage point to take a shot. We can stay undercover until the last few hundred yards, and hopefully, he will not be looking our way; otherwise, he will have a clear shot of us both. Here, take a handful of cartridges."

* * *

They followed the track through the woods. Dawkin was unfamiliar with the terrain, and the dense woods made it difficult to assess where they were heading and how far away Crombie might be, but Dawkin thought he should be as quiet as possible. Every step seemed to make some noise, either a twig snapping underfoot or a branch swishing as he moved forward through the wood. He concentrated on the ground and could see Slater was moving silently and further ahead every time he looked up. Dawkin was impressed with how fit Slater appeared to be. Dawkin moved as quickly and quietly as he could. Panting and sweating profusely, Dawkin eventually reached a clearing and flopped down beside Slater, who was peering at the hill through a pair of binoculars. The landscape in front of them had changed. There were no trees to hide behind, just ground covered with tufts of grass and heather sloping up the side of a hill. From where Dawkin was lying, the top of the hill looked relatively flat. This must be where Slater thought the killer was positioned. Dawkin lay very still in the grass and tried to get his breathing into some normal rhythm.

Dawkin took the binoculars that Slater passed to him and peered at the hill. It took him a moment to work out what he was looking at through the lenses, but slowly he moved the binoculars until the top of the hill was in view. Slater leant across and whispered, "I can't see anything up there; suppose I'm wrong?"

"I hope not, having come all this way," panted Dawkin.

"Okay, we are directly facing towards the loch. I'm hoping that the killer is still watching the house and not in our direction," said Will, "we should approach him from different routes, so he won't be able to kill us both at the same time."

"How very reassuring to know that he will only be able to kill us separately," replied Dawkin.

"Okay, I'm going to move to the right. When I wave my hand, we move towards the hill as quickly and as quietly as possible. If he appears, we shoot and make as much noise as possible. Remember, don't run in a straight line; keep weaving from side to side."

"Think I know a bit about this; I'm a policeman," retorted Dawkin, as he watched Slater shrug his shoulders and slip back into the woods. A few moments later, Slater appeared again on the edge of the clearing about fifty yards further to Dawkin's right.

A dribble of sweat trickled down into Dawkin's eye; he wiped it away with the back of his hand. He had been a policeman for many years, and he had been in some tight situations, mainly when he had been a bobby on the beat, but he always had the comfort of knowing back up was not far away. Now he was stuck in the middle of a moor, about to charge a gunman, with only a shotgun and a lawyer as his wingman.

Dawkin saw Slater indicate towards the hill with his arm; he acknowledged with a flick of his hand and rose somewhat awkwardly from his prone position. Sweat was now pouring down his face, and he wondered if he should have taken off his raincoat. Too late now. He manoeuvred himself into a low position, trying to make himself as small a target as possible, and started to move towards the hill in a crouching run. He kept his eyes fixed on the crown of the hill expecting a head to appear or, more likely, a barrel of a gun. Out of the corner of his eye, Dawkin could see Slater travelling quickly over the coarse grass and hummocks of heather. Dawkin was already puffing, and the cold air caught in his lungs and made him want to cough. An ache crept down his back and into his calves. He made a mental note to join a gym when he got home; if he got home.

A chill breeze had sprung up, and it whispered through the

long grass as it swayed one way and then the other. Everything else was quiet, except the rasping from Dawkin's lungs which appeared so loud that he thought it could be heard on the other side of the loch. Even the birds had stopped calling, unseen eyes high up in the trees watching the unfolding tableau below. Dawkin estimated that he had travelled about a quarter of the distance towards the target when strangely, the image of his wife entered his brain, snipping away at some old biddy's hair. For a moment, he wished he was back home reading the newspaper. His thoughts were interrupted by excruciating pain shooting up his legs, caused by his crouching run. Each step was like walking through treacle. He was now finding it difficult to pick up his feet, and on a slightly higher tussock of grass, his toe caught in a root of heather. He tried to step forward to regain his balance, but his legs had lost all power, and he just pitched forward slowly, face-first into a patch of gorse. The stinging pain from the scratches on his face was sharp, but he managed to stifle his cry of discomfort. As he scrambled up, legs screeching, eyes fixed on the summit of the hill, he reached down for the shotgun. The barrel of the gun had become entangled in another patch of gorse, and as Dawkin tried to pull it free, his finger twitched on the trigger and a round ploughed into the ground about twenty feet from where he was again sprawled. A black cloud of rooks awoken from their reverie rose into the sky, complaining, with a cacophony of coarse and raucous cries.

"Shit, shit," he cursed, his eyes still fixed on the top of the hill. A head appeared at the summit, and then the rest of the body kneeling and aiming directly towards where he was struggling to get up. His fingers felt like giant sausages as he tried to get his index finger into the trigger guard. He had to fire, and he had to move in that order. Dawkin raised the barrel towards the crest of the hill, but as he braced himself, he felt his front foot slide in the mud and fell forward, firing again into the ground a few yards in front of him. Now lying flat, he fired again. Nowhere near the target, but he thought he saw the shooter duck. Then, as he looked towards the hill, he saw the shooter arise again and aim at him. No time to reload, so he rolled himself to the left, but as his body came to a halt, he could see that the shooter had just slightly adjusted his line of sight. Dawkin could sense the tightening of the shooter's finger on the trigger. He had only ever been shot at twice before and never hit. Dawkin realised that he would feel the bullet before he heard any noise from the gun if he heard the noise.

Two shots rang out.

Dawkin lay flat on the ground; he had heard the noise, he was still alive. He couldn't feel any pain, so he couldn't have been shot. Dawkin looked up to see if the shooter was going to take another shot at him. But he had swivelled his gun sight around towards Slater, who was now charging up the hill, shouting and firing, weaving, and rolling alternately.

More shots from Slater's gun.

Dawkin watched Slater dive to his left, roll over and fire again. Dawkin scrabbled in his pocket and stuffed three more rounds into his gun. He fired two in the general direction of the shooter.

Two more shots from Slater, and Dawkin saw that the shooter had disappeared. He felt an adrenaline rush, partly from the relief of not being dead but more from anger and the need to catch the shooter. He started to charge up the hill, shouting and hollering.

Dawkin reached the hill's summit and flopped down next to Slater, who was crouching, getting his breath back and reloading his gun.

"Look, there he goes; he is heading towards the water sports centre. We've got to stop him before he can do any more damage," exclaimed Slater.

"You saved my life. Thanks for that," Dawkin panted.

"I'm sure you'd have done the same for me. Come on; we need to get down to the Centre and catch him."

“We should wait for the armed response team; they must almost be here by now.”

“Can’t wait for them. We have got to catch him before he hurts anyone,” and Will got up and started down the side of the hill towards the Centre and the loch.

Dawkin sighed, pulled two more cartridges from his pocket, pushed them into the gun and rose stiffly, his body complaining with every step. He could see Slater lolloping after the shooter, and he set off again at a more languid pace.

CHAPTER THIRTY-SIX

A frown formed on Roddy Neath's ruddy complexion as the noise of gunfire rang out from the hills. He thought that it might be Mack. More shots, shotguns, quick-firing, must be more than one gun. He could hear shouting too. It was all coming from the hillside behind his building. What the fuck is going on?

Roddy was used to shooting as it was not unusual. It happened either as a necessity or recreationally. Still, Mack always warned him so it didn't disturb any of his patrons at the Centre. Roddy was annoyed that he hadn't been informed in advance. The veins in his neck started to pulsate as annoyance turned, first to anxiety, then to rage. But Roddy felt something else. The hairs on his neck stood up for no reason. Red patches from rising blood pressure appeared on his neck and face. Instinct, experience, call it what you like, but Roddy knew something was not correct. No sportsman shot and shouted at the same time in the same place. He exited the reception area with deliberate strides and headed towards the back of the building, where he could see the hillside. As he stepped around the corner, he saw a man in army camouflage racing down the hill. It was that idiot boy from Sandhurst, a pistol in his hand and a rifle strung across his back. In the distance, he saw two other figures following; both had shotguns in their hands. One looked like Slater.

Roddy couldn't understand what he was witnessing. Incensed with having men with guns running about near his Centre, rage pounding through every pore of his body, something suddenly clicked in Roddy's head. He was back in Afghanistan, and one of the Taliban was running towards him, and he had to be stopped for interrogation. Roddy looked down, searching for the rifle in his hand. Nothing. He was unarmed. He had to stop the Terry, at all costs, even at the expense of his own life. Roddy looked around for a weapon. On the ground, there was an old metal railing partly covered by fallen leaves. Roddy picked it up. It felt good in his hands; he fingered the hard, cold metal; it reminded him of the barrel of a gun. Roddy stepped back behind the corner of the building and waited. He had trained for this. It was his skill. He waited and listened. First, the sound of undergrowth tearing as the man descended through the bracken and long grass, then the sound of breathing. Roddy stepped out into the man's path.

"What the hell?" exclaimed the shooter.

Roddy, his face now puce, the veins pumping at the side of his head, waved the metal bar in both hands and screamed at the shooter, "I'm going to kill you, you stinking Taliban Terry."

"Have you gone mad? Get out of my way, you idiot, or I'll kill you," howled the shooter.

The shooter started to raise his pistol towards Roddy as he went to push by, but Roddy was past all rational thought; his brain had shut off, he was in another land fighting against another enemy. Acting on instinct against an armed man, he heaved the metal pole down in a deadly arc towards the shooter's head.

Roddy could see the sudden look of realisation rather than fear etched in the shooter's face as the pole made its inexorable journey downwards. The shooter ducked away from the descending bar and flung up his left arm to protect his skull. Two things happened almost simultaneously, the sickening crack of the shooter's bones as they shattered on contact with the metal bar and a shot from the shooter's pistol.

Roddy felt the pain in his side and the warmth of fresh blood as it oozed down the inside of his trouser leg. He slipped to the ground, his hand clutched to his side as blood ran between his fingers. "Bastard Terry, bastard Terry," he screamed.

CHAPTER THIRTY-SEVEN

Crombie could see bone protruding from the wound in his arm; he vomited down the front of his camouflage jacket. He could hear the noise of the two men that followed him. The idiot who had attacked him lay in a pool of blood, screaming obscenities.

Perhaps he could get off a shot at his pursuers. His left arm hung useless at his side, and he was now shaking violently. No, he had to escape; he turned and ran towards his car parked in the lane outside the Centre. The pain from his arm was unbearable; he needed oxygen, he felt light-headed, couldn't control his legs, and the ground seemed to rush towards him and then blackness.

* * *

"Got the bastard Terry," Roddy thought, knew I would. He kept pressing at the wound. It will be okay, not fatal, as long as I don't lose too much blood. I need help.

A shadow blocked out the sun; someone was standing above him. Neath recognised the shadow. "Is that you, Sarge? Get me off this bloody road and undercover. Field dressing is in my pack over there by the armoured car." Neath felt something being placed over his nose and mouth, some material; he struggled, "can't breathe, Sarge, something is over my face, you're suffocating me, Sarge, can't breathe..."

CHAPTER THIRTY-EIGHT

His trousers were heavy from the wet, and the mud as Dawkin slithered on his bottom down a steep part of the hill. He had lost sight of Will.

A pistol shot.

"Shit, I hope that's not Slater." But then he caught a glimpse of Will still charging down the hill, still a few yards away from the Centre.

Dawkin eventually reached the bottom of the hill and stepped around the corner of the reception building. A red-haired man was lying close to the building to his left, blood coming from a side wound. To his right, a little way off, he could see Slater standing over a prone man, whom he assumed was the shooter.

"Is he dead?" asked Dawkin.

"No, think he's just passed out; his arm is in a hell of a mess."

"So, this is Justin Crombie."

"How do you know it's him?" asked Will.

"I have seen his picture; there's no doubt. There's another bloke back there who looks in a bad way too. Do you know him?"

"Yes, that's Roddy Neath; he owns this Centre."

"Go and check on him; there must be a first aid box in the office; see if you can find it."

Dawkin watched Slater scurry off as he pulled out his phone to dial for assistance.

As Will hurried back, Dawkin, in some agitation, said, "something very strange has happened. I have just dialled 999 and asked for another team to meet me out here, and they say that they haven't had any previous requests - nothing about an armed response unit needed or even an ambulance. I don't understand. They called from the house. I saw that Crombie woman on the phone."

"Something else is a bit strange," said Will. "Roddy Neath is dead. I couldn't find a pulse. He was shouting and cursing when I got down from the hill. The wound was serious, and he's lost a fair amount of blood, but I wouldn't have thought he would have died so soon, if at all. Perhaps he had some other complication, dodgy heart or something, and the shock killed him."

"Perhaps," replied Dawkin, "the post mortem will tell us. Anyway, we've got this bloke for murder now." Dawkin looked down at the inert figure of Justin Crombie. "However, I think we may have another problem. If no emergency calls were received, then the Crombie woman didn't make the triple nine call. Why? Too much of a coincidence that she should have arrived today. You had better get back to the house as quick as possible, but take care."

"Aren't you coming too?"

"I can't leave until the police get here. It is not my jurisdiction. There will be a lot of explaining to do with a dead body and a badly injured man. Tavish will try and throw the book at me as it is, but leaving a serious crime scene..." Dawkin paused, "I asked for assistance at the house as well, but that will be on its way after the first lot arrives here. But you," he said, pointing at Will, "I think you should get back to the house now. I have the feeling that all is not right there. Take a shotgun; you may need it." Dawkin leant down and felt in Crombie's pockets. "Here, this is his car key. I reckon it will be just outside. Take it. I'll cover for you here, Slater. Go, go now!" Dawkin watched Slater scuttle out of the gate, and a minute or so later, he heard a car start and move away.

Crombie began to stir, "arrh… The pain, water..."

Dawkin looked around; a few people from the Centre were huddled together at the corner of the reception building, peering out at the scene.

"It's okay, I'm a policeman, and everything is over. Can someone bring me a bottle of water for this injured man, please?"

A young woman brought a bottle over.

"Thanks, luv. Get back with the others, there's more police arriving, and they will want to take statements."

"I work here," the woman said, "can I help Roddy?"

"I fear nothing can be done for him, Luv."

"Oh my God, he's not dead?"

"Yes, I'm afraid so. Look, just pop back and sit down and wait, please."

Dawkin knelt and fed Crombie some water, "there's an ambulance on its way."

Crombie spluttered, dribbling a lot of the water down his front.

Dawkin bent closer to Crombie, "why did you want to kill Slater?"

"He ruined our lives. He deserves to die."

"You had plenty of opportunities to do that before now; why didn't you do it?"

Spittle had formed at the corners of Crombie's mouth, his breathing was shallow, and his words came out as grunts. "I promised, wouldn't do it, not yet."

"But you fired at him outside the house."

Blood had drained from Crombie's face, and the skin had

become translucent. “He wasn’t the target. That woman was. Slater will die, I promise that.”

“What do you mean? What woman? Mrs Slater?”

Crombie grimaced. “Not her, although she deserves to die as well. She should have died in the accident. No, not her, my mother, the bitch. She killed my father. Just shot him dead. Why would she want to do that? Ha, only to protect herself from being found out.”

“Found out about what?”

“You’re the policeman; you work it out yourself. You should have done that a long time ago.”

What should he have worked out? What had he missed? “Anyway, you are going away for a very long time for murder.”

“I haven’t killed anyone yet.”

“I’m afraid you have; that man who you just shot is dead.”

Crombie coughed and grimaced again, “can’t have; it was only a flesh wound to get him off me.”

“Well, that’s not the case.”

“The pain, it’s terrible, my arm,” Crombie closed his eyes and seemed to pass out again.

Dawkin looked at his watch; where the hell was the ambulance and back up. Who would live in a place like this?

Dawkin paced around the inert figure of Crombie, metaphorically scratching his head. What did he mean, *Slater will die*? Did he mean he would attempt it again? No, that was not the meaning; it was more of a statement that ‘Slater will die.’ Therefore, someone else was going to kill him.

CHAPTER THIRTY-NINE

Sara watched as Jay and Lena made Sergeant Pearce as comfortable as possible on the couch.

"How are you feeling, Sergeant?" asked Jay.

"Fine, please stop fussing; I'm fine."

"Okay, but just lie still until the ambulance gets here. Concussion can be serious if not treated." Jay said, "Sara, you still haven't told us why you are here. I would like to know right now."

"It's like this," said Sara, producing a pistol from her handbag, "Will has got a lot of money that belongs to me. I had hoped I could do it without all this fuss, but it looks as if my idiot son has screwed this up."

"You," indicating to Mack with the barrel of her gun, "sit down there next to this nice policeman. And you," to Lena, "keep sitting there and don't make a move. I have a few things to say. But first, pass me your radio, Sergeant."

Pearce unclipped his shoulder radio and passed it to Sara.

"Your mobiles, please. I imagine you have one too, Sergeant, please." Pearce delved into his side pocket and complied with the request.

Sara looked across at Lena, "and your's dear."

"Haven't got it with me. It is in the kitchen. Shall I go and get it?" Lena replied.

"No, just sit down and keep quiet."

Sara scooped up all the devices and dropped them into a large flower vase full of water.

"Now, what we are going to do is wait for Will to return and then he is going to transfer all the money that he stole from me."

"But that wasn't your money," said Jay. "It was all to do with terrorist activities and your husband's involvement. I mean, you even killed your husband because of what he had done."

Sara rocked back on her heels and laughed. "Do you know why I killed that poor inept bastard? Not because he had tried to kill Will, and he couldn't even manage to do that. No, I knew that once Will had wounded my husband, he would try and wriggle out by saying I was behind the whole operation. I couldn't afford that, so I had to silence him. He was an awful man anyway. It's just a shame someone hadn't done it earlier in Afghanistan or Iraq. There's no justice in the world."

"But why would he implicate you?" asked Jay.

"Because it was all my idea from the start," said Sara.

"I thought Michael Bore and one of your other business partners were the masterminds behind it all?" said Jay.

"You know what men are like, puff out their chests, think they are running the show, even say they are, but I was the power." Sara shook her head as if to remember where she was in the story. "Anyway, as I said, Peter deserved to die. He was not very brave even though he was in the army. Just a big bully; I calculated that I would only get a couple of years inside for the manslaughter of a terrorist. Better than doing fifteen or more for terrorism. I didn't think Will would be allowed to keep all the money, so when I heard he had, I hatched up a plan to relieve him of it."

"And to think Will had a soft spot for you," said Jay.

"It might have all been different had he married me, and I hadn't married Peter. It might have been him and me up here," she said, holding both arms out wide and looking at Jay. "Anyway, I'm not a greedy woman, you can keep the house, but I want what is left of the rest. I suggest you get your husband to make the transfer when he gets back, and I will walk out of this house forever."

"What happens if Will returns with a whole load of policemen? How are you to deal with that?"

"Well, you're correct; I hadn't planned for that idiot London policemen to be here or my son to cause so much trouble just as I arrived. So, there may be a problem. In which case, I will execute my escape plan, but you can be sure that will not be the end of it. I will have Will's money one way or another. Now, shut up before I put you in a wheelchair permanently." Turning to Pearce, Sara asked, "have you got any handcuffs, Sergeant?"

"Yes, on my belt."

"Okay, pass them over to this man," she said, pointing, "what's your name? Mack?"

"Aye, Mack," he replied.

"Okay, Mack, put one cuff around your wrist and the other around the Sergeant's ankle."

"It's a bit awkward," replied Mack as he tried to get in a position so he could get his wrist near enough to Pearce's ankle.

"Just sit on the floor and put your arm up. That way, neither of you will be able to move too quickly. Right, just toss me the keys, please, Sergeant."

Pearce delved into his uniform pocket again and threw a key ring onto the floor in front of Sara.

"Thank you," she said, picking them up. "Now, we just have to wait for a short while."

"This is stupid; the ambulance and the police will be here very soon," said Jay.

"Ah, but you see, I only said I called them. I never dialled the number. So, there should be no interruptions for a while," smirked Sara.

CHAPTER FORTY

Sweaty palms, shaking hands, and a strange car made the winding roads to Gaur House seem even more challenging than usual. Each blind bend potentially concealed a vehicle coming the other way at speed. He thought about phoning, but he didn't want to warn anyone that he was on his way. A helicopter flew overhead, and in the distance, he heard sirens. They got louder, and through a gap in the trees, Will could see an ambulance preceded by a police car. They were travelling fast, and Will didn't want to meet them at the next blind bend, so he pulled into a passing place by the side of the road and waited for them to go past. He didn't have long to wait. As the vehicles passed, a man in the police car's back seat gave Will a long and hard stare. He was sure it was Inspector Tavish.

Will was unsettled by what Dawkin had said. Why would he need to be careful? Justin Crombie had been caught, so there was no danger from that quarter. What about Sara? Why had she turned up? She hadn't given her reason before Will had dashed out after her son. Perhaps they were working together? That would make sense. She was capable of anything. Dread lay heavy on his shoulders as he thought of Sara with the incapacitated Jay at the house. But Pearce was in the house, injured but still a policeman, and Mack. No one would take liberties with him. Why did he feel apprehensive?

He decided not to enter the house by the front door. An element of surprise would be good even if everything were normal. Will drove on until he was about half a mile from the house. Stopping the car just off the road, Will walked a few yards into the woods and looked about him in a small clearing at the edge of some trees. The trees and undergrowth all looked the same. He took a few further steps deeper into the woods; a tree caught his eye, thicker than the rest. He had seen this tree before, but on which walk and on which track? He couldn't see the road or the car anymore. He had to decide. He walked around the base of the tree; the ancient and craggy trunk felt rough and ragged on his hand. There it was, the track, Will was sure it was the right one as there was something familiar with the pattern of the trees. He set off at pace with the shotgun in his hand. He followed the track, convinced that it would lead him to his destination. After about ten minutes, he spotted the large boulder that marked the entrance to the tunnel. If there was some trouble in the house, he was going to enter unseen.

A CCTV camera was pointed at the tunnel's entrance, but he didn't want to set off an alarm in the house. Will looked around and found what he needed, a large fallen tree branch still in leaf. He hoped Mack had been correct and that small animals and the like would not set off the alarm. Approaching from behind, Will manoeuvred the branch in front of the camera so the thick leaves would entirely cover its view of the tunnel's hatch. He entered the tunnel, which was still open from the earlier hasty exit, and then disappeared into the ground.

The lights were movement-activated but had an override switch to allow quicker movement through the tunnel. Will flicked the switch and set off back to the house. The floor was still uneven, and he was careful not to trip and fall, but he hustled on as fast as he could.

Climbing the ladder at the other end of the tunnel, he pressed his ear to the panel that led into the billiard room. There was just a faint wisp of air through the gap but no voices. Closing his eyes to accentuate his hearing, he listened again. No voices, but was there any movement in the room. Perhaps someone was waiting for him to appear through the tunnel. Difficult to tell - gently, he pushed the panel open. Still, nothing, although he thought he could hear voices further into the house. He opened the panel fully and climbed out. There was no one in the room, so he made his way across to the door and again listened. He could hear voices coming from across the hall in the lounge. Peering out around the door of the billiard room and still seeing nobody, he carefully made his way to the open lounge door. He felt a bit foolish doing this in his own house. There might be nothing wrong. However, the tone of the voices told him otherwise and warned him not to rush in. He pressed his back against the door lintel and listened. He could hear Sara; she sounded very agitated and aggressive.

'Where the hell is he?'

"He'll be here soon, and then Will can make the transfer to you, and you can get out of our lives for good," replied Jay.

So that's it, thought Will. I was correct. She has come for the money from the terrorist activities. He had been fooled into believing that Sara was innocent. The only one of his three business partners not involved. Would it have been possible for her not to have known what her husband was up to? Had he been so naïve? The more he thought about it, the more her involvement made sense. He snapped back into the present. Jay and the others must be held under duress. He had to see into the room before he could decide what action to take. But he was on the wrong side of the door. From the other side, he could have seen through the door jamb. He needed to peek around the edge of the door. Carefully Will laid the gun on the floor, and by lying flat, he thought he might be able to peak in without being spotted. He inched towards the opening and cautiously peeped around the corner.

"Ah, there you are, Will," said Sara, who had been standing facing the open door and spotted Will the instant his head appeared. "Why don't you join us?"

CHAPTER FORTY-ONE

Dawkin watched as the police helicopter descended from the sky. When it was within inches of the Centre's car park, four occupants dressed in black emerged and fanned out, facing the centre's buildings, backs to the loch and two on either flank.

"Armed police, do not move. You," shouted the man in front to Dawkin, "on your knees with your hands in the air."

Dawkin complied with some difficulty as most of his muscles were seizing into a solid state. "I'm police," he shouted out as a police car screeched to a halt just inside the gates to the water sports centre. Two other armed police rushed out from the car and crouched, looking in every direction.

"Police," called out Dawkin again, "everything secure. One dead and one injured. Need medics."

The back door of the police car opened, and out stepped Inspector Tavish. "Yes, he's police; let the ambulance in," said Tavish.

Dawkin watched Tavish stride towards him; his face was red, which Dawkin imagined would match his temper. He waited for the verbal assault with a degree of equanimity.

"What the hell has been going on here, Dawkin, and why are

you on my patch again? I told you before, none of this has anything to do with you. I shall be complaining to your superiors about this intrusion as soon as I get back to the station. I won't tolerate it. Do you hear me?"

"Yes, Inspector, and I can appreciate your anger, but I had justification."

"Justification, justification, looks like a scene from the OK Corral," said Tavish turning his head to look around the yard. "You had better tell me what has happened and pretty damn quick, or I will arrest you."

Dawkin could appreciate Tavish's anger, but he couldn't let Tavish distract him from his pursuit of the truth in the Slater case. He had waited too long to give that up now. "I discovered in London that Slater was a person likely to be the target of an assassination attempt, probably from that man there," said Dawkin pointing to Justin Crombie. "I couldn't warn Slater because I had no proof or any motive, apart from perhaps revenge. It was when I discovered that Crombie's mother had been released on bail a few days ago that I put two and two together. I had to warn Slater and thought the only way he would take me seriously was if I came in person. I only just got here in time as Crombie there, took a shot at Slater as I arrived." He was not going to mention who the target was. "Slater insisted on chasing Crombie. As the senior policeman on site, I knew I should go with him. We chased Crombie off that hill, and he ran into that man down there, Roddy Neath's his name, who I assume tackled Crombie, breaking his arm, before Crombie shot him dead. By the time Slater and I got into the car park, Crombie had collapsed from his wounds."

Tavish shook his head as if having difficulty believing the story. "Unbelievable, when will the killing stop? It has been the same ever since that blasted man and his wife arrived on my patch. And you're no better. You should not have allowed Slater to leave the house and called us directly, and then that man," pointing over to Neath, "would still be alive."

"We did dial 999, well, I thought Sara Crombie did, but I discovered that she didn't for some reason."

Tavish was silent for a moment, "what about Pearce? Why didn't he call it in?"

"Well, he was injured when Crombie fired at us all. Not shot, but he hit his head quite badly, and by the time we had got him comfortable, the Crombie woman had already supposedly made the call."

"And where is Slater?" said Tavish looking around the car park.

"Because of Mrs Crombie's strange behaviour in not calling the police and her sudden appearance up here, I thought Slater should get back to the house as soon as possible to see what was going on. I dialled 999 and asked another unit to go to the house."

"I thought it was him driving a car that we passed on the road up here. If I had been sure, I would have arrested him there and then for leaving a crime scene."

"That is my fault, Inspector; I let him go, which I think is now probably a mistake as I think he is in extreme danger. We need to get a car there as soon as possible, Inspector. Couldn't you get one of your lads to drop me back at the house?"

"Inspector Dawkin, have you forgotten all your police procedures or is this the way the Met operates? I have what would appear to be a murdered man, the suspect and a whole batch of witnesses, and you want me to leave all this behind and go to a local house where you believe that a man might be in danger. A man, I will remind you, that you let leave the scene of the crime. Not just some petty crime scene but a murder crime scene. Your senior officers might turn a blind eye to that sort of thing, but mine won't. In any case, Sergeant Pearce is there for some reason not yet established, as I can't seem to get hold of him. He will be able to take control of any situation that might or might not have developed."

Dawkin knew if he were going to get back to the house, he would have to do it under his own steam, "would you mind if I made my way back there myself, I could give my written statement later at the nick, unless you are arresting me?"

Tavish looked down his nose at Dawkin as if he had found something unpleasant in a plate of food that he was about to eat, "quite frankly, Dawkin, I don't care a fuck about what you want to do; just get out of my sight and let me get along and do my job."

Dawkin took that to mean he could leave. But how would he get back to the house? He would never find his way back across the hills, and in any case, he could barely take a step. He looked around and saw Crombie being carried into the back of the ambulance. Seeing that Tavish's attention was now elsewhere, he strode over to one of the paramedics waving his warrant card, "could you give me a lift? I'm here without a vehicle, all the guys are tied up, and I need to make another urgent visit."

The paramedic looked unsure, "not our job to ferry the polis aboot; we no' supposed to stop on route until we get to the hospital."

"What's up," said the other medic peering down from inside the ambulance.

"This polisman wants to be dropped off doon the way. Say's it is very urgent."

"Come on, Stew, won't do any harm; the patient is stable."

"Okay, pal," said the first paramedic, "jump up beside me and let me know when you want to get oot."

CHAPTER FORTY-TWO

Will stood up and looked around. Mack was sitting on the floor joined to Pearce by handcuffs, Jay was sitting on the settee, Lena sitting on a chair close to the door and Sara standing in the Centre of the room waving a pistol.

"Where is that idiot son of mine? Thought you and that fat policeman Dawkin might have brought him back."

"I'm afraid he has met with a rather nasty accident, Sara, so he won't be joining this little party of yours. The only joiners will be the police, and they are on their way," replied Will.

"What happened? Is it serious?" asked Sara.

"His arm is a bit of a mess, but that is the least of his problems as he seems to have killed one of my neighbours, Roddy Neath." Will heard an intake of breath from Jay and Mack.

"My God, he is an idiot. Why would he do that?" Sara paused and waved her pistol in Will's direction, "you know he wanted to kill you? I tried to persuade him that getting the money would be preferable, but he wouldn't listen. Said you needed to be repaid for what you had done to our family. He watched you in court. He was there every day. He couldn't believe that you hadn't been arrested and were only there as a witness. He blamed you for everything that happened. All I could do was persuade him to wait until I was out on parole. He agreed, but he wasn't going to wait much longer. So, I thought I had better get up here quickly after my release, get the money and then bang; you were dead too. I hadn't realised how advanced he was in his planning to kill you. You were lucky that he missed you earlier," Sara paused, "as he can't do it now. Perhaps, I should kill you instead. Maybe I should have killed you and not my husband when I had the opportunity. Anyhow, I want my money first, and then I'll decide what I'm going to do with you and this lot," she said, glancing around the room.

Will could see Jay was watching closely, her eyes flicking back between Sara and him. He knew that sign. She was weighing up her options; even though she was incapacitated, Will suspected she would do something. There was no doubt that Sara was dangerous with or without the money. As Will looked across at Jay, she gave a slight nod.

It was a sign, Will was sure. He had to keep Sara's attention. He was unclear what Jay might do in her condition, but Will would give her the best chance.

"This is planned like a military mission, every piece thought out in advance. This was not your work in prison. You don't have the connections," Will paused. "There have been many deaths so far, and I wonder if you will be the next. You're just an amateur; the thing is, Sara, I think you are expendable, sort of collateral damage. That's what happens in war, someone gets killed, but that doesn't matter, provided the result is achieved; means to the end stuff."

"Think you have said enough, Will."

"So, what was the plan, Sara? How were you planning to get away with us all here? Kill us all and then drive down the A9 to freedom?"

"Huh, you think you are so clever, don't you. You always did. Back when we all worked together, we were never up to your standard. It didn't matter how well we did the work or how many fees we brought in; you were always better than us. Well, the tables are turned, Will. I have the upper hand now as I have the gun. Indeed, I wasn't expecting so much company, but I reckon it makes no difference. I'm going to lock you all away until I have gone. My escape route is planned, and a few hours' start is all I need. What I hadn't expected was for Justin to screw it all up. Just like his father, incompetent. Bloody soldiers can't do anything without someone giving them an order. Anyway, enough of this talk, this will be simple, Will; you're going to finalise an electronic transfer of all your money. Then I shall leave you all in peace."

Will could see Jay edging towards the end of the settee, so he went on, "how are you going to get the money?"

"As I said, it is simple; I have all the information from the camera watching your computer screen. All I need is your finger-print. Now I can do that while you are alive or use it once you are dead. It's your option, Will."

Will was still not sure what Jay was planning, so he kept going.

"So, what about the Eastern Europeans that attacked me. Did Justin cut their brakes?"

"I don't know what you are talking about. I know nothing about any Eastern Europeans. I know nothing about cutting brakes. Perhaps he did it for a joke. He loved messing around with cars. I don't know. As far as I'm concerned, all the Eastern Europeans are either dead or in prison."

"Seems to be a lot you don't know about Sara. Are you sure this is your plan? Who is really behind all this, the brains?"

"That's enough, money transfer time."

"Come on then, through to the study," Will made to leave the room.

"Wait, not so fast," said Sara.

Will knew that this was the moment; With Will moving

towards the door, Sara had just momentarily lost control of the room; the group was more spread out, and Sara couldn't watch everyone without turning her head. Her concentration was fixed on Will, and at that moment, Jay launched her attack; in one movement, she picked up her crutch and flung herself at Sara, crashing the crutch down on Sara's arm. The pistol flew across the room towards Lena.

"Quick, Lena, pick up the gun," shouted Will,

Lena swooped bird-like onto the pistol.

"Well done, give it to me, Lena," demanded Will, but he stopped. The likeness, he remembered it too late.

"I don't think so, Will," she replied, pointing the gun in the general direction of the rest of the room.

"What's going on, Lena? What are you doing? Give me the gun now," exclaimed Will.

"Give Will the gun, Lena," shouted Jay from her prone position on the floor.

"Well done, luv," said Sara clutching her arm to her chest, "can I introduce my daughter Chloe Crombie?"

Lena gave a slight nod in recognition of the disclosure of her identity.

"I should have realised it earlier. I knew there was something about you that I recognised,"

"Yes, Will, I'm Chloe Crombie."

"You have been here to spy on us all the time," chipped in Jay.

"Yeah, that was the plan until Mum got out of prison, and we could take revenge on what you did."

"It was you who planted the bugs and cameras, wasn't it? It all makes sense," said Jay propping herself up on one arm.

"Sure was. I wanted to put a camera in your bedroom too, but Mum said no. She's delicate like that. Probably didn't want to see what she had missed all these years, Will."

"You're a little bitch," screamed Jay.

"Shut up, and I'm glad I won't be bossed around by you anymore. Just a pity you didn't die in that crash. That would have made all this much easier."

"You knew I wouldn't be driving the BMW. You heard us talking. So, you could get your brother to cut the brakes? You deliberately tried to kill Jay and Lucy," said Will.

"Oh yes, I thought it would do you good to know what it was like to lose someone close," replied Chloe.

"Okay, that's enough, Chloe, pass me the gun, and we'll get Will to make the transfer, and then we'll leave," said Sara.

"No, I think we should kill them all, especially these two," said Chloe indicating to Will and Jay. "They have ruined all our lives and continue to do so. There has to be revenge."

"That was not what we agreed, Chloe," said Sara. "We can walk away and hide, and no one will look for us after a while, as we have just taken some money due to us. Will won't pursue us."

Will could see a look in Chloe's eyes. She was no longer rational.

"As you said, Mother, we have the option of a live Slater or a dead one. I rather like the second option." Chloe pointed the pistol towards Will's head. "I think he deserves more punishment than just taking his money. Anyway, I don't want his tainted money. I want revenge."

"Your Mother makes sense, Lena, Chloe, just walk away while you can," said Will.

Chloe laughed, and as her finger squeezed on the trigger, the room filled full of the noise of a helicopter that dropped onto the grass between the house and the loch.

"As you said, Will, military precision. That's our exit route, not the A9," said Sara and laughed, "come on, Chloe, let's get this done."

CHAPTER FORTY-THREE

The ambulance dropped Dawkin on the main road at the end of the long lane that led to Gaur House. As he ran down the track, Dawkin pulled his mobile phone from his pocket and redialled 999, explaining who he was and that he needed immediate armed assistance. He hoped that the control would not feed the request back to Tavish, the nearest unit. Now panting and sweating profusely and in acute pain from every muscle of his body, he skirted around the rain-filled potholes hoping that his hunch was correct; otherwise, he reckoned he would be a bobby on the beat again next week. As he got near the house, he cut off the track and entered the woods to remain undetected for as long as possible. He hoped that the kitchen door was unlocked. He recalled that the main living rooms faced the water, so he approached the other side.

Edging his way around the side of the house, Dawkin approached the kitchen door. The metal was cold in his hand as he turned the handle and pushed it open. The door creaked, and Dawkin stood back from the opening in case someone was armed inside. Nothing. As he stepped into the kitchen, he could hear

Slater and a couple of women's voices. They seemed to be arguing. As Dawkin got nearer to the commotion, he could tell the voices were loud, excitable, and high pitched, indicating extreme tension. If only he had a gun. As he looked around for something he could use as a weapon, he spotted Will's shotgun on the floor on the opposite side of the lounge door. He needed an element of surprise if he were to defuse this situation, but it would be impossible to reach for the gun and step into the room without first being seen. However, his thoughts were drowned by a thunderous noise from outside. It was a helicopter landing on the lawn. He doubted the police had arrived so quickly, but he hoped all heads would be turned towards the noise. He stepped across the opening, picked up the gun, flicked off the safety and stepped into the room. He immediately took in the scene, and nearest to him was a young woman, who he hadn't seen before, holding a pistol and pointing it in the direction of Slater's head.

In a mollifying tone as if he were addressing some unruly schoolchildren, Dawkin said, "right, we need to all calm down. Young lady, please drop your gun on the floor. If you point it at me, I will shoot you."

Everyone turned in Dawkin's direction, including Chloe. Everyone was perfectly still, not a sound, just the noise of the waiting helicopter.

The peace was broken by Chloe, who shrilled, "who the hell are you?"

"I'm a policeman; more are on their way, so please put your gun down."

"Fuck you."

Everything appeared to move in slow motion: a bead of sweat dribbling down Lena's angst face, the tightening of her finger on the trigger, Slater diving to cover his wife on the floor.

The steel trigger of the shotgun felt cold and stiff against Dawkin's finger as he pulled. The recoil from the gun drove the stock painfully into Dawkin's shoulder. The air was thick with

Gunsmoke as the noise rebounded off the walls subsiding into a hum in his ears. Eventually, through the gorse of deafness, Dawkin heard the pitiful sound of sobbing.

Sara was weeping over the body of Chloe. A shotgun cartridge from twenty feet was always going to end in one outcome. He could see that Mack, Pearce and Sara had been out of the arc of the pellets. Slater had protected his wife and had also escaped the blast.

The helicopter took off, and Dawkin watched through the shattered terrace doors as it headed down the loch passengerless.

Dawkin stepped across the room and picked up Sara's pistol. He then helped Will move Jay into a chair. He released Mack and Pearce from their manacles and then stood in a state of shock at the event that had just unfolded. In the distance, to everyone's relief, they heard the sound of sirens.

A few moments later, the front door crashed in.

"Armed police," came the shout from the hall.

"We're in here," called out Dawkin, as he laid Sara's pistol and his shotgun on the floor in front of him, "I'm police, all clear, no guns."

"On your knees," came the voice from one of the Kevlar clad policemen. Dawkin was just about to protest on behalf of Jay when Inspector Tavish burst through the lounge door.

"It's okay. He's a policeman," indicating towards Dawkin.

"That's Sara Crombie, Justin's mother, and that's her daughter Chloe," said Dawkin indicating the gruesome spectacle on the carpet, "otherwise, we are all okay, I think."

"My God," said Tavish shaking his head, "I can hardly believe it. One death after another, and all seem to involve you, Mr Slater, accompanied by Inspector Dawkin here. What are you, horsemen of the apocalypse?"

"We couldn't…."

"Shut up, Dawkin. I will hear all your statements in due

course, but for the moment, this is a crime scene, and I want you all out of this room, pronto."

Mack pushed Jay's wheelchair, Dawkin, head down, shuffled beside them while Will detoured into the study to reappear a few minutes later.

CHAPTER FORTY-FOUR

During the next few hours, everyone gave their statements. Sara was arrested, and Dawkin knew that he would face an investigation for the shooting of Chloe. The lounge was sealed off, but Tavish allowed Will and Jay to remain in the house. Mack had drifted home, which left just Will, Jay and Dawkin alone in the kitchen.

"Does anyone want any more tea?" asked Jay.

"I think we should have something stronger. Who wants a whisky?" said Will jumping up from his chair.

"The Crombies, what a shower," said Dawkin shaking his head. "You would be hard-pressed to find so much evil in another family. All four of them potential killers. Quite astonishing. Pearce tells me Sara Crombie admitted to being the brains behind the whole terrorist affair last year. You know, right up until yesterday, I still thought you were really behind it all and had cleverly hoodwinked us and even kept the money. I owe you an apology, Mr Slater."

"Apology accepted, but what made you change your mind?"

"I was convinced that you were the second person whom that crooked bank manager, Justerini, was instructed to call. When a bloke from the Financial Securities Authority in the Virgin Islands phoned to say that the second phone number had been answered, I thought it must be you; still, surprisingly, it was something my Sergeant said about children. I began to think about who else might have picked up that telephone and answered the call. I think the phone went missing for a while somewhere in the Crombie household after all the turbulence, but then it was discovered and answered probably by either Justin or Chloe. I visited Crombies' home and discovered that Justin had taken many long-distance photos of you and this house. I know that didn't prove you innocent, but I was now wondering if there was something that I had missed. The only link I had between them was the army; Bore, Crombie and Justin were all in the army. Not a huge link," said Dawkin shaking his head, "but a link and I just had a feeling, call it the policeman's nose. Then there was a number scribbled at the Crombies' home, which I eventually realised was a date, not a time, and it was today. Sara Crombie came out of prison on parole just two days ago, and it was all too much of a coincidence. The one thing I did get wrong was Justin Crombie's target."

"What do you mean, Inspector? I thought I was his target?" said Will.

"While I was waiting for the ambulance after you had left to go back to the house, he recovered a little, and he admitted you were not the immediate target. He said the target was 'that woman.' I thought it must be Mrs Slater," turning towards Jay, "but Mrs Slater wasn't outside when he fired. There was only one woman outside, and that was his mother. He wasn't going to kill you then, Mr Slater, he was going to take revenge against his mother for killing his father. I guess they were close, both having been at Sandhurst."

Everyone was quiet for a few moments taking in what Dawkin had just imparted.

"I hear what you say, Inspector, but there are still a lot of questions that have not yet been answered. It feels like a jigsaw. I can see the picture in the middle, but I have a few pieces left, and they don't fit, and until they do, I can't complete the bloody puzzle."

"What pieces had you in mind, Mr Slater?"

"Well, why would Justin kill his mother in Scotland? He could kill her anywhere, and why before the money transfer? Who would have dealt with that if she were dead?" asked Will.

"This made the obvious place to kill her. Crombie was under-cover and could get away quickly. He would have planned to catch the helicopter too. Chloe was in the house and would have been in control if her mother was dead," replied Dawkin.

"So, do you think Justin Crombie was going to kill me too? "

"I think he was going to kill you and his mother. It was pretty clear that Lena, or Chloe or whatever she calls herself, had issues with you being alive when her father wasn't. So, I doubt that they would let you or Mrs Slater live after they had the money. They were difficult to assess completely, as they both appeared to be mentally unstable, but, yes, on balance, I think they would have killed you. Sara had the plan to get the money and leave, but that wasn't the children's plan. They wanted revenge. I'm not even sure they were worried about the money. However, we must not forget there has to be someone else involved. Sara couldn't have arranged this all from prison, she wouldn't have had the connections, and I can't see either of the young Crombies' being capable. So, they all had to live with whoever planned this operation up to a certain point, which I imagine was the money transfer. Then they could all improvise as they saw fit."

"But why was Justin watching me? He could have walked in here with his mother, dealt with the transfer and killed us all. Job completed," said Will.

"They couldn't do that. They had to know the house, your movements, who was living on-site and then they had to wait for Sara to be released from prison. Otherwise, they could all have waltzed up here and found you away on holiday. No, this was planned like a military operation, and that is exactly what it was."

"So, if someone else is involved, who do you think that is, Inspector?" asked Jay.

"I can't be sure yet, but I think Michael Bore."

Will thought for a moment, "yes, that could make sense, and perhaps slots in another piece of the puzzle. Would he have had the clout to have had the Boss killed in prison?"

"Oh yes, I had forgotten about him," added Jay.

Dawkin sat up in his chair, "what's that? Who was killed?"

"Sorry, Inspector, I thought you would have known. The Boss, as he was known."

"Yes, I know who you are referring to."

Jay replied, "he was murdered in prison a couple of weeks ago. One of my former colleagues from SO15 informed us. He thinks that it was to stop the contract on Will's life."

"I hadn't heard, but that all makes sense now. Bore hears there's a contract out on your life, tries to persuade the Boss to drop it, he doesn't, so he is killed. I bet if we look hard enough, we will find someone else ex-army that was in the same prison as the Boss who did the deed," replied Dawkin.

"Okay," said Will, "so Bore is pulling strings from prison and has put together a team on the outside. So far, that all fits together, but all supposition."

"Then there was the person who attacked you in the kitchen before we even owned the house," said Jay.

"I think it was Justin who attacked me. Now I have seen him close up; he fits the build. But why was he in the house in the first place?" asked Will.

"Once again, I can't be sure, but I reckon he was just reconnoitring. He had been watching you from a distance taking pictures," said Dawkin.

"You said that you thought someone had been watching you," added Jay.

"Okay, that's plausible. Then who cut the car brakes of the Eastern European intruders? Sara Crombie said she didn't know anything about that, and I believe her. Presumably, whoever cut the intruders' brakes, did so to ensure they couldn't do me any more harm. I suppose that was Justin Crombie," said Will.

"It could have been Justin Crombie, he had the technical knowledge, but I think it might have been someone else as it was a different modus operandi. The tampering of the brakes on your car, Mrs Slater, was more sophisticated so that the warning sign didn't show up immediately you started driving. That I think was Justin Crombie; he had several car maintenance manuals at his home." chirped Dawkin.

"Therefore, if it was not Justin who tampered with the Eastern Europeans' car, it means that there is someone else involved who hasn't been caught yet."

All three were silent for a moment assimilating this new thought.

"Okay, let's park that one for a moment," said Will getting up to refill their glasses. "The next missing piece is who killed Walter Gordon? You are probably not aware of this part of the story, Inspector. When we first moved in here, we found a body in the tunnel. It turned out to be the owner of this house. Walter, the owner's brother, first killed and then impersonated him to sell the house to us. Walter was convinced there was ancient treasure hidden in the house but didn't have time to find it. So, he broke in on two occasions, looking for it. On the second occasion, Mack and I had just discovered and accessed the original hiding place of the treasure. Walter had a gun, and I was convinced he was going to kill us both. But Jay and I reckon someone must have been listening, and when they realised that Walter might kill me, whoever it was, slipped into the house and shot him."

Dawkin looked stunned for a moment and said, "what do you mean, listening?"

"Ah yes, that is another thing you will be unaware of. Lena

admitted that she had bugged the house with both listening devices and cameras. The cameras mainly watched my computer screen and obtained my bank account passwords. The guy we had to sweep the bugs said that the end listener could be anywhere and impossible to trace. However, there was only a short time between Walter surprising Mack and me, threatening to kill us, and him being shot. So, whoever was listening either mobilised someone pretty quick or came himself."

"Either way, whoever was listening must have been relatively close?" interjected Dawkin.

"Yes, precisely, Inspector."

"What about the alarms and CCTV? Didn't you pick up the killer on that?" asked Dawkin.

"No, that was strange. The alarms went off when Walter entered the house; I just didn't hear them, but nothing when the killer entered. Whoever killed Walter knew roughly where the cameras were as they weren't activated. The camera by the back door can easily be negotiated if you approach from the loch, where we have no alarm trips."

"So that confirms there is someone unaccounted for," said Dawkin thoughtfully.

"Couldn't the killer be Justin or Chloe?" asked Jay.

"I'm certain it was a man; he was tall and moved like a man. I don't think it was Justin; it just didn't look like his build."

"Okay, so we still have to be on our guard," said Dawkin.

"Surely, they won't try again after today's shamollocks?" said Will.

A black cloud of despondency hung over the kitchen table while all three sat silently, considering the consequences of this possibility. The only noise was the tapping of Will's fingers on the wooden kitchen table.

CHAPTER FORTY-FIVE

Muttering to himself, Dawkin slumped further down into his chair, swallowed up by his voluminous coat hanging over the back.

Suddenly Dawkin shot up, "I have an idea, assuming my theory about the army is correct," thrusting his hand into his coat pocket to retrieve his phone. He tapped in a number.

"Edkins, I need you to look up something now!"

"Evening Guv. Nice to hear from you."

"Shut up, Edkins. You remember I said that I thought there might be a military connection in this Slater case? Well, I'm convinced there is. Get on the internet or army records or the Ministry of Defence, find out what regiment Peter Crombie was in, and see if you could find out who might have been stationed with him. Who was in his platoon, or whatever they call them? You know the sort of thing. Get back asap."

"It's late, Guv, not sure who will still be around."

"Just wake people up, Edkins, if you have to; it is a matter of life and death."

"Okay, Guv, will try."

Dawkin sighed and slumped back in his chair again; this time, his shoulders relaxed, his face uncreased, and a slight smile developed on his lips, but he was not going to tell the others what he now believed until it could be proven.

"I think we should have some supper while we wait for your Sergeant to call," said Jay.

CHAPTER FORTY-SIX

An hour later, Dawkin's phone rang, and he strode into the hall. "Yes, Edkins, tell me what you have found out."

"I was in luck, Guv, found someone still at the Ministry; they were extremely helpful. Had all the information on his computer," Edkins paused as if seeking some congratulations.

"Get on with it, Edkins."

"Well, first this bloke found out what regiment Peter Crombie was in and then he looked up where he toured. He was in the Falklands, Iraq and Afghanistan. He was in a long time. Must have loved it."

Another pause.

Dawkin sighed in irritation. "Get on, Edkins, for fuck's sake."

"Right, in the Falklands, Crombie was a second lieutenant and guess who was his Company Captain?"

"Edkins, I am in no mood for guessing games."

"No less than Captain Michael Bore."

Pacing up and down the hall as he listened, Dawkin nodded, "yeah, yeah, makes sense."

"Well, Guv, Bore retired after the Falklands. Crombie was promoted to full lieutenant but seemed to have got stuck at that rank for a long while. I think there was some trouble. The bloke at the MOD didn't want to elaborate. In Iraq, he was in charge of a platoon and by Afghanistan, he had been promoted to company captain. We crossed checked names between his platoon and his company, and there were only two names that were in both."

"So, who were they, Edkins?" interrupted Dawkin.

"A Corporal Roderick Neath and a Sergeant Hamish MacInnes."

"Well done, Edkins, good job, thanks. Hopefully, I will be back in the smoke very soon."

With a self-satisfied expression, Dawkin strode back into the kitchen, "got it, told you my hunch was correct. Serving with Peter Crombie in both Iraq and Afghanistan was a Corporal Roderick Neath. Bore would have known that, and I suggest, Mr and Mrs Slater, we have found our missing soldier and hopefully the last piece in your puzzle, Mr Slater."

"So, Neath cuts the intruders' brakes and then, after the bugging is in place, hears Walter Gordon threaten us and kills him. Ex-soldier, guess he could easily do that," said Will nodding in agreement with himself.

"That's about it, I reckon, Mr Slater," said Dawkin, still looking pleased with himself.

"But why did he attack Justin Crombie? They were in the same team?" asked Jay.

"We may never know the answer to that question, but Neath helped us out catching young Crombie."

"Yes, yes, he did, and think you are correct that may have completed the puzzle," said Will, "I think we should all have another drink."

The enlightened mood in the kitchen was terminated by more shrilling from Dawkin's pocket.

Peering at the phone screen, he said, "excuse me while I take this call," and walked out into the hall.

Head down and again muttering to himself, Dawkin walked

back into the kitchen very slowly this time, his former hubris burst like a bubble in the air. Eyes scrunched and deep lines etched across his forehead, he lowered himself back into his chair, picked up his glass of whisky and stared into it.

"Bad news, Inspector?" asked Will.

"I don't understand it?" Dawkin muttered again.

"What is it?" asked Jay in a concerned tone.

"That was Tavish on the phone; the Procurator Fiscal's office, which is the same as the coroner in England, has made some initial findings into the death of Roddy Neath. They thought Tavish should know immediately. Neath didn't die from the bullet wound; it was not fatal."

"Heart attack?" queried Will.

"He was suffocated. Someone deliberately stopped him breathing. They found some fibres in his nose and mouth from a piece of material. They haven't worked out what material yet."

"My God," exclaimed Jay.

"You said he was dead when you got to him, Mr Slater?" asked Dawkin.

"Yes, you don't think I…?"

"No, no, I might have a while ago, but not now. Very strange, why kill Neath?" mused Dawkin.

"Never mind the answer to that question; what it means is that there is still someone else out there, the person who murdered Neath," said Will.

Dawkin thought for a while and asked, "tell me did you have all the bugs removed?"

"No, we didn't, as we thought it would warn the listeners that we were onto them," said Will.

"Probably a very good idea. I need to make one quick call and will be back," said Dawkin.

* * *

Will looked across to Jay, shrugged his shoulders, curled his bottom lip and stared at his glass of whisky.

Two loud raps at the back door had Will springing out of his chair, "who's that?' said Will.

"Only one way to tell," replied Jay, and Will walked across and unlocked the door.

A voice floated out of the darkness, "hello, Will."

"Hamish, how are you? Come in. What brings you here at this time of day? Who's manning the bar?"

"Lydia, as there is no one in for dinner and after all the commotion, I wanted to come down and make sure both you and Jay were okay."

"That's very kind, Hamish. Let me get you a whisky. I'm afraid we are banished to the kitchen after our little shoot out earlier."

"Hello Hamish, yes, thanks for popping in," echoed Jay.

"So, all the police have left now?"

"Well, yes, except for Inspector Dawkin," said Will, "he's in the hall making a call; he'll be back in a minute."

CHAPTER FORTY-SEVEN

Will stood up as Dawkin strode back into the kitchen, "you don't know each other, Inspector Dawkin; this is Hamish MacInnes; he runs the local inn on the main road."

Will could see the look on Dawkin's face.

"Good evening, Mr MacInnes," said Dawkin. "I have been expecting you. I'm glad you didn't disappoint us."

Wide-eyed with surprise, Will's head swivelled between the two men as MacInnes produced a pistol from his pocket and indicated for Dawkin and Will to sit down.

"Okay, there's no point in playing games. You know who I am and what I want. Let's make this easy. Put your phones on the table, please."

Will and Dawkin thudded their phones onto the wooden surface, almost in unison.

"I'm afraid mine is still in the flower vase next door, but I expect you know that already, having listened to everything unfold," said Jay.

Will saw a thin smile appear on MacInnes's lips. "Now we are all going into the study where Will is going to transfer his money into my account. Why don't you push Jay in the wheelchair, Inspector? We'll follow."

Will took up his place in the little coterie that passed through the hall and into the study.

"Okay, Will, these are the details where to make the transfer," said MacInnes sliding a piece of paper across the desk. "Don't be clever, Will; I know your account and have your password; all I need is your thumbprint to open the account and transfer the funds."

Will logged on to the online portal of his Swiss bank account and typed in the password.

"Okay, that's good so far," said MacInnes peering over Will's shoulder, "now the thumbprint, there, they are asking for it now."

Will placed his thumb on the anointed place, and the account opened up. In large green text, the balance on the account shone out from the screen.

Zero.

"What, what," screamed MacInnes, partly at Will and partly at the computer, "that can't be; where has it gone? I saw you checking the account only yesterday morning before Sara arrived. You have tricked me."

"I haven't tricked anyone, it's my money, and I moved it this afternoon. You must have missed the film show, too busy watching the horror movie on the other channel."

"You think you are so clever; well, you can just transfer it back now."

"I'm afraid I can't do that as I transferred it into the clients' account of my solicitors and have no control over the money now."

Will pushed his chair back from the desk and looked up into MacInnes' eyes, trying to establish what Hamish might do next.

"I should kill all of you; you all deserve it."

"I don't think we do, Hamish. You were a soldier; you trained not to kill innocent people. We are innocent people, Hamish.

Michael Bore has tricked you and Roddy. The money you are trying to recover came from terrorists, the very people you spent much of your army career trying to stop. Put your gun down before it gets any worse for you. Think of Lydia."

A sense of calmness descended on Will. It was strange; it was as if the house was giving him strength. He could see that Hamish was shaking and that the scenario could go either way. It didn't worry him; he had had enough of all the killing, the attempts on his life, the effect on those who he loved. He had finished fighting this battle whichever way it turned out. Que sera, sera, he thought.

The silence was palpable. No one even breathed as MacInnes's eyes flicked back and forth between Will and the other two. Then in the distance, there came the familiar cry of police sirens.

"It's all over, MacInnes," said Dawkin, "the police are here, and there's no escape. Just put your gun down on the desk and walk away from it, please."

MacInnes' body crumbled as if his skeleton had broken up inside him, his face creased, and his legs started to wobble as he dropped the gun onto the floor. Will leapt up and pulled MacInnes onto his chair before he hit the ground. Dawkin swooped in and snatched up the gun. "Why, Hamish, why did you get involved in this stupid plan? You had a good life without all this."

"I had to; it was my duty."

"What do you mean your duty?"

"For the Regiment, the Company or old members in it."

"How does that all work?"

"You get a signal."

"What do you mean a signal?"

"If a member of the regiment or, more precisely, a platoon or company member was in trouble, there was a signal sent. It started in the Falklands and then went on from tour to tour. If we were under attack, a signal was sent. After the wars, this developed into a text message - a code, time, and place to meet. An assignment was given, and whoever received the signal was responsible for carrying it out. The help required were simple tasks, alibis for cheating spouses, frightening off a debt collector, collecting the odd debt, that sort of stuff. It all sounds a bit stupid now, but it was an honour sort of thing. Then I got this one last year from Michael Bore. It was a very sophisticated assignment. Normally, no payment is given, but I was offered a considerable sum of money because of what was involved. The inn wasn't doing so well, and it seemed fairly risk-free. There weren't meant to be any killings. I was told that you had stolen a lot of money from Peter Crombie, my old company commander and that the plan was to get it back. I should have done some research, but I just needed the money. There was a lot of reconnoitring to be done, and I couldn't do it all by myself, so I co-opted Neath into the team. I was then instructed that this lad, Crombie, Peter's son, would also help watch. I put him up here in the Inn, and he and Neath watched. He was very keen and did most of the work, which pleased Neath, who couldn't stand the boy. I had to keep them apart or ruin the mission. I think it was because the lad bunked Sandhurst. Neath thought he should have seen it through like a proper officer. I always felt the assignment meant more to the lad than just the watching brief, but he did his job well, so I couldn't complain until the end." MacInnes paused in thought, "the lad Crombie introduced his sister into the team to work on the inside. We needed information about your bank accounts. She placed all the bugs and fed us any information we didn't get from the devices."

The sirens were very close now, and out of the corner of his eye, Will saw Dawkin inch out into the hall to let in the new arrivals.

"But what about the Eastern European intruders who came to kill me?" asked Will.

"We didn't know that there were going to be others out there trying the same thing. I got a message to say that there was a contract out on your life and a couple of thugs from London were looking for you. That was before the bugs had been planted, so Neath and Crombie's role was to watch out for you."

"So, it was Neath in the woods the night the intruders had their car brakes cut," said Will.

"Yes, he was only meant to scare them as I was told the contract on your life would be withdrawn. Anyway, collateral damage, as we say."

"I'm guessing that their boss wouldn't withdraw the contract, so he was dealt with too," interjected Jay.

"I don't know much about that, but we had some good contacts inside, other ex-military men, so it was sorted. The plan had always been to get better intel from inside the house; hence the girl planted the devices. Didn't like her one bit, an absolute hard case. Like her brother, she seemed to have some hidden agenda. As it happened, the cameras turned out to be useful when we had to deal with that idiot after the treasure. Neath and I took it in turn to listen and watch. It was just luck that I was listening the evening Gordon turned up. We couldn't watch and listen all the time; most was recorded, which we caught up on at intervals. Anyway, I couldn't believe it when Gordon turned up with a gun. I didn't know what he was going to do and couldn't risk him killing you. Although we had all the bank details, we still needed your thumbprint, and although we could still use it if you were dead, Bore's plan was not to kill you. I called Neath and told him to get over here quick and deal with Gordon, but he was tied up with something, so I turned up. Fortunately, you had explained how to get into the house without triggering the alarms. However, I thought that I would have to break in but found the kitchen door unlocked. I knew roughly where you all were from the camera on the first landing. So made my way up to the next floor. I listened for a while and heard him ranting and raving, and then I realised he would kill you, so I had to act. He shouldn't have been there. He had his payoff and was supposed to be back in Oz. Once again, collateral damage," said MacInnes, shrugging his shoulders.

The sirens had been switched off, but the swirling blue lights cast shadows as they reflected around the room. Will could hear subdued voices at the front door, but he needed to get as many answers as possible before Hamish was arrested and taken away.

"So, did you know young Crombie wanted to kill me?" asked Will.

"No, his mother said that you would be okay, and he wouldn't kill you even after the money had been transferred. Bore was also adamant about that. I didn't even know he had tampered with Jay's car until much later. I was livid. As I said, I thought he had another agenda, but we had to accept it, even though Neath didn't like it. He felt that the lad was unstable and could compromise the whole assignment at any time. Ironic because poor old Neath was even more unhinged. Mind shattered by constant pressures of combat."

"Why did you kill Neath?" asked Will.

"I would rather not have, but he was starting to get funny, you know, mental stuff to do with Afghanistan. I was his platoon Sergeant. He was the medic, tough job, dealing with his dead mates or worse when limbs were blown off. I was with him the day he cracked. He couldn't move a muscle - complete breakdown. I had to stretcher him out under fire from the Terry. Quite frankly, it was all enough to send anyone..." He made a circular motion with his finger towards his head. "I think it was the killing of the thugs that did it. We used to sabotage Terrys' vehicles by cutting the brakes. Neath was good at that, used a scalpel. I was also listening when Sara arrived, as I knew she was due that day. I organised the chopper to get them all away. When I realised things were not going to plan, I headed over to Neath's place because that was Crombie's escape route. I thought I might be able to help. I got there just too late, and Neath and Crombie had already clashed. When I saw, what Neath had done to Crombie, I knew he had gone native and that he would talk even if it incriminated himself. He had taken a bad hit, and I thought that if he were dead, at least for a while, everyone would assume the shot had killed him, and it would give us extra time to complete the assignment."

"So, it was Michael Bore who gave you the assignment."

"Yes, Captain Bore, and he continued to give instructions to the end."

"It must have been for more than honour and money that you killed all these people. Surely, there has to be a limit to this honour thing," said Will.

"You see, Lieutenant Crombie, Justin's dad, saved my life in Iraq, almost got killed doing it. A bloody hero should have got an award, but he didn't; I think it was because he had such a dodgy record. Anyway, Bore, who served with Crombie in the Falklands, must have found out about me, and knew a debt was due for honour. So, I got the signal."

"My God, some honour," chipped in Jay.

"So, Sara Crombie arriving at my house was all part of the plan," said Will.

"Oh yes, it was part of the plan. But she was only told what she needed to know. I think she thought it was her plan. She was just a pawn, expendable, if necessary, as was the case. She was not going to keep the money, or at least not much of it. Bore loathed her even though she was Peter Crombie's wife. In fact, he much preferred you, which is a bit ironic."

"I think I have heard enough," said Inspector Tavish as he sidled around the study door, followed closely by Dawkin, who had on his self-satisfied smirk again.

"Hamish MacInnes," Tavish continued, "I am arresting you for the murder of Roderick Neath, acting in conjunction with others to murder Walter Gordon, Marius Vassily and Christophe

Wesinivic and the attempted murder of Mrs Jay Slater and her daughter. Illegally planting listening devices and trying to illicit money by false pretences. You are not obliged to say anything, but anything you do say will be noted down and may be used in evidence. Do you understand?"

"Yes," mumbled MacInnes.

"Do you have anything to say?"

MacInnes shook his head.

"Right, get him out of here," said Tavish to two burly policemen. "Okay, Mr and Mrs Slater, looks like more statements are required. We will soon be able to bind them up to make a book. Assuming you continue to live on my patch, I sincerely hope this is the last of the mayhem and pain you will inflict on me and my team. It has been a challenge. As for you, Inspector Dawkin, I have found your presence here extremely intrusive, annoying and downright rude. However, I have to admit that there may not have been such a successful outcome without your intervention. I shall relay that information back to your boss and hope your investigation re the shooting goes okay."

Tavish nodded slightly to no one in particular, and Will thought there was almost a smile on his lips as he performed his dapper turn on his heels and followed the others out to their vehicles.

The intercom buzzed in the study.

"Is everything okay, Will? Saw the police are back again," said Mack.

"Yes, everything is fine here. We just had a visitor, Hamish MacInnes, and as they say, he is now helping police with their enquiries. He was Walter's killer."

"Hamish? Not sure how he got to the house without triggering one of the alarms."

"Don't worry, Mack. I think that was my fault, as I remember telling Hamish that we couldn't cover all access points and there were no alarm trips if someone came via the edge of the loch. I will fill you in tomorrow. Goodnight."

Will turned to Dawkin, "I think I have to thank you, Inspector. Without your perseverance, well, who knows what would have happened."

"What a plan and what organisation," said Dawkin.

"Yes, I suppose the final missing piece in the puzzle for me was why here, and why this house? But I suppose it had to be somewhere close to where Bore could use some of his old comrades. What I didn't realise was how much you could organise from prison," said Will.

"Provided you got money and connections, you can pretty much do anything on the inside. Captain Bore is going to be extremely upset, especially with you, Will," said Dawkin shaking his head slowly in an almost apologetic manner.

"Well, I guess we will have to live with that. There is a price for everything."

"I had better get going. I thought I would get a taxi back to Glasgow to be on the first train tomorrow morning. I want to keep my job and my wife if possible."

"Let me phone for the local taxi; I'm sure he will be pleased with the fare."

"Okay, thanks. I have one question for you, when did you transfer all the money to your solicitors?"

"As you, Mack and Jay went into the kitchen after the police got here, I nipped into the study and did it then. My solicitors will have kittens tomorrow morning," Will looked at his watch, "I mean this morning when they see they have had an unauthorised transfer of many millions into their clients' account. I have a final question for you, too, Inspector. I assume you called the police when you went out just before MacInnes arrived, but how did you know he would come?"

"It was when I asked you whether the bugs were still in place. After the extraordinary events of earlier, I reckoned, the missing team member would be tuned in and likely to visit. I didn't know it would be MacInnes. His name was on the same list as Neath, having served with Crombie in the Middle East, but I'd never met him, but as soon as you introduced us, I realised who he was."

Will nodded his head, "well, thank you again for all your help Inspector and if there is anything I can say to help you, just let me know, anytime."

"Thank you, Mr Slater. I'll get my cab now." Dawkin shook both Jay's and Will's hands, inclined his head to recognise something unspoken, turned and left.

"Wow," said Jay.

"Absolutely," replied Will, still thinking about the likely rancour of Michael Bore.

The End

Will Slater and Inspector Dawkin will be back.

Made in the USA
Middletown, DE
03 December 2022

15982561R00156